THE GUARDIANS OF TRUTH

A JAKE SCOTT MYSTERY

BARRY FINLAY

Published by Keep On Climbing Publishing

Copyright ©Barry Finlay 2022

(613) 240-6953

info@barry-finlay.com

www.barry-finlay.com

Cataloguing data available at Library and Archives Canada.

ISBN: 978-1-7771395-4-4 Paperback

ISBN: 978-1-7771395-5-1 eBook

REMOTE ACCESS

AN INTERNATIONAL POLITICAL THRILLER

"While grounded in reality, Remote Access is a must-read with a singular sense of escapism rare in a political thriller." – **BestThrillers.com**

A PERILOUS QUESTION

AN INTERNATIONAL THRILLER AND CRIME NOVEL

"Written with a compassionate, knowledgeable voice, the book is an excellent story of mystery and intrigue." – **RECOMMENDED by the US Review of Books**

THE VANISHING WIFE

AN ACTION-PACKED CRIME THRILLER

"The pace grabs hold. Whether the mild-mannered accountant Mason Seaforth could actually pull off what's at stake depends on the colour, the energy and dialogue of the story telling. The Vanishing Wife is convincing." – **Donald Graves, Canadian Crime Reviews**

KILIMANJARO AND BEYOND

A LIFE-CHANGING JOURNEY

"The book reads like a journal and the writing is warm, familiar and humorous. 'Kilimanjaro and Beyond, A Life-Changing Journey,' will challenge all who read it to consider how they too can make a difference, not only for others, but for themselves as well." – **Reader Views**

I GUESS WE MISSED THE BOAT

A TRAVEL MEMOIR

"This is an exhilarating read." –– **Grady Harp, Amazon Hall of Fame reviewer**

ACKNOWLEDGEMENTS

It has been eleven years since my first book was published, and I have come to realize that one of the most enjoyable aspects of writing for me is the research required before actually sitting down to create the story. It involves internet searches and speaking with subject matter experts. Each book has allowed me to broaden my knowledge about subjects I previously knew little or nothing about, thanks to the people who have helped me. In-depth research was required once again as *The Guardians of Truth* follows retired reporter Jake Scott on the trail of various clues to find a missing friend.

The research for this book delved into the subject of cults. It is estimated that hundreds of thousands join a cult each year. According to *Psychology Today*, "No one joins a cult; they are recruited by systematic social influence processes." It's a fascinating, yet terrifying, subject.

As part of my research, there are various experts I lean on for advice. I'm fortunate to have a paramedic in the family that I can go to for guidance. Thank you once again to Doug Finlay for answering my questions about first responders. Various members of Ottawa Police Service and the Ontario Provincial Police generously gave me their time, but I especially want to thank Staff Sergeant Cory Robertson who educated me about hostage negotiation. Of course, any errors or embellishments in paramedic practices or police procedure are mine.

Once the research is done and the writing starts, it takes many people to bring a book to fruition and I owe a big thank you to each of those involved in the process.

Katie Baker did an amazing job of editing, and it is a better book as a result. Mirna Gilman at Books Go Social designed the cover, which I think nicely reflects the feel of the book. Chrissy Hobbs at Indie Publishing Group performed her magic with formatting. I am grateful to all of you.

I deeply appreciate my readers who keep me writing. The reviews and feedback provided are always appreciated. Before the book is ever published, the members of my Advanced Reader Copy team provide valuable feedback. For that I am grateful.

For those who help by telling your friends and family about my books, thank you very much. Making people aware of a book among the millions available is always a challenge and I appreciate everyone who helps.

Finally, a special thank you to my wife Evelyn, who always reads the earliest versions of the manuscript, and provides the invaluable comments, encouragement, and inspiration to keep me going.

CHAPTER ONE

S HE PLANNED TO expose him for the fraud he was. Nothing about him was real.

It couldn't be.

She had witnessed Julian's diatribes for weeks now. At first, he had her convinced. His sincerity. The conviction with which he spoke. The vivid neon-like blue eyes and the charismatic voice. All very compelling. But now she was positive of the identity and motivations of the man who held over 100 followers in the palm of his hand. He was the worst kind of fraud.

Cassandra Wright, or Cassie, as her friends called her, peered at her companion who drove the car. He stared straight ahead; his countenance was as inscrutable as a Buddha's. She studied the chiseled features of Robert Weatherby's handsome face and recalled how they had met a few weeks ago, and what had led them here.

Cassie first became aware of Robert while idly skimming profiles on a dating site. She was attracted to his photo, but she also learned that he practiced psychology. She contacted him and they dated a few times. She eventually sought his professional help to stave off feelings of depression. The sessions started with Cassie detailing her anxiety and sleepless nights. Over time, he seemed to help her, and her attraction to him deepened. Cassie thought Weatherby sensed the connection, too, so she wanted to take things to the next level.

She wore her prettiest dress, emphasizing her shapely figure, for a dinner date. They ordered exquisite steaks with lobster at a high-end restaurant and, halfway through, Weatherby leaned in and asked about her religious beliefs. She informed him she would describe herself as "uncertain." Since she enjoyed being with him and didn't want to risk offending on the topic, especially that night when she had other plans, she let him lead the conversation.

He continued by describing an organization with a charismatic leader that met every Monday night, or more frequently if deemed necessary, on a farm west of the city. He called the organization the Guardians of Truth. The attendees thought organized religion had let them down and that their freedoms were under assault from repeated intrusions by the government. Simply put, they had become disenchanted with the institutions and people they had trusted. To Cassie, they sounded like a dissatisfied group of people looking for something better, which she had to admit defined her. Left to raise a teenage daughter on her own, life had been a struggle lately. She worked in a dead-end government job. Recently, despondency had settled over her, so this might be what she needed.

She laughingly suggested the organization sounded like a cult, which produced a frown and an immediate defensive denial from her companion. The night she had planned fizzled out, as Robert became more and more insistent that she should attend a Guardians of Truth meeting. The kindness and gentleness he had displayed seemed to develop into an obsession to convince Cassie to attend a session. He assured her it would be the answer to everything she needed.

He described the group's arduous admittance process. Only certain people and true believers were allowed to join. Cassie's curiosity rose. *What did they truly believe in? And why were they so secretive?* Robert had told her how they vetted everyone through a questionnaire, and that she would have to sign a non-disclosure agreement, or NDA. She ignored the red flags and agreed to go through the process to please him.

Eventually, she passed the screening and Robert delightedly invited her to an assembly, as Julian referred to them. Any hint of a romantic connection with Robert evaporated like moisture on a hot sidewalk, as he insisted Cassie's treatment must remain professional.

They had traveled in silence as they left the suburbs of Ottawa, Canada's capital, and headed west. As they drove, the wipers fought to clear the windshield from a torrential downpour that had occurred sporadically throughout the day.

The weight of the silence in the car wore Cassie down.

"Aren't you going to say anything?" she asked.

Even in the vehicle's gloom, a crimson tide washed over Robert's face from the neck up. He grew angry when Cassie had warned him as they left Ottawa that she intended to speak with Julian. She had considered it for weeks but wanted to be sure. Tonight was the night, but had she miscalculated by revealing her suspicions about the man to Robert? She told him she planned to expose Julian as a fraud and demanded a face-to-face meeting with him. Robert wouldn't have any of it. His eyes narrowed, and his voice sounded flat and threatening.

"You're making a big mistake. Why can't you let it go? Julian has given so many people hope and will ultimately save them from what's coming. You can be one of the saved ones. I'm begging you not to do this."

Cassie's frustration mounted. She realized she didn't know Robert as well as she had thought. "Save them from what? A comet that's going to miss earth by millions of miles? All people have to do is follow the science to realize it's all BS. How many people have died because he told them vaccines implanted microchips in their bloodstreams? How many more people will he kill because of his stupid ideas? Besides, I'm confident the name he uses is fake. I think I know who he is, and if I'm right, he's nothing but a charlatan."

"You signed an NDA," Robert growled.

"So what? It's worth nothing if Julian is doing something

illegal. At the very least, he's doing something unethical. The NDA means nothing."

The rest of the ride passed in stony silence until they arrived at their destination, where cars sat scattered like marbles in the farmyard and into the adjoining field. The recent heavy rain left the ground spongy, so stones picked up by the tires ticked against the undercarriage of the car as they skidded through the mud to a vacant spot. They entered a dilapidated barn, but the outside appearance foretold nothing about the interior. A red carpet on natural stone tiles ushered the attendees inside. Chandeliers hung on long wires from the roof. Spinning ceiling fans cooled the room, and rows of occupied oak benches faced the front, where a red velvet curtain separated a raised stage from the gathering waiting patiently for something to happen.

Cassie and Robert asked a couple to squeeze together, so they could sit in the only space available. The couple nodded but stared straight ahead as they shoved over without a word. As usual, an unnerving silence hung in the room. At precisely seven o'clock, the lights dimmed, and the silence shattered like glass hit by a boulder, as raucous rock music blared from two enormous black meshed speakers on either side of a raised stage. The performance was about to begin. Theatrical fog streamed from machines under the stage, obscuring the front of the room. The bench vibrated under Cassie from the music's thundering bass, and the crowd stirred. Cassie did an inward eye roll at the spectacle.

The front of the raised platform remained dark, save for one strategically placed brilliant spotlight that created an eerie shimmering glow in the remaining dry ice cloud at the center of the stage. The music stopped, and the crowd quieted until the man of the hour magically appeared and started speaking. His sonorous voice soothed the masses. It surprised Cassie when Robert wandered away for a few minutes. *Perhaps he went to the bathroom*, Cassie thought.

She examined the faces staring at the front of the room. They hung on every word, enraptured by the man speaking. But something about the man had always bothered her. She listened closely again, as she had done for a few weeks. The face didn't match the familiar voice, yet she knew this man. She recalled her shock when she had recognized something at one assembly as his sleeve inadvertently rode up on his arm. It confirmed her suspicions.

When Robert returned, Cassie stared at the man on stage, even though his gloomy dissertation barely registered. As he wound down, she glanced again at the attendees. Some closed their eyes, others wrung their hands, while still others raised their arms to the ceiling, their lips silently acknowledging every wonderful word Julian spoke. While she didn't consider herself an expert by any means, she understood people brought together by anxiety and lack of trust could be led to a common goal, almost like hypnosis. That's what was happening here. Robert interrupted her reverie when he reached for her hand and squeezed it, until she pulled away from his painful grip.

The room became stifling hot. Some attendees appeared to be on the verge of fainting. Young women passed through the crowd offering bottled water at seven dollars a pop. Then, Julian masterfully lowered his voice to a medium level, saving the best for last.

"We can all be saved if you will continue to support building the underground bunker here on our farm. You will be the ones to carry forth a civilization that can start over and make things right. We need young people to ensure civilization continues. We need older people who lived their lives when things were good to teach the young people." Then, with his voice barely above a whisper, he said, "You are the chosen few. Give everything you can. We don't have a lot of time, folks. God has spoken to me directly and Doomsday is coming. We'll have another meeting on Sunday to discuss it more. We can all be saved if you give generously. An underground bunker will keep us safe from the catastrophic event that will end the world as we know it."

The crowd murmured, and some shouts echoed through the enclosed space. The same young women who sold the extravagant bottled water passed through the audience again, and the sound of whirring credit and debit card machines filled the air as attendees poured their life savings into Julian's words. When a pretty teenager of about seventeen arrived in front of Cassie and Robert, Cassie shook her head, which caused the teenager to frown.

"Don't you want to be saved?" she breathed.

Cassie replied, "Save yourself by getting out of here." The girl gasped and moved on.

When the spectacle ended, and the crowd filed out of the building, Cassie turned to Robert and said, "I've had enough. I'm going backstage to confront this fraud."

Robert's chest heaved with a heavy sigh. "Wait," he intoned. He sat expressionless with his arms crossed as the last of the crowd made their way through the exit. Cassie glanced around, thinking that only the two of them remained. She didn't see Robert motion to someone behind them. He said icily to Cassie, "I'll tell him you want to meet with him. You wait here."

As Robert stalked away, Cassie sensed movement behind her. Before she had a chance to turn, a sharp pain shot through her neck. Everything became fuzzy in an instant. The room blurred as it closed in on her. She grabbed at her gasping throat, desperately trying to draw a breath. She reached out to hold on to something, anything, to stabilize herself, but her hand grabbed at empty air. Her legs buckled. It was as if a hole opened in the floor, and she couldn't prevent her boneless body from sliding in.

For Cassie Wright, everything faded to black.

CHAPTER TWO

MONDAY.

Jake Scott consistently disliked Mondays, especially since his retirement. As the week went on, he always looked forward to the Saturday breakfast gathering with his buddies at Brew and Buns, the restaurant down the street in his Westboro neighborhood. The camaraderie even carried forward to Sunday. But Mondays. Ugh!

Today had been especially boring. The lyrics from a song he remembered from the early seventies skipped through his mind as he swiped a soapy cloth across his dinner plate. *Rainy days and Mondays always get me down.* He peered through the kitchen window. Raindrops continued to slither down the glass, as they had all day, blurring the glistening sidewalk in front of his house. He sighed as he tossed the cloth, landing it half in and half out of the sink. He dabbed the plate with a towel before setting it on the table, where it would sit with the cutlery until he had to use it the next time. At least the day had almost ended.

He opened the door and, as usual, the start-of-week stack of flyers lay beyond reach. He hurried into the rain to retrieve them, wiping away a giant drop from the eave that hit him square in the eye. A plastic bag protected the flyers from turning into a soggy, unreadable mess. He returned inside and unsheathed the stack, quickly scanning the flyers before opening the inside door to the garage to throw the ones he had no interest in into the blue recycling bin. One remained as he poured a cup of coffee and headed for his recliner in the sunroom. Sadly, reading the Canadian Tire flyer would be the highlight of his day.

He had learned to pace himself during retirement, especially since his beloved wife, Mia, passed away. The rain sidetracked the day's big plan of mowing the grass. He *could* do things when it rained, like clean the basement, but he had passed the time watching a John Wayne movie, reading a Raymond Chandler novel, and having a nap instead.

He set the cup beside a stack of magazines on the side table and pulled the cord to open the vertical blinds on the patio doors. Everything appeared blurred through the glass doors that were mottled by the rain and drops dappled the puddles already lying in the garden. Shortly after he settled into his chair, a tabby cat wandered down the hall and hauled himself onto Jake's lap. Despite the cat's protracted diet, he still wouldn't be winning any feline races, or even turtle races for that matter. Jake kneaded along the cat's ribcage. The vet had told him the padding shouldn't feel thicker than that on the back of Jake's hand. "Well, Oliver," Jake said, "it looks like you and I will have to diet a little more." The cat grumpily hissed and thumped back down to the floor as if the word 'diet' had been too much for his sensitive ears.

Jake remained seated, sipping his coffee, and flipping through the flyer. The usual layout of weekly deals in colorful ads greeted him, but nothing of interest. He tossed it on the floor on top of the day's Ottawa Citizen, where a headline blared about trouble in the Middle East. There would never be a lack of sensational problems to write about. He had done his share of describing the worst of humanity during his days as a reporter for the paper. Oh, there were happier stories too, but they didn't sell newspapers as effectively.

Jake rested his head on the back of the chair. Just as he dozed off, the doorbell chimed, jarring him awake. As he wandered down the hall, two shadowy figures became visible through the sidelight. Laughter drifted from the other side of the door. *Possibly some kids selling something.*

When he opened the door, he found two teenage girls, one of whom he recognized. Emilie was the daughter of his friend, and fellow breakfast attendee, Dani Perez. The second girl appeared to be about the same age as 16-year-old Emilie. Both looked like they had wandered through a car wash as they shivered on the doorstep.

Emilie had become comfortable with Jake as his friendship with her mom plodded toward something more serious. She spoke first through chattering teeth in her usual rapid-fire style as she used her sleeve to mop up random drips from her face. "Hi, Jake, we got caught in the downpour. This is my friend, Haley Wright. Haley, this is my mom's friend, Jake."

Jake stepped aside to let them enter. He regarded Haley, whose bright red rain-slickered hair hung in forlorn strands down one side of her head, while the other side was shorn, practically bald. She wore shapeless pants, and a shirt wet enough to cling to her, despite being about three sizes too big. Emilie sported her usual stylishly ripped and faded jeans, now blotched by the rain, and a sodden tee shirt featuring a logo for a band completely unfamiliar to Jake. Her normally curly, raven hair hung limply down her neck. Both wore saturated, muddy running shoes, which they removed at the entrance. Socks, that may have once been white, followed, plopping onto the mat like wet dishrags from the sink.

"Nice to meet you, Haley. You two can have a seat at the kitchen table while I find you a couple of towels."

The girls laughed noisily at something that tickled them as he hurried down the hall to the linen closet. Emilie called out, "Jake, there's nothing in the fridge again." Now he remembered what else he had planned to do today. He had eaten the last TV dinner and had planned to shop.

When he returned, he handed the towels to the girls, which they used to pat their hair dry, as Oliver sat perched on Emilie's lap, where he usually sat when she visited. Jake invited the girls into the sunroom, where he started the gas fireplace, even as the air conditioner cooled the inside temperature. The girls sat cross-legged in front of the fire, and

Oliver, who had followed them down the hall, wormed his way onto Emilie's lap again.

Jake said, "I can't offer you dry clothes, at least anything that would fit, but the fire will help you dry out. Why are you out in this weather? Wait, it's Monday. No school today?"

Emilie cast a sideways glance at her friend.

"It's summer, Jake. No school, remember?" She turned to Haley and shrugged. "Jake went to school a very, very, very long time ago." Her friend smirked and nodded knowingly.

Jake's face flushed as an image of him riding to school in a horse-drawn sleigh flashed through his head. He might be old, but not *that* old. He suspected they thought he'd had to chisel his homework on stone tablets. Of course, they didn't attend school in the summer. He tried again. "So, what brought you out in the rain?"

Emilie glanced at Haley again before responding. "We stayed overnight at Haley's. She lives two blocks over. Her mom's been acting weird, so Haley asked me to stay last night. We've been hanging out with friends all day, and we're on our way back to my place. Haley's staying over tonight."

Jake glanced at Haley and noticed her lips turn down at the corners as if she agreed, but the subject of her mom made her uncomfortable. He moved on.

"Well, I can offer you some toast with peanut butter, and the milk in the fridge is still good. Interested?"

Emilie absent-mindedly stroked Oliver's fur as she regarded her friend, who had so far said nothing. Finally, Haley responded. "No, I'm okay, thank you. We ate at my place. Our fridge looks like yours, Mr. Scott, but we had some crackers and cheese. Em said she had food at her place. My mom's divorced, and she's been acting a little crazy. She's never around."

"Hmm. Is this something you should talk to your dad about, Haley?"

Haley's eyes never left a dark spot in the woodgrain of the hardwood floor.

"I don't even know where my dad is. He walked out three years ago, and we haven't heard from him since. I wish Mom would just tell me what she does all the time when she's away. She won't talk to me about it. She said she joined a group and attends their meetings. They meet every Monday, so she's probably at one tonight. She's been acting weird ever since she told me that."

Jake glanced at the patio doors. "Okay, well, here's what we'll do first. It looks like the rain is slowing down. Since you can't live on crackers and cheese, let's go out and get you fed. You choose the restaurant."

CHAPTER THREE

MILIE AND HALEY waited under the roof of Jake's porch as he backed his Subaru Outback out of the garage. The rain that had let up moments ago, once again came down in torrents, and the large drops tattooed a steady drumbeat on the car's roof as Jake edged it into the elements. The girls giggled as they raced toward the car. Haley's feet slipped from underneath her in a puddle on the driveway, but she managed to grab the back door handle as she began to fall. Emilie turned with a huge grin to look from the front seat as she buckled her seat belt. Haley climbed into the back seat and mumbled, "That was close," prompting another round of laughter.

Water rushed down the sides of the street, before pouring into the sewer grates. The car splashed through the puddles on the way to the restaurant. A truck traveling too fast in the opposite direction hit a pool of standing water, swamping Jake's car with a wave large enough to make a surfer drool.

Jake pulled into a parking lot, and the threesome hustled to the entrance of Harvey's, the restaurant chosen by popular demand. Haley and Emilie devoured their juicy, all-dressed burgers with french fries. They both wiped their mouths with a napkin and drew noisily through the straws of their milkshakes. Emilie's empty cup hit the table with a clack as she set it aside with a deep sigh of satisfaction.

Haley had polished off her meal in the blink of an eye. The girl must have been famished. She wiped a dab of mustard from her mouth with the back of her hand. A familiarity about her nagged at Jake. He tried to look past the dyed red hair, but the time or place he had seen her eluded him.

When they finished, Jake asked, "So, what are you two going to do now?"

Haley glanced up, but Emily answered. "Mom said Haley can stay at my place, so we were hoping you would drop us off. We have land training for ringette in the morning, so we'll take the bus there."

Then Jake remembered. Lately, he thought he still had a good, but very short, memory. "Now I remember where we met, Haley. You and Em were on the same ringette team last winter, right? I'm pretty sure I met your mom. She's blond, about your height, and wears glasses? Very pretty. If I remember correctly, she wore a team jersey. She had a cowbell that she rang every time your team scored, and she carried a big sign with 'Go Hawks' on it. Does that sound like her?"

"Yeah, that's my mom. She embarrassed me, but I wish that person still lived at my house. She's somebody else right now. Mom used to help me with my homework, but lately, she's always distracted when she comes home. She won't be home until late tonight. She never is on Monday nights. That's why I'm staying at Em's place." Haley's eyes glistened, as the words poured from her lips. Jake sensed she needed to talk. He felt sorry for the young girl.

Haley continued. "Mom came home one night and said she would be busy for a while and that I would have to be an adult and look after myself. I reminded her I'm 16 years old, and she said she had some-thing important to do. That someone she thought she knew might hurt people, and she had to stop it. She came in late last night and left again before I got up this morning. She hardly said anything, but she looked upset. I'm worried about her."

An uncomfortable apprehension slithered up Jake's spine at the mention of someone hurting people. "Well, can Emilie's mom help? Em has probably told you she's on the police force."

Haley nodded. "We talked about that, but I don't want to get my mom in trouble."

Jake rested his elbow on the table with his chin in his hand. His finger tapped his upper lip as he absorbed the information. He asked, "Did she tell you how she thought this person might hurt people? It sounds serious, but it seems like your mom is trying to do the right thing. You can be proud of her for that."

"She didn't say anything more. She wanted me to go along and 'be an adult.'" Haley used her fingers to punctuate the phrase with air quotes, but the tone of her voice revealed her true feelings.

Jake rested a comforting hand on the girl's shoulder. "Well, I'm sure once your mom deals with whatever is bothering her, she'll be back to normal. Sometimes people need time to sort things out. In the meantime, you and Emilie are welcome to drop in any time you like." He chuckled before adding, "I promise to have more food in the fridge."

The thought of Haley's mom trying to stop someone from hurting people sounded ominous, but Jake couldn't do anything about it. When Haley nodded, he turned to Emilie. The girl looked so much like her mom, with her olive complexion and fiery, dark eyes.

"How's your mom, Em? I'm meeting her for coffee tomorrow, but it's been a while."

A smile broadened the 16-year-old's lips. She was conscious of the attraction between Jake and her mom. Sometimes her observation skills seemed to Jake to be more like those of a 30-year-old, than someone about half that age.

Emilie said, "Mom's doing great. She's working on that murder that happened about a week ago. She says it's gang-related."

Jake frowned at the thought that a teenager should have to think about such things, but Emilie lived in that world, and Jake would also if he got too involved with Dani. Jake wanted to see more of Em's mom, and he imagined himself dealing with Dani's job as a homicide detective, but it could be dangerous work. Horrifying thoughts crept into his mind without warning. It had taken him three years to start recovering from the devastating ordeal of losing his wife, Mia. What if something happened to another loved one? And Dani had her demons from a failed marriage. Jake wanted to take it further, but so far, their respective previous experiences held them back. They had agreed to take things slowly.

He grabbed his rain jacket from the bench beside him and said, "Well, ladies. Ready to go? There's a bad-tempered cat that will be even grumpier, if I don't go home and feed him."

CHAPTER FOUR

JAKE WOKE A few minutes before eight the next morning, showered, fed Oliver, and headed out for his breakfast date with Dani. As he'd told Emilie, it had been too long since he had spoken to his friend.

Friend? he asked himself. She seemed more than a friend. They just needed to deal with their baggage before taking it further.

As he sauntered along the tree-shaded sidewalk, he still had to skip around a few puddles, but they were evaporating in the morning heat. Bright blue from horizon to horizon had pushed out the menacing clouds that had dominated the skies the previous day. The forecast called for a hot day, which the morning delivered in spades. The leaves on the trees lay unmoving, and Jake could not detect even a hint of a breeze. A trickle of sweat drizzled down his spine as he strolled along the sidewalk.

His destination lay dead ahead on Wellington Street. Brew and Buns had become the local favorite breakfast restaurant of the Saturday morning group. The corner of the restaurant was visible from his house, and while it didn't look like much from the outside, it offered a source of comfort. The weekly breakfasts with his friends provided one of the few bright spots in his life until recently, when Dani had changed his attitude. He examined the restaurant as he drew nearer. The plain, light brown, all-brick building had a small patio and a large window overlooking the street. A neon sign hanging on the wall above the window announced the name in clean, tall, straight lettering.

Regular patrons knew the restaurant's unusual name referred to the amazing coffee and delicious cinnamon rolls for which it was famous. The men of the breakfast group used to tease the previous owner that Brew and Buns would be a good name for a strip club, but they wouldn't dare say the same to the new twenty-something-year-old proprietor, Amanda. She told the breakfast group she had purchased the restaurant with a loan from her parents. The group supported and cheered the young woman for her entrepreneurial spirit and marveled at her guts to take on the challenge, as the restaurant industry gradually dragged itself from the hole created by the pandemic.

Jake loved the industrial look of the place with its exposed pipes. The converted warehouse featured long, thin light fixtures hanging on chains from the ceiling. Modern art adorned the vivid yellow drywall that ended about two-thirds of the way up. A built-in, linear electric fireplace near their table provided an amazing amount of heat in the winter. The blended industrial and contemporary décor appealed to the regular patrons. It pleased Jake that the new owner hadn't changed the décor, although granted, she still might change it as well as the name.

Amanda exited the restaurant to deliver two coffees and cinnamon rolls to an olive-skinned Venezuelan woman sitting at a table on the patio. The woman wore a casual business outfit, featuring a white blouse with tan slacks. Her pitch-black hair was pulled back from her face and held with a clip so that the tail cascaded to her shoulders. Jake had seen the style on her before and loved the way it highlighted her facial features. In her early fifties, she was so indisputably striking that she drew admiring glances from men, younger and older alike. The woman, Daniela Perez, worked as the staff sergeant in charge of the homicide division with the Ottawa Police Department and had been the one person who had somehow pulled Jake from the doldrums following his wife's death. She had divulged to Jake that she and her husband had endured an ugly divorce two years prior. Her mouth broadened in a wide smile when she noticed Jake.

Amanda greeted Jake as he entered the patio area. "No need to place your order, Jake. It's already done. No diet for you today." She chuckled as she bustled away to serve others. Although she had recently taken over ownership of the restaurant, Amanda had learned well from the previous owner and still served the same great coffee and cinnamon rolls.

Eight white tables with blue umbrellas and seating for four occupied the patio's interior, while identical, but smaller tables with seating for two sat beside the fence separating the enclosed area from the street. Planters with brightly colored flowers decorated the fence. Jake smiled as he approached a table for two along the fence where Dani sat.

Dani followed his progress as he strode toward her, then slid her chair back to wrap her arms around him in a big, long-lasting hug. "It seems like a long time," she breathed against the side of his face. Jake enjoyed the hug and wanted it to last as long as possible. When they reluctantly let go, he dragged the empty chair back and sat. Jake noticed that too much work had darkened the flesh beneath Dani's eyes. But those eyes. Bright. Intelligent. Kind. Yet, Jake had seen first-hand how they turned stone-cold when something angered her.

They enjoyed their coffee and rolls, but the conversation even more. They leaned close to each other as they exchanged casual tidbits about their daily lives. While the conversation wouldn't have meant anything to anyone else, it held meaning for Jake and Dani. They spoke about Emilie and Haley's visit to Jake. Then, keeping the conversation light, Dani said, "Did Emilie tell you she has her G1 license?"

Jake had long ago lost track of the process inexperienced drivers must go through to earn a driver's license. He vaguely recalled his daughter, Avery, achieving hers some 12 years earlier. Jake hadn't given it a second thought since.

"Wow, to me, Emilie is still a kid, not someone about to get a license. She must be happy. She probably forgot to mention it because of concern for her friend. What's involved? I've forgotten everything about it."

"I know. Not that long ago, Em hovered in that awkward stage between a youth and a teenager. Young enough to do kid things, like eat cotton candy or ride on the tilt-a-whirl, but too old to admit it was fun. Now, here she is getting her license. First, she had to pass an eye exam and a written test. She sailed through both, so now she has 12 months to practice. As long as there's an adult with a license in the car, she can drive."

A warning sign went up for Jake. Dani had a reputation for driving at least as fast as conditions allowed. "Will she be taking, uh, private lessons?"

He shielded his eyes from the sun peeking around the umbrella as he waited for the answer. He decided now would not be the right time to sip from his coffee cup in case the answer made him spit it out.

Dani said, "She will, but I'm teaching her the ropes."

Jake gulped. That's what concerned him. He had ridden with Dani many times. She loved the accelerator, while the brake remained foreign to her. The 'oh, shit' handle above the passenger door of Dani's car had borne the brunt of Jake's tensed fingers during his many rides with her. Her car had two speeds, fast and faster, and he wondered how that would translate into lessons for her daughter.

Dani burst into laughter. When she regained control of herself, she said, "You should see the look on your face. It's priceless. She's signed up with a private instructor starting next week. I'm showing her where everything is in the car, so she isn't at a complete loss when she starts. I'm aware, I sometimes drive a little fast."

Jake tried not to show his relief while he joined in the laughter. His thoughts focused more on Dani's term 'little' when a tune playing from her cell phone on the table interrupted them.

She glanced at the phone. "I better take this. It's Em."

Dani composed herself as she listened to her daughter. Emilie's unusually loud and excited voice echoed through the phone's receiver. Dani's face transformed before Jake's eyes, going from an open-mouthed laugh to a closed-lipped smile, to a taciturn frown. Her eyes narrowed as she listened, and her face changed into the one belonging to Detective Daniela Perez, Head of Homicide.

Most of Emilie's side of the conversation reverberated unintelligibly to Jake, but the clear implication sent a shiver racing down Jake's spine. Haley's mother hadn't returned home.

CHAPTER FIVE

D ANI SAT LOST in concentration when she hung up. Her brow furrowed, and she stared at something unseen on the table as she set the phone down.

"That conversation, or at least what I perceived, didn't sound good," Jake said as he reached out to put his hand on top of Dani's. She acknowledged the gesture by caressing the top of his hand with her thumb. She glanced at Jake.

"Hard to say what to make of it. Emilie says Haley's mom seems to have gone off the deep end. Haley intimated the same to you. I don't know the woman. Haley and Em are on the same ringette team, so they became friends. In Haley's words, her mom has been acting weird. Haley stayed over last night because they had land training this morning. They stopped at Haley's place to pick up her equipment, and it looked like her mom hadn't been home. She said her mom hadn't made the bed and had left no note for her, which Haley insisted was very unusual. She called her mom's office, but she didn't show up for work either. It sounds like the kid is worried sick."

Jake picked up his cup and sipped, grimacing as the remaining cold drops landed on his tongue. He peered through the window to see

Amanda behind the counter. He resolved to hail her for a refill when she returned to the patio. Recalling Haley's troubling comment from the night before, he said, "Did Haley ever mention anything to you about her mom trying to stop someone from hurting people?"

Dani's frown returned as her dark eyes zeroed in on Jake's.

"No, what do you mean?"

"Haley said she didn't want to get her mom in trouble by talking to you. Em told her you are a detective. I took the girls for something to eat, and Haley told me her mom wanted to stop someone from hurting people. She also said her mom joined an organization. That's all she told me."

Dani's frown deepened. "I'm going to talk to Em about this. I thought she would talk to me about anything now. She hasn't been mad at me every day recently, which is an improvement. But why didn't she tell me? Am I the big, bad authority figure she can't confide in?"

It pleased Jake that Dani still held his hand. Usually, she would have pulled away by now. He hadn't experienced such a tingling in his body since his first date with Mia. He said, "I might offer a reason. Having raised a daughter, I can tell you they have their secrets with their friends. It's important to them. Telling parents is sometimes the last resort. You're not the big, awful authority figure, but Haley seemed to be worried that it would be trouble for her mom if they told you about it. I assume she swore Em to secrecy. There are many plausible reasons for her mom not coming home, right? Maybe she came home and left again. Business meeting or something?"

Dani fiddled with her napkin as she considered Jake's question. "Em said Haley realized from the way the apartment looked that her mom hadn't come home. Also, there's the note, or lack thereof. It's possible. Everything has its place in my condo, and I would notice anything out of the ordinary."

Jake pictured his disheveled house and acknowledged to himself he couldn't say the same.

Dani continued. "The reason that always comes to mind is that she found the love of her life and slept over. That often turns out to be the case. You would think she would at least call her daughter, though."

Jake shook his head. "On the surface, it sure makes no sense. I saw the mom at Haley's ringette games. You would have seen her, too. She wore a team jersey and carried a sign. She rang a cowbell. Haley meant everything to her."

"I remember her now that you mention it. I think she embarrassed Haley, but you're right, she seemed to be a doting mother last winter. Things change, though."

"So, what happens next, Madame Detective?"

Dani regarded Jake before she responded. "If it looks like her mom is missing, I'll turn it over to the Missing Persons Unit, but I want to talk to Haley myself first. Want to come along?"

CHAPTER SIX

JAKE PICKED UP the tab, and he and Dani hurried to Dani's silver Hyundai Tucson, which she had driven to breakfast since she planned to go to work after. As they walked, Dani filled Jake in more about the phone call. Emilie had told Dani that she and Haley had finished their land training and returned to Dani's condo after leaving Haley's place. Haley had repeatedly called her mom with no answer and no response to the messages she had left.

When they arrived at the car, it became clear Dani had parked in a hurry. The vehicle's front end sat about two feet from the curb, while the back was three feet away. Dani started the car to allow the air conditioner to cool the interior and left the door open while she called her office. Jake slid onto the hot passenger seat and adjusted the vent, so the air blasting from it didn't hit him directly in the face.

He fastened his seat belt, while Dani finished her call. When she hung up, she said, "I have pressing files at the office, but they'll have to wait a few minutes. I need to find out how Haley is and whether they've heard anything." She started the car and mashed the accelerator, missing the fender of the car parked in front of hers by inches, while pressing Jake back in his seat. Dani had told him once that she had never had an accident. A few speeding tickets, yes, but no accidents. She clarified afterward that she meant no accidents for which the authorities blamed her. Still, Jake compared the likelihood of that happening to everyone in Canada winning the lottery three days in a row. He believed her, but it was an incredible statistic. He considered it a testament to her driving skills… or dumb luck.

Dani wheeled the car into her parking spot in the underground garage of her condo building. She and Emilie lived in a spacious two-bedroom condo on the 12th floor, overlooking the Ottawa River and the Gatineau Hills. The building sat just a few blocks from Jake's house, close enough to walk to Brew and Buns. The light gray brick building carried the name in stylized cast iron writing on the front. She had mentioned to Jake once that she worried the rent may someday be out of reach, but for now, it remained affordable.

They rode the elevator to the 12th floor, and when they entered the condo, they found Emilie and Haley talking quietly on the sofa. Haley looked pale; her eyebrows drawn together in worry. The sun shining on the girls through the window created a stark contrast between Haley's pasty skin and her electric red hair. Dani joined them on the sofa, sitting beside Haley. Jake sat in an opposite chair.

"Any news about your mom, Haley?" Dani asked.

Haley's lower lip trembled as she said, "Nothing. I'm so scared something has happened to her. She didn't answer her cell phone. I left a bunch of messages, but she hasn't returned any of them."

Dani leaned forward, drawing the distraught girl into her confidence. Emilie threw her arm around her friend's shoulders.

Dani searched Haley's hazel eyes. "Could your mom have gone to a meeting today, earlier than usual, or stayed with a friend?"

"She wouldn't do that without calling me or leaving a note. Anytime she left before I got up, she would always put out a plate, knife, and fork to remind me to eat. She would always leave a note to tell me to have a nutritious breakfast. She always said breakfast is the most important meal of the day, especially when I'm training for ringette. Even though I stayed with Em, she would have left a note for me or called, just to tell me to have a good day. She didn't leave a note this morning. If she stayed with a friend, she would have called. It makes no sense." Haley stifled a sniffle before she mumbled, "I'm sure something has happened to her."

"Okay, Haley, can we go to your place to look around?

Haley nodded glumly, and they left the building and piled into Dani's Hyundai to make the short drive to the apartment the young girl shared with her mom. Dani drove at a reasonable speed, at least in Dani's world, and they soon reached Haley's building. Jake stared out the window at the cars parked on the street as questions about the events of the last half hour slammed into each other in his head. He felt so sorry for Haley. Nobody should have to go through this, let alone a 16-year-old.

They took the stairs to the condo on the second floor of an older, red brick, three-story building. What the apartment space lacked in size, it made up in personality with its light gray walls adorned with family pictures. Many of the photos displayed Haley in various uniforms as she graduated from one level of ringette team to the next.

Dani said to Haley, "I'm just going to have a quick look around, okay?" When Haley nodded dejectedly again, Jake followed Dani into the kitchen where, as Haley had said, the table lay completely bare. Dani opened the door to the dishwasher where clean dishes sat untouched. The empty fridge reminded Jake of his place.

The compact, tidy bedroom appeared well kept, save for the unmade bed. An eight-by-ten inch picture of Haley smiled from the four-drawer wooden dresser, where Cassie would see it when she went to bed or woke up. The entire apartment seemed normal to Jake. No sign of a purse or cellular phone. Nothing out of place. An apartment where a woman and her daughter lived, and one to which a mother should have returned last night to be with her 16-year-old. For some reason, she hadn't.

They returned to the living room, where Emilie and Haley sat quietly on the sofa. Haley sat with her hands between her knees, staring at the front door, as if willing her mom to walk through.

Dani said, "Haley, where would your mom keep your suitcases?"

Haley frowned at the question before answering. "They're in the storage locker."

"Can you show me?"

Haley and Emilie rose from the sofa. Haley removed a key from a drawer in the kitchen and led the solemn group to the door to exit the apartment, when Dani stopped her and pointed to a closet. "Please check to see if your mom's jacket is there. The one she would take for a cool evening."

Haley opened the door and shuffled the hangers aside, before pointing to a lightweight hooded jacket. "She loves that jacket. It's so soft." She rubbed the fabric between her thumb and finger. "Mom wears it all the time when it's cool outside. If she planned to be gone for long, she would have taken that jacket."

Dani thanked her, and Haley led them to a staircase at the end of the hall that descended to the basement. A musty smell tickled Jake's nose when they entered a dark space lit only by a few low-wattage bulbs. Jake suspected the landlord did it to conserve energy, but he had seen some brighter back alleys at night. Darkness enshrouded corners of the hallways where anything might be lurking. Rows of steel mesh cages, many crammed from floor to ceiling, held the apartment dwellers' belongings.

Haley murmured, "I hate this place. Mom won't let me come down here by myself, and I don't want to."

Jake understood why. It was downright creepy.

Haley turned on the flashlight on her phone and aimed it toward a cage about halfway down a corridor, where two red expandable suitcases lay on top of a small washstand amid other paraphernalia. The light brightened the area straight ahead but deepened the shadows on the sidelines.

They wandered closer, brushing cobwebs away as they walked.

"Does anything look different?" Dani asked.

Haley examined the pile before responding, barely above a whisper. "No, we came down here a couple of days ago to look for a portable radio Mom stored when we moved here. You probably noticed it on the kitchen counter. She wanted to hear the news when she worked in the kitchen. We found it, and everything else looks the same."

Fingerprints on the dusty suitcases confirmed someone had moved recently among them, so Haley's explanation made sense. Dani nodded, and they returned to the apartment.

"Here's what I'm going to do, sweetheart," said Dani. "I'm going to report your mom missing to the woman in charge of the Missing Persons Unit at my office. She may wait a while to see if your mom returns, but she's going to want to talk to you. Her name is Maria Allard. If you can put together a list of all your mom's friends that you remember, it would be very helpful. Jake mentioned your mom talked about an organization she joined. If you have any information, or can remember her saying more about it, please pass it along to Maria. She will also want to look at your mom's social media, so she will want to see her computer. She may even want to borrow it for a while. It's nothing to be alarmed about. She's just doing her job. Maria's very nice and easy to talk to. You can be a big help to her by doing everything she asks, okay?"

Haley gasped as she inhaled. Her eyes misted over. Jake sensed that reporting her mom's disappearance to Missing Persons just made things much more real for the teenager.

Dani continued, "Do you have anyone you can stay with, Haley?"

Jake noticed Emilie's eyes imploring her mom to let her stay with them, but Dani stood steadfastly, waiting for an answer.

"I can probably stay with my aunt until you find my mom. I've stayed with her before. You *will* find my mom, right Mrs. Perez?"

"Let's have a chat with your aunt. You should stay with her until we get this sorted out. We'll find your mom, Haley. Don't you worry."

To Jake's ears, Dani didn't sound convinced.

CHAPTER SEVEN

HALEY'S AUNT KATHERINE lived in the historic neighborhood of Rockcliffe Park, a short drive from Westboro. As they drove down the tree-lined residential streets, past rocky outcroppings, Haley explained that her aunt married a senior executive with a high-tech company. The name of the company escaped her.

"But we're happy where we are," she added, as if she felt compelled to justify the neighborhood in which she and her mom lived compared to her aunt's luxurious surroundings.

They parked behind a Mercedes in the circular driveway of an awe-inspiring brick house with a multiple-car garage. Dani suggested Jake and Emilie wait in the car while she and Haley went inside to speak to Katherine. Haley grabbed the backpack she had thrown some clothes in before leaving the apartment and trudged behind Dani. A tall woman with platinum hair and wearing a white pantsuit greeted the pair at the door.

Jake and Emilie sat in the car, waiting. Finally, Emilie interrupted the silence, asking quietly, "What do you think happened to Mrs. Wright, Jake? Why didn't she call Haley? Do you think she's okay?"

"I'm sure your mom and her team will do everything they can to find her, Em. There has to be an explanation for her disappearance that makes sense."

"Did you ever write about missing people when you were a reporter?"

"I did."

"Were they found?"

Jake hesitated, recalling the missing person cases he had reported on. Sometimes they didn't turn out well, but he didn't want to worry Emilie more. Often, missing people are disoriented and eventually turn up. Or, they are victims of foul play and are found dead, or never seen again. He replied, "I remember one case when a four-year-old vanished from a campsite, and it took two weeks to find her. They found her unharmed in someone's house. They arrested the man. That case turned out well."

"It must have scared the parents."

"It terrified them, but it just shows you can never give up hope. And with the team they have at the Ottawa Police Department, I'm sure they'll find Haley's mom."

Dani soon exited the house and climbed into her car. She started it and wheeled out of the laneway.

Jake asked, "Is everything okay in there?"

"Yes, the news shocked Haley's aunt, but she recovered quickly enough to be a steadying influence. Haley seemed reasonably confident her mom would turn up. It'll be difficult for everyone until we find her."

Emilie listened quietly as Jake asked for the second time in a few hours, "What happens next?"

"I've already alerted Maria that Cassie didn't come home last night. I mentioned to you she's in charge of Missing Persons. She will plan with her investigators. The first thing they will do is to ask Haley and her aunt for a list of Cassie's friends and places she frequented. They'll investigate her social media, financial transactions, phone calls, her health card activity, those kinds of things."

Jake kept his eye on the traffic as they slowed for a light beside the granite pedestal and arch of the National War Memorial on Wellington

Street. Emilie, who was developing a keen interest in her mom's work, asked from the back seat, "Don't they need a search warrant to do all that?"

"Not anymore, sweetie. The *Missing Persons Act* that came into effect in Ontario in 2019 changed all that. Even if there is no criminal investigation underway, if certain criteria apply to a missing person, we can request information with an urgent demand as long as it is written on the appropriate form."

"What if you don't find her right away?"

"The file is never closed, honey. We'll keep looking."

They arrived at Dani's condo building, where Emilie got out and blew a kiss to her mom. Dani continued to Jake's house, where they pulled into the driveway. She glanced at Jake as he undid his seatbelt.

"You've been quiet, Jake. The gears must be turning."

Jake flashed a half-hearted smile. "I'm just worried about Haley. I hope her mom turns up soon. Is there anything I can do?"

Dani's face brightened. "Yes, there is something you can do. You can take me out for dinner. Oh, wait. Am I being too forward?" Her lips widened as she waited for a response.

"I would be happy to. When you get a chance, check your calendar, and tell me what day suits you. My schedule is pretty open."

They hugged each other before Jake walked into the house. He marveled at Dani's ability to switch gears and suggest a dinner date, when she had just found out about Cassie's unusual behavior. He understood that's how she coped as a homicide detective. She couldn't get too close to a case, especially when she knew the people involved. Otherwise, it might destroy her.

Oliver greeted Jake at the door with a loud meow.

"So, Oliver, I guess you think your throat's cut. I'm kind of feeling that way myself. I haven't eaten since breakfast."

Jake rectified Oliver's situation by pouring a generous helping of cat food into his bowl. The cat munched it down like he hadn't eaten in months, barely taking a breath to look up when his owner returned to the kitchen from the bathroom.

Jake retrieved his grocery list from the kitchen table and headed to the door once again. He checked for his keys and, as usual, they were in a different pocket than he expected them to be. This time, he didn't attribute it to a failing memory. No, this time, the list of friends and acquaintances the police would ask Haley and her aunt to put together distracted him. He understood the reality—that the Ottawa Police, like any other in North America, had severe staff shortages. From speaking with Dani, he understood the Missing Persons Unit comprised a sergeant and two investigators who handled over 2,500 cases per year. The list of persons reported missing grew with each passing week as the aging population developed dementia.

He sat at the kitchen table watching Oliver and considering how to use his investigative skills to assist, recognizing the fine line between helping and interfering. Haley worrying about her mom, and the effect the situation would have on Emilie, left a rock-like lump in his stomach. If he wanted to help investigate why Cassie Wright didn't return home, the first thing would be to get his hands on that list.

CHAPTER EIGHT

THE TICKING CLOCK in the empty house sometimes drove Jake batty. It only survived because his wife Mia had loved it, and it had been easier to tolerate it when he was younger. They paid a small fortune for the vintage metal-framed beast that occupied more than its share of space on the wall in the sunroom. Its gaudy silver and charcoal Roman numerals attracted Mia enough to convince Jake to buy it, but he never paid much attention to it when she was alive. Since then, it seemed louder, and he had stopped himself from donating it to the local Value Village on more than a few occasions. Guilt always overtook him when he thought about getting rid of it, but it remained on very thin ice.

5:28.

5:29.

Jake left the room to distract his mind from the clock and to throw together a broccoli frittata. The simple groceries he purchased restocked the pantry and refrigerator and allowed for meager meal preparation. The usual supply of TV dinners had a special place in the refrigerator. He had mastered the cooking time for the frittata, thanks to a few failures. He would probably starve if it weren't for eggs, although the doctor had warned him that his weekly intake contributed to the rise in his cholesterol. They had pills for that.

Now he sat in his recliner, trying to ignore the clock. It seemed especially loud in the quiet house tonight. Oliver had disappeared to another room, likely because he didn't want to listen to the damned ticking either. Jake regarded the last photo taken of his wife facing his recliner in the sunroom. He said, "Mia, would you mind if I get rid of the clock?"

The photo offered no response.

The picture showed the happy couple celebrating their 33rd wedding anniversary during a Caribbean cruise. Mia, in her floppy, multi-colored sunhat, dark one-piece bathing suit, and golden-brown complexion, beamed at Jake from the photo with the stark white, luxury liner in the background. Not long after the cruise, she succumbed to an aneurysm. He loved the picture and often talked to it during the loneliest of times. He had even sought the picture's approval to date Dani. Although the picture never answered, Jake sensed Mia did, and her reply told him she didn't want him to be alone.

He anticipated Dani's phone call, so they could schedule their dinner date. The clock's second hand ticked inexorably toward infinity. He debated with himself about calling Emilie for Haley's contact information. Finally, he did it. Even though the clock's ticking drove him mad, it also reminded him that time marched on. Too much time had already passed since Cassie hadn't returned home.

Emilie answered the phone with an upbeat tone. She told Jake she had been drawing something inspired by the *Divergent* books in her sketchbook. Jake had no clue what the *Divergent* books were, but promised to look at her latest drawing when he had a chance. The detailed charcoal sketches always amazed him, although he had to admit he didn't understand some of the recent ones.

She readily supplied Haley's contact information and told him that Dani was still working. Jake thanked her and wished her well with her driving lessons before hanging up.

Oliver wandered into the sunroom, glanced at Jake with a stern look and a rather dispirited silence, and settled in front of the unlit fireplace. If the cat had more prominent shoulders, he would have shrugged.

Jake dialed Haley's number, and the subdued girl answered on the first ring.

"Hi, Haley. It's Jake Scott. How're you doing?"

"I'm okay, thanks, Mr. Scott. The police sent over a list of questions that we answered as much as we could. Things like names of friends, where she worked, and stuff like that. Aunt Katherine and I met the police at our apartment. They took Mom's computer and looked around the apartment a lot like Emilie's mom did. We gave the investigator some pictures from the wall and mom's computer. They asked my aunt and me some questions. We just got back. We gave them the list of names they asked for. It had a few people on it. It feels like a waste of time, because my mom is going to come back."

The girl sniffed, and the faint rustle of a tissue whiffed through the phone.

"I'm sure she will, but right now, it's tough. Stay strong, Haley. The police will do everything they can to find your mom. It's in expert hands. You should continue your daily routine to help keep your mind off things. I'd happily give you a ride to a practice or games or anything."

This time, a sigh came through the phone's receiver.

"That's what the police officer said, to keep up my daily routine. I don't know if I could concentrate on practice. I'm so worried. The Ottawa Police missing persons' site online has pictures of a bunch of people. One poor lady has been missing for over 40 years! My mom will come back, but I can't imagine what it's like for that poor woman's family."

"Well, just let the police do their job, Haley." He realized what he wanted to ask her would contradict his suggestion. He asked anyway.

"Listen, Haley, would you mind sharing the list you put together for the police with me? A scan of a photo of your mom, too? I'll talk to people on the list to see if I can uncover anything. The police will talk to all of them, but perhaps I can help. As you know, I used to be a reporter, so sticking my nose where it doesn't belong is part of my nature." He hoped his attempted humor would put Haley a little more at ease.

"I'll attach it to an email and send it right away. There isn't much on it. Mom didn't talk about her friends much. I don't know anything about the organization she talked about. Aunt Katherine doesn't either."

"Okay, thank you. I appreciate it. You take care." Jake recalled from his reporting days that one source often led to another, and a list such as the one Katherine and her niece cobbled together would eventually expand.

"I will. Oh, and Mr. Scott, I want to help too. If there's anything I can do, please tell me."

Jake promised to keep Haley informed and hung up. Within seconds, a notification showed up on his phone announcing an email message in the inbox. The email had the list, and a scanned photo was attached. As Haley said, the list wasn't long, just five names. No phone numbers, just names. Two had the name of Cassie's workplace noted beside them. The names of a friend and a fitness instructor followed. The fifth and last had nothing beside it, but the name made Jake raise his eyebrows. He printed the two documents, set the list on the end table, and slid the folded picture into his wallet.

The clock ticked loudly toward nine p.m. Jake pondered his next move. The police would make their round of calls and check social media for Cassie's recent activities. If Cassie hadn't returned by morning, he would start his inquiries.

CHAPTER NINE

MORNING BROUGHT NOTHING new. Oliver remained grumpy, Jake still rattled around the house by himself, and the clock still ticked noisily. Dani hadn't called to schedule a dinner date. And Cassandra Wright had not returned, according to Haley's Aunt Katherine.

The time had come.

Jake used Canada 411, Canada's online phone directory, to track down the first person on the list, Noah Kirkland, Cassie's colleague at a large government institution downtown. Jake had a vague idea about who the government departments served. This one had something to do with managing the government's finances. The purpose of the department didn't interest him.

While Jake expected an administrative assistant to pick up the phone, he guessed times had changed as Kirkland answered the call himself.

After the introductions, Jake asked Kirkland if he knew Cassandra Wright. He replied he did, and that the police had informed him his colleague had disappeared. Jake asked if they could meet for coffee. He always wanted to watch a person's face when he asked questions. The face frequently reveals secrets that a voice expertly conceals.

Kirkland said, "Who are you again?"

"I'm a former reporter and a friend of the family." Jake paused, thinking the statement might be a bit of a stretch. He added, "The police are doing their job. Based on my reporting days, I sense that the Missing Persons Unit is short-staffed, so I'm just doing what I can in the background. I promise I'll pass anything I learn to the police. I'd appreciate it if you can spare a few minutes for me."

Kirkland agreed to meet at Starbucks downtown. Jake checked the man's Facebook profile so he would recognize him. The pictures made him look tall and athletic, his posts depicting him in various sports activities. Jake considered the man's face more beautiful than handsome. He had shaped his eyebrows, and his nose seemed narrower than the average man's.

After driving through the shimmering heat and parking, Jake reached the Starbucks entrance simultaneously with a man dressed in a golf shirt and dress pants. He noted the photos didn't lie. Noah Kirkland towered a good three inches above Jake with a lithe runner's frame. Jake noticed he walked with the effortless grace of a ballet dancer as they moved to the counter to order their coffees. Jake selected a cinnamon raisin bagel warmed with butter, while his former personal trainer's voice in his head chastised him for the irresistible 270-calorie delight. His companion ordered coffee. The only blemish Jake saw on the man was a small raised, purplish birthmark on his forearm that peeked from beneath his sleeve when he reached for the milk.

They found two empty armchairs, and Jake started the conversation by asking how long Noah had known Cassie. He replied they had worked together for about five years.

"Did you know her well?"

His voice sounded deeper than Jake expected. "We regularly had coffee together. The police asked me the same question. If you're asking if we did more than that, the answer's no. I'm merely interested in women as friends, if you know what I mean." His somber eyes penetrated Jake's.

Jake hadn't expected an answer to this unasked question. A little defensive, but Jake interpreted it as a pre-emptive strike to deflect any notions of a romantic connection linking him and Cassie.

"When did you see her last?"

Noah sighed. "Friday. A day like every other. We had coffee together as we normally do."

"Anyone else ever join you for coffee?"

"Yeah, the boss sometimes, Kevin Hall."

Jake remembered the name from the list. "I'll talk to him. Did Cassie seem any different lately?"

Kirkland's thin eyebrows drew together. "You sound like the detective. There were issues. I noticed her demeanor changed, more withdrawn, like she was depressed. She didn't talk about her daughter as much. The divorce had been difficult for her. She often griped about her job, and she'd recently missed out on a promotion. I think everything just got to her lately."

"Do you think she might have harmed herself?"

This time, Noah's eyebrows rose as his eyes widened. He made a harsh sound of derision through his nose. "Cassie? Not a chance. She'd never leave her daughter alone. She loved her too much. Likely she met some guy, and she will turn up. She did the online dating thing."

"That's interesting. The police will discover that when they get into her social media. I'm sure they'll investigate it."

"Don't misunderstand me, Mr. Scott. I like Cassie, and I hope she shows up soon. There's nothing more I can tell you. Sorry, I wish I could."

They chatted a few more minutes until Jake decided he had learned as much as he was going to. The meeting clearly annoyed Noah, as he repeatedly stated he had answered all the questions before, but Jake sensed the man wanted to help. Jake asked, "Is your boss in this morning? I'd like to talk to him."

"He was there when I left." Noah took out a pen and scrawled a number on his soiled napkin, then slid it across the table to Jake. "Call him. I think he'll have some useful information," he said as he turned on his heel and glided to the door.

Pleasant fellow, Jake thought facetiously as he considered the dating site angle and dialed the number for Kevin Hall. He resolved to check the site when he got home. Hall answered himself, just as Kirkland had done. The voice sounded raspy, like a long-time smoker.

Jake explained the reason for his call and received an even more defensive reaction than he had from Kirkland. Hall explained the police had already interviewed him, and he had no interest in rehashing his responses to a reporter, let alone a former one. Even though Jake pleaded for a few minutes of his time, Hall remained adamant, even belligerent. *What's with these people Cassie works with?*

Jake wondered if Kevin Hall had reacted the same with the police. On one level, he understood. Admittedly, it had only been one workday since Cassie disappeared, and this guy had an important job to get back to. On another, he didn't understand why someone wouldn't want to do everything possible to find an employee who everyone agreed had done something completely out of character.

With any luck, Cassie Wright had already returned home with a logical explanation. If not, something about this man's attitude blipped on Jake's radar and set his investigative juices flowing. Now Jake had two things to investigate—the dating site angle and everything he could find about Kevin Hall.

CHAPTER TEN

WHEN JAKE ARRIVED home, Oliver greeted him at the entrance as he usually did when he heard the garage door open. The cat had few needs: food, milk, the occasional pet, and sleep. His master provided three of the four. Sometimes Oliver's simplistic life made Jake a little jealous.

He fed the cat and contacted Jessica Davis, who Katherine and Haley had identified on their list as a friend of Cassie's. Jessica's voice sounded pleasant, and Jake imagined her to be older than Cassie, although he conceded trying to guess age by a voice could be problematic. She seemed eager to get together, but unavailable until the next day. He posed questions like those he had asked Kirkland and Hall. She supplied similar answers, most notably, that Cassie seemed despondent lately. Noah Kirkland had used a similar word. He referred to her as "depressed." A theme was developing.

A thought occurred to Jake as a beep sounded on his phone, indicating another call. He ignored it. "Jessica, were you aware that Cassie used a dating site?"

"Yes, I told the police that. She and I use the same site. It's called Cupid's Choice."

"Do you know if she met anyone through the site?"

"I can't be certain. A few months ago, she seemed happier. There could have been several reasons, but one might be that she met someone. I asked outright, but she wouldn't respond. She kind of played coy, as if she preferred not to reveal the information. I get it. I met someone and blabbed about it to everyone. The guy was a complete jerk. He talked endlessly about the hours he spent in the gym. He would point out his biceps to anyone who showed any interest, and many people who didn't. Sorry, it still pisses me off. At some point, Cassie became unhappy. I don't know what happened. She didn't talk about it."

"I assume you would sign up for this Cupid's Choice site online. Show your likes and dislikes? That kind of thing?" Jake recalled looking into one at his daughter Avery's urging, but that was as far as it went.

"Yes, exactly. There is no actual contact with a human being unless there's a match that interests you. It's up to you to connect with the person. I wish I could tell you more about Cassie's involvement with the site, but that's all I know."

"I appreciate your time, Jessica. Would you mind if I contact you if I have more questions?"

When Jessica said she didn't mind, Jake hung up. He checked his messages to find one from Dani asking him to call. When he did, she answered with, "Hi, handsome. What have you been up to?"

A niggle in the corner of his brain urged him to tell her about questioning Cassie's friends and colleagues, but he ignored it for now. Instead, he told her he hadn't been doing much of anything.

She said, "If you're still interested in dinner, I have some time tonight."

A twinge of excitement raced up Jake's spine. "I've been waiting for your call, and I would love to have dinner tonight. How about seven o'clock at our favorite Italian restaurant?" They agreed and hung up, so Dani could go back to work.

Jake wandered into his office, sat, and searched out Cupid's Choice on his computer. Based in New York, it boasted millions of users and an exceptional rating. He wouldn't know if Cassie had met someone on the site unless he could access her computer. The police would have already gained access to Cassie's social media through the *Missing Person's Act* and would likely know Cupid's Choice. He decided he might talk to Cassie's sister Katherine about it.

Next, he searched for Kevin Hall's name on Facebook. The senior government manager's profile picture showed a man with a thin face and pale blue eyes. He combed his hair straight back, perhaps not the best style for a man whose nose came to a point. A half-smile completed the picture of the man Jake spoke to on the phone. One post displayed an expensive watch on his wrist, half covering a scar. The caption noted he had been saving for years to reward himself. Most of his posts grumbled about lost freedoms, and in one, he grudgingly admitted to being vaccinated to keep his job. A review of his Twitter account revealed similar rantings and some retweets of conspiracy theory memes Jake considered offensive. Not enough to get Hall fired, apparently, but they made his views clear.

Jake spent the rest of the afternoon examining the social media accounts of the people on the list and making notes. He confirmed his suspicions that Jessica was older than Cassie. Possibly, none of his findings had anything to do with Cassie's failure to return home.

The time came to prepare for his date with Dani. He pulled on a lightweight pair of gray pants and a blue sport shirt with a floral pattern. He glanced in the mirror, grimacing at his choice, thinking it might look like an old man's shirt. In his mind, it complemented his deep blue eyes, but what did he know? His hair seemed grayer every day, but at least he remained thankful he had some. Like his late father, the receding hair at the front would someday meet the bald patch at the back. He was in no hurry for that to happen, but it was just hair. His dad always said cheerfully, while patting his nearly bald head, "It's what's under the hair that counts." He straightened and pulled his shoulders back to take advantage of his five-foot ten-inch frame. Better. He silently thanked his trainer for showing him exercises to tighten his spongy stomach muscles, although a lot of work remained in that department.

Satisfied, he headed out to pick up Dani, happy they agreed he would drive. She greeted him downstairs at her condo, dressed in a red silk wrap dress. She could wear a burlap sack and still appeal to Jake. After a brief hug, they set out for the Italian restaurant on Wellington Street that they had frequented a few times. They ordered wine and laughed when they both ordered the tortellini gorgonzola, even though the menu offered plenty of other choices. It reminded Jake how their tastes merged on so many things. They amicably chatted about inconsequential subjects. The conversation eventually veered to Dani's work, as it often did. Jake suspected they did that to avoid the elephant in the room, their relationship. This time, though, he wanted to know if the Missing Persons Unit had made progress on finding Haley's mom.

Dani said, "They're following the procedures, checking with friends and family members, looking at Cassie's recent activities, including her credit card usage. I'm confident they're doing everything they can. So far, nothing significant has turned up. They found out she had been using a dating site and may have found someone of interest." She stopped chewing and cocked an eye at Jake. "Since we're on the subject, I understand you've been doing a little investigating into Cassie's case on your own and probably already know all this."

Jake sat back with a gulp. To the casual observer, his mouth formed an "O," but it was actually half of an "uh-oh" as he waited for Dani to unleash her world-famous scolding. He managed, "How do you find out about these things?"

Dani finished chewing before saying casually, "I'm a mom and an investigator, remember? I know everything."

Jake couldn't help but stammer. "I'm… uh… just trying to help where I can. I know the Missing Persons Unit is understaffed, so I'm looking into a few things. If I uncover anything, I'll tell them. I promise."

"Uh, huh? Make sure you do, Jake Scott." Dani emphasized the point by waving her fork at Jake's chest. Then she said, "This dish is delicious. No wonder we aren't adventurous when we come here. I could eat this every day."

Thankfully, Jake survived relatively unscathed, and they continued to chat through their meal, neither one broaching the history of their respective previous relationships. Jake reasoned they should just let things develop organically. He was about to ask Dani's opinion, when her phone rang. He thought, *people probably finished conversations before cell phones came along.*

Dani answered with a cheery hello, before her face transformed into investigator mode. She posed questions like "when" and "where." An uneasy feeling rested on Jake's shoulders, as if he had put on a pair of lead-lined football pads.

When Dani hung up, she said, "Sorry, Jake, but I'm going to have to forego dessert. A hiker discovered a body in an area around Mer Bleu Bog on Anderson Road. It's a Caucasian woman in her forties. It could be Cassie Wright."

CHAPTER ELEVEN

DANI DIDN'T WANT to waste time retrieving her car, so Jake drove his Subaru east from Ottawa toward Anderson Road. Dani encouraged him to speed up more than once, and Jake considered pulling over to let her drive. The 18-minute drive took 14 minutes through the back roads suggested by Jake's GPS.

Thoughts collided in Jake's head like popping corn as he considered the consequences if the body turned out to be Cassie Wright. It would devastate Haley, her aunt, and any other family members and friends. There would be repercussions for Emilie. The meal he enjoyed with Dani rested like a lump of coal in the pit of his stomach.

They turned onto Anderson Road toward the Mer Bleu Bog, where the unmistakable red and blue flashing lights designated the crime scene. Several police cars sat parked haphazardly on the road, along with a paramedic vehicle, an ambulance, and the medical examiner's car. At the perimeter, Jake recognized the uniformed police officer holding up his hand. Dani had once introduced Constable Davidson to him, but Jake didn't remember the officer's first name.

Dani leaned across Jake to speak to Davidson as they rolled to a stop. "You remember Jake Scott, Constable?"

He nodded at Jake before addressing Dani, "Yes, I do, Staff Sergeant. The body is along the trail, about half a mile. The reeds and cattails hid it a few feet off the trail, but a hiker noticed the sun reflecting off her watch. She hasn't been there long." He glanced at Dani's dress and leather slip-on loafers. "Uh, you might want different clothes to go in there, Staff Sergeant. I have an extra Tyvek suit in the Explorer up ahead, if you would like to use it. It's the second vehicle from the left."

"Thanks, Constable. I'll take you up on that." She turned to Jake. "Drive as close as you can to the trailhead, and I'll walk from there."

Davidson stepped aside to allow Jake room to pass, and he angled his vehicle in beside a Ford Explorer with the lights flashing on the pulled-down visor. He stared into the setting sun at the bog with trepidation. The area was declared an internationally significant wetland in 1995, but it looked more typical of the Arctic Circle, than the Ottawa Valley. Normally, the reeds and grass waving gently in the evening breeze would provide a sense of calm, but tonight the crime scene tape and long shadows of people milling about in the distance had an eerie effect. While hikers and skiers enjoyed the trails in the winter and summer months, tonight it offered something unspeakable. Someone's loved one lay dead in the marsh, and it could be Cassie Wright.

"You can stay in the car." Dani's quiet voice snapped Jake to attention.

"No," he replied. "I think… I think I want to go with you."

"Okay, you know the drill. Stay well back. Touch nothing."

Dani found the polyethylene suit in the Explorer and pulled it on over her dress. Jake flushed as the suit tugged at the bottom of the dress, exposing her leg to mid-thigh. Although paper-thin and disposable, the suit offered some protection from the marsh. Tossing her shoes in Jake's car, she pulled on a pair of booties next, and handed a pair to Jake. "There might be usable prints on the boardwalk," she explained. She asked for a pair of latex gloves from an officer as she exited the car. She tugged them on and strode down the boardwalk, with Jake following.

Jake had seen bodies during his lengthy career as a reporter. It had bothered him at first, but he learned to disassociate himself. It became part of the job. No one relished it, but it was something that had to be done. Dani dealt with it in the same way. Remaining detached became the defense mechanism used by professionals to hang on to some level of sanity while seeing the worst humanity offered.

This time was more personal, as he expected Dani would confirm that Cassie Wright lay in the bog. Jelly seemed to have replaced the muscle tone in his legs as he trudged after his friend. He had to know, but the thought of what he might see weighed like an anchor. He continued to follow until they reached the location. The soft patter of their bootie-covered shoes on the boardwalk seemed incongruous with death.

When they arrived near the crime scene, Dani instructed Jake to stay well back. The police had scattered evidence markers in various places. The gathered officers, along with the height of the reeds, obscured Jake's view. He glimpsed the body lying fully clothed like a rag doll, half-submerged in water about ten feet from the boardwalk. Crime scene investigators had trampled the surrounding reeds that would have hidden it from hikers, although carefully enough to secure the scene itself. The perpetrator must have waded into the shallow water carrying the body.

Dani nodded to a man whose tie peeked out from beneath white coveralls. Jake assumed him to be the medical examiner, and the man confirmed it when Jake strained to hear him say, "I did a cursory examination. There's an unusual mark on the side of the neck. It looks like a needle mark. The only reason I noticed it is because of the surrounding bruising. You'll see it looks similar to someone taking a blood sample and missing the vein on the first attempt. Might be that someone poisoned her. Don't quote me," he added quickly. "Nobody else has touched the body. Your crew has been gathering evidence and taking pictures."

"Time of death?"

"I can't be certain until I get it back to the morgue, but based on the state of secondary flaccidity of the body, I would say she has been here from one to three days."

Jake sucked in a quick breath. He was familiar with the term the doctor used. It meant the body had reached maximum rigor mortis, and the muscles had loosened because of the chemical changes that take place after death. The time fit with Cassie's failure to return. He tried to get a better look through the reeds. The woman lay face down. Blond hair, about the same length as he remembered Cassie's, fell around her shoulders, and obscured her face. Her dusky pink, square-neck sundress rode up her thighs. Jake's dread weighed heavier by the second.

He glanced back at Dani, who waded into the murky, ankle-deep water. The medical examiner followed in his rubber boots. They splashed through the muddy water, shoving aside the thick reeds that impeded their progress and scaring up a flock of indignant blackbirds watching from a distance. Dani leaned over the body when they arrived, the minutes silently ticking away as she did her examination. She focused on the woman's neck. Eventually, she nodded to the corner. He reached underneath the body to turn it over.

Jake sucked in a breath, wanting to avert his eyes, but unable to, as he strained to see if the body belonged to Cassie Wright.

CHAPTER TWELVE

THE MEDICAL EXAMINER tugged on one shoulder of the body to turn it over. Jake heard him grunt as he pulled it free from the mud, which seemed to have a firm grip. Wet, blond hair flopped across the woman's face, still concealing Jake's view. A sigh of frustration escaped his lips as the medical examiner leaned over the body, and Dani turned away from him to observe. Not knowing surely weighed more heavily than learning the truth.

It seemed like hours, but it took a little over a minute before Dani turned and shook her head. The body didn't belong to Cassie Wright! Jake's shoulders sagged at the relief Dani's head shake triggered, but it was short-lived. The woman would have a family of her own, just as desperate to find out what had happened to her. The realization soon overtook the solace of knowing that Haley's mother didn't rest in the bog.

After a few minutes, Dani waded back to the boardwalk. Jake offered his hand, which she accepted and hoisted herself up on the wooden planks, her booties muddied and dripping from the ordeal. Water from the material of her coverup splattered onto the wooden walkway. She motioned with her chin toward the vehicles on the road, and they silently headed in that direction. After removing the Tyvek suit and booties and depositing them in a black plastic garbage bag, which she threw into the back of the Explorer, she found a towel and dried her legs before putting on her shoes. She smoothed her dress and fluffed her hair with her hand. Glancing down, she said, "Well, it doesn't look too bad, considering I've been wading through reeds and muddy water. I need to change and go to the office to organize the investigation. My crew will gather the evidence. I'm sorry our date ended this way, Jake."

"It's okay, Dani. I understand." His mind wandered as he walked to the driver's door. Did he understand? Did he *really* understand? If he and Dani became more involved, there would be more situations like this. Could he handle being interrupted in the middle of something good by an investigation that could take her away for days? He had just experienced it firsthand. Perhaps he was being selfish to want all her time, when others needed her to investigate what had happened to a loved one. He shook his head and opened the car door.

They rode quietly back to Dani's condo building, until Jake broke the silence. "At least we don't have to give Haley bad news." He glanced at Dani, surprised by her pensive nod. "What's up? Something is bothering you. Care to share?"

"Of course, I'm happy we didn't find Haley's mom, but I talked to Maria, and so far, there have been no breaks. For every bit of good news, there's bad news. Somebody is missing a mom, a sister, a daughter, or all three. Cassie is still out there somewhere, and we need to find her soon. We don't know the identity of the woman in the bog, but the resemblance to Cassie is uncanny. Same blond hair, roughly the same height and build ..." Her voice trailed off.

As Jake drove into the circular driveway in front of Dani's building, he said, "Are you thinking there's a connection?"

Dani opened the door. "I'm not ruling anything out. You learn there aren't a lot of coincidences in this business, so my mind is wide open." She leaned across the seat and kissed Jake on the cheek before closing the door and hustling inside.

Jake met very few cars as he returned to his house, but people crowded the streets, enjoying the humid evening. The bugs hadn't become plentiful yet, and people enjoyed being outside, especially since the pandemic numbers had lessened. A twinge of jealousy hit him when a pair of young lovers walked past, hand-in-hand on the sidewalk. He cared for Dani, but possibly that part of his life had passed him by with his wife's untimely death. He trudged into the house with a heavy heart.

Oliver met him at the door with a loud admonishment, surely related to the lateness of his dinner. Jake did as he was told, pulling food from the cupboard and pouring an extra helping into the dish, despite the hefty cat's diet.

Jake's stomach grumbled as he poured Oliver's ration. Wishing he and Dani had asked for their unfinished meals from the restaurant to-go, he made himself toast with scrambled eggs and wandered with his plate into the sunroom. He settled into his lounge chair and flipped through the channels with the remote, until he found the Toronto Blue Jays tied with the Baltimore Orioles at the top of the sixth. His lips curled in a smile, since he knew what would happen next.

He guessed correctly. No sooner than he turned the channel to the ball game, did Oliver amble down the hall to settle in his favorite spot, equidistance between Jake and the TV. The list of things that soured Oliver's mood grew daily, but two things made him sit quietly. One was the daily battle between a loud blue jay and a persistent black squirrel in the front yard over the food in the bird feeder. Oliver observed the clash for bird feeder supremacy around the same time each afternoon. Jake assumed Oliver did daily calculations on what it would take to eat either, or both.

The cat also enjoyed baseball. Oliver would sit as if he had paid for premium seats, until the game ended. It didn't matter who won. It just mattered that a ball sailed back and forth on the screen. Jake suspected that in Oliver's cat mind, the ball, the squirrel, and the bird would all be his one day.

Jake finished his meal and set his plate and other utensils on the stack of magazines on the floor. He picked up the list from the side table. A few names remained. Tomorrow, if Cassie still had not returned, he would talk to her fitness instructor, Stephanie Taylor. He regarded Oliver, who was so intent on retrieving the ball, that he seemed oblivious to the fact Jake still occupied the chair. Jake drifted off into a deep sleep. His last conscious thought before everything went black turned once again to the disappearance of Cassie Wright.

CHAPTER THIRTEEN

J AKE WOKE AROUND midnight to sportscasters running down the nightly scores, and no sign of Oliver. The cat would have pulled up stakes when the ball stopped darting across the screen. Jake turned off the TV and went to bed.

The next morning, he awoke refreshed and still thinking about Cassie. He carried out his morning routine and settled at the kitchen table with some cereal, while Oliver practically swallowed his bowl as he demolished his ration. When Jake finished, he found one empty spot in the dishwasher to slide his cereal bowl into. He located a detergent pod in the hall closet and started the machine before retreating to the sunroom.

The morning sun blazed into the room, so he closed the blinds. A glance at the oversized clock told him it was too early to call Stephanie Taylor, the fitness instructor, so he tried his daughter, Avery, in Toronto.

She answered cheerily. "Dad, I thought of calling you today. It's been a while. Is everything okay?"

"Yes, honey, everything's fine. I've just been a little busy."

"Busy chasing Detective Dani, I hope."

"No, we're taking our time." He realized the words came out a little sad and hoped his astute daughter didn't pick up on it.

Avery's voice sounded exasperated. "Taking your time? What are you waiting for? Dad, she's lovely. I saw when I was there in the winter that she cares for you. And her daughter thinks you're pretty cool too. Somebody else will sweep her off her feet, if you don't make a move soon. If it's mom you're worried about, you and I both know, she wouldn't want you to be alone. C'mon. Get on it."

Feeling properly scolded and wishing to move on, Jake opted for the modern term to describe a situation where people don't want to put the effort into making something work. "It's complicated, honey. A case has us both tied up. The mother of one of Emilie's friends didn't return home a couple of days ago, and no one knows where she is. A hiker discovered a body that could have been the mom, but turned out to be someone else, thankfully." A wave of guilt washed over him as he remembered that someone, somewhere, must have loved the dead woman, too. "It means that the girl's mom, Cassie Wright, is still missing."

Avery's voice turned skeptical. "What do you mean by 'a case has *us* tied up'? Have you become a private investigator or something in the few months since we last talked?"

"No, but the Missing Persons Unit is short-staffed, so I'm speaking to a few people to see if I can turn anything up. Just trying to help. There isn't much I can do."

"Dad, I know what you're like. What makes you think you'll discover anything the police haven't already considered?" She didn't wait for an answer. "You'll jump in with both feet, like you did when you wrote that book. You almost got yourself killed. Just be careful, okay?"

Jake winced at the mention of the book he wrote about a previous case he had become involved in. He wanted to get off the phone before his daughter tried harder to convince him to leave the case alone. He promised he would be careful and asked about Avery's boyfriend, Nick. They chatted a little longer about Nick's recent activities in the high-tech world before Jake announced he had some errands to run. After more encouragement from Avery to pursue Dani, they hung up.

Jake picked up the sheet of paper with the list of Cassie's contacts and tracked down Stephanie Taylor. A breathless woman answered. When Jake told her the reason for the call and asked if they could meet, she had the same reaction as the others so far, although she seemed a little more willing to help.

"Sorry … I'm out of breath … I teach a virtual high-intensity fitness class, as well as the in-person one we just finished. Cassie takes one of my in-person fitness classes in the evenings. At least, she does now that the government lifted the pandemic restrictions. But I already talked to the police and told them everything I know. We can meet, but I don't know what help I can be. I feel so sorry for her daughter. It must be horrible not knowing where her mom is. If you think I can help, though, let's meet."

They agreed to meet around three o'clock at a Tim Horton's in Billings Bridge shopping mall, about halfway between her studio and Jake's home.

Jake checked the list again, and his eyes zeroed in on the fourth name. Residents had voted the man in as a city councillor, and he repeatedly made the news by passionately defending his ward and the residents there. He was in his thirties and wore a permanent tan, even in the winter months, when the prolonged snow and ice had turned most inhabitants pasty white. Based on Jake's reading of local politics, while many on the Council voted with the mayor on various subjects facing the city, this gentleman frequently sided against her, mostly with convincing arguments.

Jake recalled interviewing the man in his first term in office. With the new councillor's relative youth, movie star good looks, and charisma, he represented a breath of fresh air to the city council. While subtle, the small Canadian flag tattooed on his upper wrist emphasized his patriotism and would be popular with the younger crowd. He spoke with measured, well-structured sentences, grabbing the listener's attention. He sat straight and gazed directly into a television camera, like a magician urging his audience to follow the swinging pendulum. Like any smart politician, he would remember something about you, even if he hadn't seen you for weeks, or even months. His charismatic charm could launch him on a meteoric rise in politics, should he choose to follow that route.

His name was Conrad Smythe, and his parents owned Smythe Homes, a construction company that had its hand in most of the major developments around town. With the rising cost of housing, and the fact the family regularly made the news for donating sizeable sums of money to various hospital foundations, Jake was sure the family had everything they needed. Not to denigrate Cassie Wright, but Jake's curiosity grew over the connection between her and Conrad Smythe.

Jake found the number for the councillor's office and dialed it. An efficient-sounding woman answered, announcing herself as Mr. Smythe's executive assistant. In response to Jake's inquiry, she said Mr. Smythe was meeting with his constituents all day. Jake said, "I'm sure Mr. Smythe is aware of the disappearance of Cassie Wright, and his name is on a list of Ms. Wright's friends. I just wanted to talk to him, to see if he might have any thoughts on the matter."

"Who did you say you are again, Mr. Scott?"

Jake was getting used to the question. "I'm a friend of the Wright family. I'm a retired reporter, and I'm just trying to help where I can." To deflect the next question, Jake said, "The police have probably already talked to Mr. Smythe, so you could say I'm supplementing their work, not duplicating it. If Mr. Smythe could spare a few minutes, I would certainly appreciate it."

The assistant said, "The police have not spoken to Mr. Smythe, to my knowledge. He's in his ward as we speak, knocking on doors. As you may have read, there have been a lot of speeders in that residential area, and people have different ideas on slowing them down. So, as he always does, he's gathering opinions on the best way to calm the traffic. Mr. Smythe always tries to do what's best for his constituents. I suggest you drive around the neighborhood, and when you see some young people in identical blue shirts going door-to-door, that will be Mr. Smythe and his volunteers."

The woman was practically swooning by the time she finished

talking. She obviously held Smythe in high esteem, or conceivably more. Jake thanked her and headed out the door to track down Conrad Smythe in the area of the ward where the enthusiastic assistant assumed he would focus his attention. After circling a few streets in the residential neighborhood, he found the swarm of young people in blue tee shirts, clipboards in hand. He idled up beside a young woman in tight, denim shorts, who appeared to be slightly older than Emilie, and asked for Smythe.

The sun had roasted her face painfully pink, but she still beamed and pointed down the street. The mere mention of the man's name seemed to unleash an outpouring of reverence. "He's at number 515. If you want to talk to him about the traffic calming, I can arrange it for you." She seemed proud of her connection to Smythe.

"Sure, I can drive you down."

The girl hopped into the car without hesitation, and Jake drove down the street, pulling alongside the curb at house number 515. Jake said, "You should stay out of the sun for a while. Your face is getting pretty burned." The girl smiled and brushed it off.

"I only have two more hours and I want to help Mr. Smythe. He's doing so much for the community, and I want to help when I can."

Councillor Smythe stepped off the doorstep as they arrived. The girl got out of the car, hustled over to Smythe, and chatted to him as she pointed toward Jake's car. Jake leaned over the steering wheel, smiled, and waved.

Smythe walked to Jake's side of the car while the young girl ran back to her previous location on the street. Jake pressed the button to wind down the window.

Smythe stood tall and had to bend to look into the driver's side window. His sonorous voice was something Jake remembered from various TV interviews. Smooth, graceful, and subtly persuasive, Smythe would sound good on a television commercial. Despite apparently spending the morning in the sun, he could have just prepared for a dinner date. Not a hair lay out of place, and no sheen on his face. If he threw on a sports jacket over the blue tee shirt and jeans, any high-end restaurant would welcome him.

As the councillor leaned in the window, a flicker of recognition swept across his face. "Hello, I'm Conrad Smythe. I understand you live in the neighborhood and have concerns about traffic calming."

"We've met before, Mr. Smythe. My name's Jake Scott, and I interviewed you for a piece in the paper when you were first elected. Actually, your volunteer might have misunderstood my reason for wanting to speak with you. I'm a friend of Cassie Wright. You may know that Cassie has disappeared."

"What? Cassie Wright? No, I hadn't heard. Resolving this traffic crisis has kept me preoccupied. This is a shock."

Jake sensed the man was lying.

"Can I ask how you knew Cassie?"

The councillor hesitated before responding. Finally, he said, "Sure, if it's the same Cassie Wright. We briefly dated a few months ago."

CHAPTER FOURTEEN

JAKE GESTURED TO the passenger side. "Do you have time to chat for a few minutes?"

"Yes, of course. I don't want to leave my volunteers very long, though. They're doing a superb job of gathering names of individuals who wish to talk to me, and the list is getting rather long." Smythe smiled self-importantly as he strode around the car's front to the passenger side. Despite the man's political acumen, apparently, he hadn't recognized Jake initially from the interview a few years back. Jake sat bemused as the councillor weighed the potential of garnering his vote.

When Smythe climbed into the car and shut the door, he leaned back and examined Jake.

"I remember you now. You wrote an exceptional piece. It introduced me to the city, and I'm positive it helped my career, especially in this ward. I never had a chance to thank you, so it's great to meet you, and thank you very much. You are a brilliant writer."

Jake batted the flattery aside. "Thanks. I'm retired now. So, I gather the police haven't contacted you yet?"

"No, why would they?"

"Your name came up on a list of friends and acquaintances that Cassie's sister and daughter put together."

A flicker of concern replaced the enthusiasm that had collected on Smythe's face during the time he had walked from the driver's door to the passenger side.

"Huh. I don't know why my name would be there. Cassie volunteered with me for a while. That's where we met. We dated for a brief time, but decided we didn't have a connection, so we parted ways. That was about a year ago. I haven't talked to her since. I hope she turns up soon. It must be horrible for her family."

Jake agreed with that statement. They chatted a little longer, but the talk left Jake thinking Smythe hadn't revealed everything. A familiar feeling deep in his gut told him the beloved councillor withheld something. Maybe no one had spurned him before. After ten minutes of conversation, Jake decided he wasn't accomplishing much, so he gave up. He thanked Smythe for his time and left him to continue dazzling his constituents.

The time of day meant light traffic, and Jake reached the Billings Bridge shopping mall in about twenty minutes. He passed some time watching people in the mall before wandering to Tim Horton's at the other end of the parking lot around three o'clock.

Stephanie Taylor had described herself as short, with dark curly hair, and said she would wear yellow exercise tights and a light sweater. The woman stood out in the crowd. The canary yellow tights reminded Jake of Tweety Bird. They clung to her short, athletic frame. Jake had a tough time imagining anyone wearing them in public, although she carried it off admirably, and he admitted his taste in clothes tended more toward frumpy. Dani and Emilie had committed themselves to rectifying that situation.

Stephanie eyed Jake's tan shorts, old t-shirt, and worn sandals. She pointed toward a vacant table and wandered off in that direction. Jake noticed male and female heads turning to watch her progress as she strutted to the table before his turn came to order. She seemed to be oblivious, or she had enough confidence that she just didn't care. He asked for a small iced cappuccino and joined her. He thanked her for her time and asked how Cassie seemed in their last class.

"She might have been a little distracted. I didn't see her put as much effort into her session as she usually did. It seemed a little lackluster, but I'm pretty hardcore, so I try not to judge others. It could have been my imagination. I teach a boxercise class, so it gets intense, and I expect my students to keep up. Cassie hadn't been keeping up in the last few sessions. I talked to her about it over coffee one night. She said she had things on her mind. What's your interest in her disappearance again? Family friend?"

"Yes, Cassie's daughter is a good friend of the daughter of a friend of mine." Jake added, "The police do a great job, so I'm just trying to offer what I can. Would you consider yourself to be a friend of Cassie?"

"We had coffee occasionally. We weren't best friends or anything, but I think fitness instructors are sometimes like bartenders or hairdressers. People like to confide in us. I guess they think it's safe, and whatever they tell us won't go anywhere."

"Did Cassie confide anything that might help the police find her? For example, did she ever date?"

"She dated a couple of people that I know of. She dated that city councillor. What's his name? Smith or something like that."

Jake said, "Do you mean Conrad Smythe?"

"Yeah, that's it. He thinks he's pretty great. I have to admit, he looks good. From the little I know, it seems the guy doesn't take rejection well. Cassie told me it upset him a lot when she broke it off."

"I assume you told the police all this?"

"Yeah, I told the police everything I thought of, but on the way over here, I remembered something I forgot to mention to them. I told them after Cassie broke it off with Mr. Wonderful, I mean Smythe, she used a dating site. There's nothing unusual about that. I use the same one. It's huge, and it's called Cupid's Choice. Some people that come up as a match are creepy, though. I don't know how they could screen better, but they should try. People lie about their profile and skate around the questions." Stephanie eyed Jake as she finished her coffee, perhaps waiting for a reaction.

Jake listened thoughtfully. This could be something.

"Did you mention Cupid's Choice to the police, Stephanie?"

"Yes, they said they would follow up with the dating site to see who they matched her up with. The part I forgot to tell them is that she received some text messages while we were having coffee one night. She looked at them and responded *while we were having coffee*, which seemed kind of rude to me. The messages seemed to upset her."

"What do you mean, they upset her?"

"Just by the way she tapped the screen when she answered, ya know? She got really quiet after."

"Did you see who sent them to her?"

"She guarded her phone pretty well, like she wanted to keep the name secret. But after the last communication she had with whoever it was, she kind of thumped the phone down on the table, like she was angry about something, and it spun toward me. She reached to grab it quickly and the screen soon went black, but I saw something."

Stephanie stopped speaking, apparently unsure whether she should divulge the information to a stranger, or perhaps just trying to build the drama. Seconds ticked by as she regarded Jake. Finally, she leaned forward and whispered, as if about to divulge the nuclear launch codes.

"It wasn't a name, just initials. They exchanged several texts, and the sender was someone with the initials R.W."

CHAPTER FIFTEEN

THE OWNER OF those initials, Robert Weatherby, stood in Julian's lavish office behind the stage. A Manhattan lawyer on Park Avenue would not appear out of place among the furnishings. Julian sat behind a harvest cherry, L-shaped desk. Behind him rose a monolith-like shelving unit constructed of the same quality of wood. Oak hardwood had replaced the original barn board floor. Expensive paneling covered the walls. Julian himself stared into a round 10-inch, lighted mirror on his desk, his eyes wide, and his mouth pursed as he peeled a fake nose, cheeks, chin, and ears from his face.

Robert amused himself by wandering to the books occupying the shelves as he waited to drive Julian back to Ottawa. He pulled a book off the shelf and read the back cover, rolling his eyes at the prophecies promising the end of the world. He flipped through the pages to discover the world would end on December 21, 2012, with the completion of one of the great cycles of the Mayan calendar. Turning to his friend, he said, "Looks like the prognosticators missed the mark by a few years on this one, Julian. We're still here. You might as well toss this book in the garbage."

Julian grunted and rubbed a red mark on his face as he pulled back another piece of prosthetic makeup. A mirthless laugh escaped his twisted lips. "I like to keep them to give me ideas. I just advance the date. Nobody remembers the details, including when or how somebody predicted the world would end. They just remember it didn't, and they're happy they're still here. I can tell my flock that the Mayan calendar cycle will end next year, and they'll believe me."

Weatherby shook his head and put the book back in its place as he continued to scan the titles. Many suggested outrageous prophecies guaranteed to scare the daylights out of anybody. Some readers would undoubtedly put together survival kits for the pending apocalypse, while others would listen to someone like Julian.

Other titles promised to educate the reader on how to convince a loved one that a theory leaned toward wacky, or how to spot a hoax before being dragged down a rabbit hole. Weatherby pulled one book from its place on the shelf and blew the dust off the cover. He showed the title to Julian. *Compendium of Ways to Debunk Conspiracy Theories.*

"Why do you keep these? Aside from being a stupid title, it's supposed to convince people that most of the stuff people like you say, is crap. What if someone broke in and saw these books? That would be the end of Julian."

Julian finished removing his makeup and began rubbing cream into his face. The words came out in spurts as he massaged around his mouth.

"No one is going to break in. Our good friend, Luke Erickson, will make sure that doesn't happen." He referred to the giant guard who patrolled the yard. "I keep the books, so I know how to dissuade skeptics. If I know every argument against conspiracy theories, I can counter them. I think I'm pretty good at convincing the doubters, don't you? The bank account is looking pretty good. We'll use the excavator to move some earth around for a couple more weeks, and then I think we'll have enough money to book permanent trips to wherever we want. Too bad for the people you're counseling, but they'll find someone else equally qualified." He examined his face in the mirror. "Do you see any red blotches? I don't know how I would explain it at work."

Weatherby glanced at the mirror. "You worry too much about your appearance. You look fine to me." He put the book back and wandered around the desk, where he plunked into one of the plush leather chairs facing the desk, slinging one leg over the arm. "There are at least two doubters you didn't convince. We took care of one. She's lying in the bog at Mer Bleu. No one will find her for a while. But what about Cassie Wright? She wanted to expose you. We can't keep her drugged forever. She didn't tell me who she thought you were, but she had herself convinced she knew."

Deep lines furrowed Julian's forehead when he regarded Weatherby's posture. "Luke made a mistake by giving the first one too much sedative. He won't do that again. I have to say, no one would believe you're one of Ottawa's preeminent psychologists, if they walked in and saw your leg draped over the arm of that expensive leather chair. Get your damned feet down. You're leaving streaks of muck."

Weatherby removed his feet and attempted to brush the muddy streaks off the chair with his hand, to no avail. He wandered to the bathroom sink to dampen a cloth.

Julian continued, "We can't risk two bodies turning up in the area just yet. The police will think they have a serial killer on their hands and get the RCMP, provincial police, and every available dog, from here to Vancouver, on the case. Keep her drugged for now. We'll keep her alive until we're ready to change our identity and get out of town. You and Erickson can dump her somewhere. Not the same place as the other one. You'll have to find a different spot."

Weatherby wiped the mud streaks off the chair before tossing the cloth back into the sink. He wandered back to his chair, this time keeping his feet planted on the floor. "You sure that's a good idea? She's a determined woman, and, if she escaped, she'd bring hell down on us. Besides that, she told me she's got a kid, and I'm sure the police are looking for her as we speak."

"She won't escape. We'll keep doing what we're doing a little longer. You just keep running your business the way you have. Take on new clients. If they're rich, bring them here. I'll look after the Guardians of Truth." His chuckle was moist and throaty before he added, "We're almost done. We've been at this for two years, and we're nearing the finish line. Trust me. In the next few meetings, I'll have the people so scared, they'll give their life savings to save their sorry asses. It's business as usual for now. Keep Cassie so doped, she won't know which end is up, and then we'll dump her and blow this place."

"What if there are other doubters?"

"I feel good about the comet approaching earth theory. Did you see how people gave at Monday night's meeting? They dug into their wallets and purses with the urgency of someone stranded in the desert, looking for water. I'll take things up a notch at the next assembly." The same moist, sarcastic laugh again.

"How did you come up with that comet theory, anyway?"

Julian closed his makeup kit and hefted it into a closet by the bookshelf. "It's not a theory. The largest comet ever seen is coming in our general direction in the next few years. It'll miss us by a gazillion miles, but it'll pass close to the sun by space standards. If anyone sees the headline, they'll believe anything I say. People are so gullible." He got up and clapped Weatherby on the shoulder. "Let's get out of here."

They were striding to the office entrance when a thump from behind a door beside the shelving unit stopped them in their tracks. Weatherby glanced at his watch, just as a blond, broad-shouldered man approached from the stage area. Luke Erickson wore jeans that strained across his thigh muscles and a lightweight polyester jacket. Curly, flaxen chest hair sprouted from his open-necked shirt. His grim face, broad nose, and small eyes peering through narrow slits added to his menacing appearance.

Weatherby thought, if they ever needed to cast someone new for Jack Reacher, this would be the guy. He said, "It sounds like our princess is waking up, Luke. Did you give her the dose I told you to give her last time?"

Concern swept across the guard's face as he clenched his ham-like fists. "I'm sure I did, Mr. Weatherby."

"Well, she shouldn't be awake this soon. Hit her with about a quarter of a dose more. That should keep her sleeping until morning. Keep an eye out for any movement around the yard and call me if you see anything unusual."

Luke nodded and yelled, "See you later," as he walked to the door to deal with Cassie Wright. Julian fretted about why Cassie was even allowed to join the organization as he and Robert Weatherby wandered away to drive back to the city and their day jobs.

CHAPTER SIXTEEN

CASSIE WRIGHT WOKE with a start. At least she thought she was awake. Her blouse clung to her skin, and she didn't think she would notice that if she had died. *Where am I? And what day is it?* Her head felt like someone had stuffed it with cotton balls. She willed her hand to move, and it did, but unnaturally slowly. Despite the fear trying to lift the fog, she giggled as the random image of a sloth inching its way up a tree invaded her brain. When her hand reached her bare leg, she pinched it and felt a measure of relief when the nerve endings responded. The tear she wiped away from her cheek provided more proof she was alive.

The intensity of the darkness scared her into thinking blindness had set in. She stared into a dullness so pervasive, it could have been a cave. She thought she imagined movement in the shadows as her body revved up for a full-blown panic attack. The symptoms were familiar. She had experienced them before. Shortness of breath, quivering like a wet puppy, stomach lurching like a rolling sea. She sat and used her arms to draw her knees to her chin. She had to quell the panic settling over her.

Think!

Cassie needed to know if she had lost her sight, before anything else. She leaned back and stared at the tops of her knees. As her eyesight adjusted, she made out the outlines of her hands around her bare legs. She shifted them to make sure her mind wasn't playing tricks on her. No, she could see them. Her body relaxed a little.

Her white blouse had become visible as her eyes adjusted further to the darkness, and she reached down to make sure she wore something on the bottom. It relieved her to feel the fabric of her skirt and, as she leaned further, a thin mattress-like material brushed against her bare legs. She reached out and touched the cold concrete floor to the side. Her fingers moved a paper plate and touched a saran-wrapped sand-wich. A hunger pain stabbed at her stomach, but she pushed the plate away. As she did so, she felt a plastic water bottle. After ensuring the bottle had not been opened, she removed the cap and initially sipped before downing the refreshing liquid.

The airless room contributed to her shivering, and for the first time, she noticed a musty odor. The shakes subsided enough a few minutes later, that she thought she could get up. At least until she tried to push herself off the mattress. Her head spun, and bile raced into her throat as she plunked back down again. Several deep breaths helped to slow the spinning, but it didn't erase the horrible taste in her mouth.

Haley sprung into her head. Her poor daughter must be terrified. She had to find a way out. *How long have I been here?* The hunger pain jabbed at her stomach again, and her mouth felt like she had eaten sand. The sandwich lying on the plate tempted her, but what if they had poisoned it? She gulped several times, trying to find enough saliva to swallow. She compelled herself to stand and wobbled on her weak knees. *Why don't I have any strength?* The realization hit her with the speed of a lightning bolt. *It's not just the aftereffects of sleep that's causing me to feel this way. They must have drugged me. But why?*

Shaking her head didn't dislodge the thick, gauzy sensation in her brain. She needed to forget about why she was there for a minute and try to find a way out. She took two paces to her right and stopped dead. *Were those voices?* It sounded like muted murmuring on the other side of the wall. She focused her attention on the sound and walked, step-by-step in the direction she thought it came from. Her outstretched hands found something soft, almost spongy. She touched it as high and wide as she could. A foam-like material covered the wall. While spongy to the touch, the material had a rough surface. Either the owners of the faint voices stood a long way off, or just beyond walls covered by noise-dampening tiles. *That would account for the texture.* By pressing her ear hard against the material, the murmuring became marginally louder, but still unintelligible. It sounded like the voices of two people.

At one point, when the tone of the voices rose, her fuzzy memory cleared. She couldn't be sure, but one voice seemed recognizable. *Am I dreaming?* It could be Robert Weatherby, the man she stupidly became attracted to. She couldn't believe she fell for his BS. The other person could be the man who called himself Julian. The leader of the so-called Guardians of Truth. *What a joke!* She spat the name out loud, as much to hear her own voice as to express her disgust. His name wasn't Julian. She knew him. If she ever got out of her cell, the first thing would be to hug her daughter. The second would be to expose that son of a bitch to the world.

But first, she had to get out. She continued feeling along the wall in the darkness, her fingers never leaving the foam covering. While the material felt solidly attached to the wall behind, she finally came to a spot where it gave a little. She pushed against it until she found edges. Judging by the dimensions, it had to be a window. Absolutely no light shone in anywhere. Maybe she could pry away the acoustic tiles to reveal the window behind. She tried to find a gap in the tiles to gain entrance with her nails, but couldn't find one. She punched the tile, which depressed slightly, but it simply sprang back into place. This required more thought, so she continued to explore.

The room turned out to be one big cube. Cassie moved slowly to her right, until she kicked an object with her foot. She bent down and touched the cold, round edges of a plastic bucket. A metal handle attached to the top hung down the bucket's side. She lifted it and felt the two holes where it had been inserted. She pulled on the sides of the handle to see if she could remove it from the holes, but they barely moved in her weakened state. She thought that once she regained her strength, and, with a little work, she could pry the handle from the bucket and use it to jab a hole in the tiles large enough to insert her fingers. Or she might use it as a weapon. Right now, it would give her immense satisfaction to drive it into the eye of her captor. The realization of why they left the bucket in the room hit her. It was her toilet. She felt along the concrete floor, and sure enough, there was a roll of toilet paper. Fatigue and despair settled over her again. She needed to lie down, but she didn't know where her mattress lay. She had become completely disoriented during her exploration. And she had never felt lonelier in her entire life.

Then, she thought, if she continued around the room, she would come across the mattress eventually, so she summoned every bit of strength she had to continue. Step by agonizingly slow step, she continued feeling along the wall. Eventually, she came across another change to the shape behind the foam. She felt up its length, across the top, and down to the floor. She had discovered the entrance to the room, or her cell as she came to think of it. Could it all be a joke? Or maybe they wanted to teach her a lesson? At least, the presence of the bucket indicated they wanted to keep her alive. Simultaneously emboldened and excited, she persevered. She pressed along the door's right side, until she found what she sought. She closed her hand around the cold, round doorknob that poked through the acoustic tile.

Slowly, she tried to turn the knob. It didn't budge. She put more pressure on it, but it wouldn't move. No way could she ever budge the door. It was solid and locked. She leaned her head against the tiles as tears welled up in her eyes. This was more than teaching her a lesson. She realized they had something worse in mind for her, and it filled her with dread. The fatigue from before dragged her down again.

She weakly lashed out with her foot in frustration and connected with the tiles at the bottom of the door. She stopped when the most chilling sound of all followed her kick.

Silence.

The murmuring beyond her walls stopped. Even muffled, the dull sound of her foot connecting with the tiles on the door must have been audible on the other side. Harrowing seconds ticked by before the voices resumed. She didn't think of them as people. To Cassie, they were just voices. They might as well have been sounds coming through the speaker in her car. But then a third one joined the first two. This one sounded slower, deeper, and even more threatening. She listened as the three unintelligible voices drifted through her walls. Suddenly, the sounds separated. Two faded, but the voice of the third, the one that chilled her to the bone, grew louder. It sounded like he was approaching the door to her cell.

Cassie calculated where her mattress should be and stumbled across the room in that direction. A key rattled in the lock. Her toe hit the corner of the mattress, and she sprawled face first, half on the makeshift bed and half on the floor. Her knee scraped on rough cement. A blinding light filled the room as the door opened. She grimaced at the pain in her knee as she scrambled onto the mattress and rolled over, pretending to be asleep. Before she closed her eyes, an immense shadow crept across the wall she faced.

CHAPTER SEVENTEEN

THE MAN CLOSED the door behind him as he entered. Cassie desperately wanted to turn and look to get her bearings, but maybe they would spare her life if she couldn't identify him. Then she realized with hopelessness that she could identify Julian and Robert Weatherly. They couldn't let her live. She remained in a fetal position, with her back to the door.

The man's strong, slow voice gave her goosebumps.

"I know you're not sleeping. A thumping sound came from this room minutes ago. You wouldn't know what caused it, would you, Cassie? Turn around."

Cassie debated whether to do as he said. He sounded menacing, so ignoring him might antagonize him into hurting her. She did as he wanted, gradually turning around, while keeping her legs underneath her and holding her skirt so it didn't ride up her thighs. She didn't know what they would do to her, but she sensed unnecessarily exposing skin to this man would not be a good idea.

As she turned, she scanned the room. As she suspected, black two-foot by two-foot foam, sound-dampening tiles covered the walls. They looked like the bottom of a shallow egg carton. She glanced toward the area where the window might be but saw no break in the covering. The same material covered the ceiling, and a stained corner tile accounted for the moldy smell. That, and the brown stain that looked like blood in the middle of the filthy, thin mattress. The floor was poured concrete. She glanced toward the door opposite her and estimated the distance in strides. There was no light switch on the inside of the room. The plastic bucket, roll of toilet paper, empty water bottle, and the sandwich on a paper plate were the only other things occupying the space.

Her eyes shifted to the syringe that the giant filled from an upturned bottle. The sight confirmed her suspicions that he had drugged her and was about to do it again. She pushed herself back against the wall and tried to find her voice. Despite telling herself to be tough, it came out in a whisper.

"Who… who are you?"

The man's narrow eyes squeezed together in concentration as he examined the level of liquid he drew into the syringe.

"I'm a supporter of Julian, and you are definitely not. You should have eaten your sandwich. You'll be pretty starved when you wake up next time."

"Don't you know he's a fraud? He's not who he claims to be. That stuff he's preaching is all lies. Read the news. Do some research. You can easily find out there's no basis for anything he says. Open your eyes! He'll go down, and he'll take everyone who supports him with him."

The man said nothing as he put the bottle in his pocket and lumbered toward her. His eyes scanned her legs before zeroing in on her breasts, straining against her blouse.

The pungent odor of sweat reached Cassie before he did. The skills she learned in her boxercise class might help, but that was more for conditioning. She pressed the fingernail on her right index finger against her thumb. She always considered herself lucky to grow long nails, never thinking that she would one day need them as weapons. If this man touched her, he better be ready for the fight of his life. She flexed her hands to get the circulation flowing. She was ready.

Cassie flinched and drew away as the man knelt on the mattress beside her and ran his hand up her leg, underneath her skirt. An ominous smile traced his lips, but he stopped just above her knee. His hand shot up to grab her left arm in a painful, vice-like grip, and he lifted the syringe. He moved to plunge it in when Cassie lashed out with her right hand. Her fingernails scraped across his rugged face, and a howl escaped his lips as she connected with his eye. He released his grip on the syringe, and it dropped to the mattress. It bounced once and rolled onto the concrete floor, but it didn't break.

Cassie leaped to her feet and raced for the door. She'd calculated ten paces to reach the closed door, but made it in six. She turned the handle, but her momentum made her crash into the door. The handle didn't turn. *How did he lock it from the inside?* The man bellowed behind her. She desperately rattled the knob until she felt it turn. The door sprung free just as she sensed his hand reaching for her.

She lurched through the door into the sanctuary where Julian conducted his services. She couldn't run at maximum speed with her weakened legs, and she stumbled her way toward the front door. Shock raced through her once again as a huge hand clamped down on her shoulder halfway down the aisle. The thought of Haley worried sick at home energized her and fed strength to her legs as she lengthened her stride. She just wanted to hug her daughter. She wouldn't even expose Julian if that's what they wanted.

The daylight from the barn's open door beckoned. She shrugged off the man's hand and sprinted for the opening. She was just about to pass through when shadows darkened the doorway. Two men turned the corner, filling the opening and blocking her path. Weatherby and Julian. She had no alternative, but to slide to a stop.

Helplessness overtook her on realizing she had failed. The large man caught up to her and spun her around. She had the satisfaction of seeing blood seeping from beneath the hand holding his eye just before his fist lashed out, and she lost consciousness again.

CHAPTER EIGHTEEN

JAKE TURNED ON his computer and clicked on the browser. The little number on the email icon at the bottom of the page showed he had messages. The inbox held two. His daughter Avery had sent him a political joke with a note saying, "Thought you might find this amusing. Talk soon. Love you." The cartoon she sent brought a chuckle. Jake's heart soared when he received an email or any other message from Avery, even if she just sent a joke. It meant he was in her thoughts.

The weekly breakfast gathering organizer, Eric Jacobson, had sent the second, but Jake chose to read it later. Other things occupied his mind. He entered "Cupid's Choice" in the search bar and waited until the site came up. He had little to go on. The initials R.W. wouldn't get him anywhere. He considered the statistics he had researched. Of the people who register on an online dating site in Canada, 40% of men lie about their job, while 20% of women don't use a current profile picture. More men than women use dating sites. The site boasted 14,000 new worldwide users every day. The chances of finding R.W. ranked between slim and none. Jake didn't know if R.W. lived in the Ottawa area, if the initials belonged to a man, or if there could be a connection to Cassie's match. A needle in a haystack came to mind.

He had to try. He resolved to pass his findings on to Dani, regardless of how much or little they turned out to be. He signed up for Cupid's Choice. It turned out to be straightforward: email address, date of birth, and password. Once complete, the site took him to a profile page to add a picture and optional information like gender, location, relationship status, the type of person who would interest him, hobbies, appearance, lifestyle, values, education, faith… The list went on and on. It even offered the opportunity to write a brief essay. It would all be relevant information if he wanted to find a match for himself. He ignored all of it.

The next page requested a credit card number to sign up for $29.99 a month for six months, with the promise of an additional half-year free if he didn't find a match during that time. That he provided.

The basic information he entered allowed him to view other profiles, but limited his search. Turning back to the profile page, he filled in a few lines, knowing that the site's computers would toss him into its algorithm to see if anyone matched his preferences. Even with the scant information he provided, a message came up alerting him that he had matches. *Great! Just what I don't need,* he thought as Dani's image jumped into his head.

Oliver wandered into his office and rubbed against his leg. Jake reached down to slide his hand along Oliver's back as the cat arched. "Have I been ignoring you, Oliver? You'll never guess what I'm doing. I just signed up for a dating site. I hope no one, including Dani and Avery, ever find out. Don't tell them, okay?"

Oliver soon became bored and sauntered out of the room. Jake suspected if the cat ever found his voice, Dani and Avery would be the first to know what he had just done.

The site's search feature offered the option of looking for a match based on physical traits and interests or inputting a specific name. Jake entered Cassie Wright's name. A recent photo of Cassie that Jake had noticed on Haley's dresser instantly showed up with her profile page. The professional-looking photo had Cassie with her arms crossed and dressed in a dark blazer and white blouse. Her blonde hair flooded around her shoulders, and her blue eyes sparkled. Her bright, wide smile expanded into apple-shaped cheeks. She looked relaxed and happy. Jake sighed, wondering where she could be and hoping she was alive some place.

He examined her profile. She mentioned one teenage daughter, her love of pilates, yoga, boxercise, going to movies, and long walks. Dancing didn't appeal to her, but romantic dinners with candles or wine in front of a fireplace did. So did movies and live music shows. The profile doubtless reflected the likes and dislikes of most people on the site. But, when Jake reached the bottom, he slumped back in his chair.

Cassie had written the optional essay where she divulged information that could have waited until she built up a rapport with her match. She mentioned looking for more satisfaction in her job and from life in general. She wrote that she loved her daughter, but that emptiness had settled over her. To Jake, the depth of her description, and the tone with which she wrote it, exposed a vulnerability and naivete that someone with the wrong intentions could easily take advantage of. He shook his head. Although he had explored the basics of a dating site before at Avery's urging, it was a world that remained alien to him. He could be completely off base, but it might have been better if Cassie had stopped before adding the essay.

He navigated back to the search feature to find that he could call up profiles of people in his physical area, but his attempt to do so only provided matches of women, the preference he had entered originally. Changing his preference to males would only produce matches of men with the same taste. He quickly realized this wouldn't work. Sitting back in his chair, he returned to the cartoon Avery had sent him. He chortled again at the not-so-subtle skewering of the current prime minister. His fingers played with his bottom lip as he studied the picture, and his mind drifted. *Avery.* Could he do this? *Should* he do this? He had to.

He dialed his daughter, who answered after the first ring. They exchanged pleasantries, and Jake thanked her for the joke. Then his daughter, ever aware of her dad's tone, said, "So, what's up? Looking for some dating advice?"

Jake understood she referred to his relationship with Dani, but the question startled him. That's sort of why he called. A hesitant chuckle bubbled up from his throat. "Yes, kind of, but not in the manner you might think."

A few seconds of dead air followed as Avery considered what her dad might be up to now. When she found her voice, she said, "Uh, okay, what do you mean?"

"This is going to sound a little strange, but I would like you to do something for me." He hesitated before charging forward. "I'd like *you* to sign up for a dating site."

"Oh, boy," was all Avery mustered.

CHAPTER NINETEEN

FTER A FEW beats, Avery found her voice. "Okay, I'll bite. What's going on? If I didn't know better, I'd suspect you didn't like Nick after all these years. Good thing you told me you're involved with some hare-brained scheme to find that woman, Dad, or I would be pretty upset right now. *Sign up for a dating site? Seriously?* If you don't tell Dani how much you like her soon, you're the one who's going to have to sign up. Oh, wait a minute, you already did that a while ago. How did that work out for you?"

Jake stopped his daughter before the temperature on the other end of the line rose further. "To tell you the truth, Avery, I already signed up for one. It's related to the disappearance. Let me explain." Jake described his hunch that the initials, R.W., could belong to someone Cassie met through Cupid's Choice, and how she had appeared upset following a text message exchange with someone just before her disappearance. "The person who upset her in the text and the person she met might be the same. I realized when I signed up with Cupid's Choice that I'll just get matches of females, so that doesn't help. I need a woman to sign up to see if we can discover something." He added feebly, "I suppose I could create a fake account, but I thought you might enjoy being part of the investigation."

"Okay, quit trying to butter me up, sweet talker. As I understand it, this Cassie person *might* have met someone on this dating site, and someone upset her, who *might* have been the same person she allegedly met on the site. And then, this person she *might* have been dating and who *might* have upset her, *could* have something to do with her disappearance. Do I have it right, Dad?"

Jake's face flushed as he said a silent thank you that Avery couldn't see him right now. His daughter had a way of cutting to the chase. He always thought she should have enrolled in law school.

"When you put it that way, it sounds far-fetched. I guess I'm grasping at straws, but I want to help the family. I thought it might eliminate something, as opposed to finding something. But you're right. We can forget this angle. I'll think of something else."

"Are you kidding? You had me at the first 'might.' I'm in, but call me back with a video call. Since you've already signed up, I'll take over your computer and sign up as me. You can walk me through the process to speed it up. Unlike some people, I've never signed up for a dating site, and I must get some work done. I have a report due today. Besides, I don't want to sign up for a dating site on my computer. They'll bombard me with advertising."

Jake was incredulous. "You can do that? You can take over my computer?"

"Sure, Nick showed me how. I'll send a link to your computer, and you just have to give me permission. Never do it with anyone else, though."

The link arrived on Jake's computer screen as Avery spoke. He hesitated before authorizing Avery to go ahead. The thought of watching someone else operate his computer, even Avery, gave him the creeps. As he clicked on the link, Avery said, "Thanks. Now, hang up and call me back on Facetime."

"Okay, give me a second." Jake had never become accustomed to video calls. He didn't like the tiny image of the elderly man in the screen's corner that repeated everything he said, at the same time he said it. But as soon as his daughter appeared on the screen, the small image smiled as defined wrinkles traced a path from Jake's nose to the corners of his mouth. He thanked Avery for agreeing to help. Then his mouth dropped open as the cursor moved across the screen, while his hand remained perfectly still on the mouse.

Jake propped his cell phone beside the computer and walked Avery through the sign-up process, even though she would have figured it out in seconds. The cursor darted back and forth across the screen as she opened and closed tabs on his computer.

As if on cue, Oliver launched himself onto Jake's lap to position himself in front of the cell phone camera. The cat turned so that his rear end filled the screen. As Jake shoved the cat off his lap, Avery said, "I think that's what Oliver thinks of your idea, Dad." Jake countered with, "Either that, or he's making a statement about the fact you haven't visited for some time. I think it's just some instinct cats are born with, to be as annoying as possible."

They laughed and agreed that Avery should enter profile information, including the essay, roughly identical to Cassie Wright's. She signed up using her credit card, after her dad agreed to reimburse her, and created the profile. Then, she entered a search for matches in the Ottawa area. He sighed when the new search returned over 4,000 profiles. How many with the initials R.W. would be in that group? When Avery scrolled through the profiles, men of all ages and ethnicity appeared. Apparently, age isn't a barrier to love. Jake thought of his relationship with Dani. There are lots of lonely people out there.

Jake and Avery discussed Cassie's essay. "What did you think when you read it?" he asked his daughter.

"I don't know. It seemed kind of needy to me. I don't know what kind of man it would attract, but I think someone could take advantage of her. She put herself out there, that's for sure."

"I agree. What kind of person would be a match for someone who considered their life unfulfilled? It probably describes practically everyone on the site, but if you read some of the other profiles, not one goes into that kind of depth. Not everyone would admit to having issues in the intimate detail Cassie did. Could it be interesting to a professional, like a psychologist or psychiatrist? Maybe it would be someone who purports to be a good listener."

Avery laughed sarcastically. "Dad, all men think they're good listeners. Let's enter it as a search criterion just for fun."

Avery typed the words into the search bar, and more than half the men came up. Jake saw the results on the computer screen, and Avery's goofy, I-told-you-so grin on his phone.

Jake smiled with a shrug and tried to put himself in Cassie's shoes. *What type of person would interest her?* Her essay made her appear almost desperate, so someone who proposed to bring excitement and meaning into her life might appeal to her. Avery entered search terms like movies, candlelight dinners, and fireplaces, which produced another slew of results. Could she be desperate enough to look for someone who could offer more on a personal and professional level? Jake asked Avery to enter the city name Ottawa and then "psychiatrist." The search rewarded them with several profiles, but after a quick review, they discovered none belonged to someone with the initials R.W.

He asked Avery to enter "psychologist" into the search bar. In a second, a much more manageable number of 30 profiles popped up. It didn't take long to scan through them. One stood out.

Jake stared at the profile picture. Women would surely consider the man's sharp features attractive. He had wavy brown hair with touches of gray in his sideburns. He had that popular, unshaven look. His profile stated he was 42 years old and that he liked many of the same activities Cassie had identified in her description. It also stated he had found a higher meaning for himself, and that a woman who would be interested in doing the same would appeal to him. It could be a coincidence, but based on her profile, this man's general likes and dislikes, and his listed occupation as a psychologist could have interested Cassie. The reference to "higher meaning" could have lured her like metal to a magnet. It could all be speculation, but the man's name flashed in Jake's brain like a neon sign: Robert Weatherby. R.W.

CHAPTER TWENTY

WHEN AVERY AND Jake finished their search and hung up, he dialed Dani to tell her about their findings. He listened to the phone ring as he checked the second message in his inbox. The sender, Eric Jacobson, mentioned that he and other members of the group had no time for breakfast on the coming Saturday and suggested they meet Friday instead. It surprised Jake, as he couldn't remember them canceling, or even postponing, a gathering before. Usually, at least two or three of the five attendees made it. Dani answered as he typed his reply, agreeing to the rescheduled date.

"How are you doing, handsome?" Dani asked when she answered the phone.

Jake chuckled, replying he had never been better. "In fact," he said, "if I was any better, I'd be twins."

They bantered for a few minutes as they usually did, leaving Jake questioning why they didn't take their relationship further. They had such a great rapport, and speaking with her enlivened him. She might want him to make the first serious move. Then, he remembered the reason for his call.

"Dani, I may be completely out to lunch here, but I think Cassie might have been seeing someone. I'm sure your colleague knows she used a dating site called Cupid's Choice." He recounted how Stephanie Taylor had told him about the message exchange between Cassie and someone with the initials R.W. "The investigator, Maria, might not have all this information, because Stephanie said she forgot to mention it. Anyway, Avery and I looked into the site today and researched Cassie's profile. She mentioned the usual stuff about her likes and dislikes, but she also wrote an essay to expand on the type of person she had in mind. The essay sounded desperate. Who knows? Maybe she was looking for a man to become romantically involved with and decided to ask him to help her professionally. Avery and I searched for psychologists and found someone in the Ottawa area with the right initials and many of the same likes and dislikes as Cassie. He's a psychologist named Robert Weatherby."

Dani remained quiet through Jake's recounting of his activities. When he finished, she blew air through her lips. Jake waited to see if exasperation that he continued to look into the case prompted the air expulsion, but she said, "I marvel at your ability to sleuth something out of nothing, Jake, I really do. I guess that's what the newspaper business does for you. The dating angle could be a coincidence, but it's worth investigating. Maria is swimming upstream right now, following various leads. She'll examine Cassie's computer, and I'm sure if Robert Weatherby is someone Cassie dated, she'll talk to him. Just because she might have dated this guy doesn't mean he might be involved in her disappearance, but it's a lead for sure. Thank you for letting me know. I think it would be best if you relay the information to Maria yourself. It's better than it coming to her third hand."

Jake wrote Maria's personal cellular phone number down as Dani dictated it. When he finished, he said, "Do you have any time in your schedule for breakfast, lunch, or dinner in the next few days? I would really like to see you." He thought he might sound a little desperate himself.

"I would love that, Jake. I'll have time in the next few days. I haven't seen Emilie much, either. Hopefully, she'll recognize me. We're trying to identify the woman in the bog at work." A deep sigh followed, and then she carried on, "I need a personal life. Sometimes I think I bury myself in my work to avoid having one. I should look for another job."

The last sentence surprised Jake. She had suggested nothing like that before.

"No, Dani. I don't think you would ever be happy doing anything else. I understand how busy you are, and I'm sure Emilie does, too. You are doing important work, and Em certainly understands that. I won't keep you from it any longer. We can talk about this when we have time."

"It might give me indigestion." She chuckled. "I'm sorry, Jake. There will be time soon, I promise. I noticed our friends have moved the breakfast gathering to tomorrow. When I have the time, I would rather have breakfast with you. Thanks for calling. Please make sure you call Maria at Missing Persons."

With a promise he would call Maria Allard immediately, Jake hung up. He dialed the number Dani had given him, and a woman with a thick, French-Canadian accent answered with, "Allard."

Jake identified himself by explaining his friendship with Dani and that he had information that might be helpful in Cassie Wright's disappearance. Maria listened quietly as he described his investigation of the dating site. Her professional reaction revealed nothing. No surprise and no suggestion that she already knew about Robert Weatherby, or the dating site. Jake expected nothing more.

Maria simply thanked him for the information and said she had experts going through Cassie's computer. She assured Jake they would follow up on the dating site angle and hung up.

The discussion left Jake questioning what he should do next. He knew one thing for certain, though.

He had to meet Robert Weatherby.

CHAPTER TWENTY-ONE

THE NEXT MORNING, Jake wandered down the street toward Brew and Buns. The sun blazed down despite the early hour, and Jake's shirt clung to him like plastic wrap in the tropic-like humidity. The brown grass along the sidewalk suffered from the heat, even though it had rained recently. Most of the heavy rain had simply run off. Jake reminded himself to water the grass in the backyard when he returned home. Vehicles halfway down the block shimmered in the heat, like they were passing through a time warp in a bad science fiction movie.

Jake noticed the rest of the group, except for Dani, at their usual table when he entered the restaurant. He caught the owner's attention after he sat. Amanda pointed to a cinnamon roll with one eyebrow cocked, just as the previous owner had done every time Jake entered the restaurant. His personal trainer's voice sounded the alarm in his head about sweets, but Jake nodded and received a full smile from Amanda in return.

Like congregants occupying their regular pews every Sunday at church, each group member had claimed a chair, and no one dared to suggest a change to the sacrosanct seating arrangement. Human nature dictated that each chair "belonged" to one of them, and a missing attendee's seat would remain vacant.

Ryan Cambridge sat in the chair to Jake's left. He liked to remind everyone he was the youngest, most successful, and the most athletic of the group. Although it invariably brought howls of protest from the others, they silently agreed with him. They had all seen Ryan capably play hockey, albeit in a beer league, and his lithe body oozed athleticism. The law firm he had started with a partner ran into difficulties, but he had successfully re-established his practice from his house. Although Ryan neared 51, there was a tiny, yet undeniable, age discrepancy between him and the others.

The paunchy, bald organizer, Eric Jacobson, sat next to Ryan and grinned as Amanda set the warm, gooey cinnamon roll and coffee in front of Jake. He was the oldest in the group, a retired bureaucrat, a proud grandfather of two, and a bass player in a classic rock band. The group wouldn't meet at all, if it weren't for Eric. Each had a connection to someone in the group, and they all became acquainted through Eric's efforts to organize the weekly gatherings. Jake considered the breakfast to be a godsend after his wife died. Until he'd met Dani, the weekly meeting remained the only thing that kept him from falling off the rails altogether.

Jake glanced at the empty chair to his right. Dani, who normally occupied the chair, would always be Jake's preferred attendee, while his least favorite had to be sitting next to her regular spot. Pierre Chevrier, a French-Canadian city bus driver, liked to use Jake as his foil, and while he always looked to the others for approval, they usually sided with Jake. Jake learned to tolerate the barbs, but the breakfasts were always more relaxing when Pierre didn't attend. The bus driver was short and stout with a fleshy face, and futilely combed his hair forward to cover his bald spot. He observed the icing-ladened roll and said, "Off the diet, Jake, eh? You were doing so nicely, too. I don't think your trainer will be happy with you." He laughed, looking at the others to jump in, but they weren't having any part of it.

Jake made a show of licking his fingers and smacking his lips as he savored a bite of the tasty delight.

Ryan asked if anyone knew what Dani was doing. While the question floated into the air like a beach ball, he regarded Jake as he asked. Jake hesitated to see if anyone else answered, but when all remained silent, he responded. He chose his words deliberately, unsure of how public the information would be.

"Someone discovered a body in the east end someplace. Dani had been working on a gang-related murder, and now this. Her workload is pretty heavy these days."

"Ah, you would know, I guess, eh, Jake?" Pierre said with a wink at the others.

Jake didn't need to look up to see the source of the accusation, but as he often did, he threw out a word that would leave Pierre scratching his head. "I think it would be helpful if you used epexegesis in your questions, Pierre."

As usual, Pierre didn't know what to make of Jake's response and remained quiet. Jake silently chuckled and thanked the morning paper for today's word of the day, which meant adding more words to a question or statement for clarification.

The group discussed the usual subjects of electric and hybrid cars, sports, inflation, and politics. The travel subject had fallen off the agenda during the pandemic. Had Dani been there, the subjects would have changed little, although they might have broadened somewhat.

Ryan suggested the group should come up with a fun name for themselves. He said, "I thought of a few. How about the Happy Timers? Or the Autumn Leaves? Or the Golden Harvesters?"

The suggestions generated plenty of eye-rolling around the table.

"How about the Old Farts?" asked Amanda, as she refreshed their coffee with a chuckle.

They promptly dismissed Amanda's suggestion and discussed the subject half-heartedly for a few minutes more. Jake suggested North of 50, which drew agreeable nods. He expected the conversation would die on the vine until a lightbulb went on, "I've got it. Eric and the Pacemakers."

The others laughed, and Jake glanced at Eric, who had remained uncharacteristically quiet throughout the breakfast. Jake thought the suggestion would please Eric, or at least it would give him a chuckle, but sweat glistened on the musician's brow. Eric swiped it off with the back of his shaky hand.

Jake's eyebrows knitted together in a frown. The room's air conditioner kept the temperature at a reasonable level, so something else had to be bothering his friend. "Eric, are you okay?" he asked.

Eric tried to respond, but his voice seemed to catch in his throat. His chest heaved, as if he had just finished running a marathon. He sputtered, "I'm not feeling well… I have to go…" His eyes scrunched tightly together as he clutched his chest. "I feel dizzy… I…" He rolled off his chair onto the floor, where he landed with a pronounced thud.

Other patrons in the restaurant gasped at the sound of Eric hitting the floor. Chairs screeched on the floor tiles as some stood to see what was happening. Amanda ran to the table from behind the counter. The other members of the breakfast group gaped in stunned silence, shocked into immobility and unsure of what to do. Jake scraped his chair back and rushed to the fallen Eric's side.

Eric's chest rose and fell sporadically, his breathing ragged as he lay unconscious on the floor. Jake turned to Amanda, who knelt beside him. "Call 911. Tell them we think Eric has had a heart attack." Amanda rushed behind the counter to retrieve her cell from her purse, but other quick-thinking patrons already had their phones to their ears. Ryan yelled at one young man, who was obviously recording.

Jake started CPR on his fallen friend. He had taken the course after Mia died, hoping he would never have to use it. It was a clumsy attempt, but he remembered the instructor saying, "It's better to try than to do nothing."

Ryan gently pushed him aside.

"Let me. I had to do this for one of the hockey players in our league."

Ryan performed hard and fast chest compressions, but the grayish tinge on Eric's face darkened, and his shallow breathing worsened. Soon, sirens sounded in the distance, and within minutes, the ambulance screeched to a stop at the front door. The clatter of a gurney being unloaded rattled through the restaurant door, which Amanda held open for the paramedics. A male first responder took over for Ryan when they arrived. "Good job on getting on this right away, guys," he breathed. "It improves his chances." He didn't have to add, "of survival."

"Civic Hospital," the young, female paramedic shot over her shoulder to Jake as they loaded Eric onto the gurney and wheeled him to the vehicle. The image of the female paramedic preparing the AED, or automated external defibrillator, as the ambulance door closed would remain burned into Jake's brain for some time. So would the wail of the siren as the vehicle disappeared down the street and around the corner.

Ryan, Pierre, and Jake stood solemnly watching the ambulance until it turned the corner. Pierre threw his arm around Jake as the sullen group walked back to their table. Jake irrationally felt horrible about the pacemaker comment. The other patrons had resumed eating, or prepared to leave. Half of Jake's cinnamon roll sat at his spot and would remain uneaten. He removed his phone from his pocket to call Eric's wife.

CHAPTER TWENTY-TWO

A FEW HOURS LATER, Jake completed the 10-minute drive to the Civic Hospital, pulled on his mask, and hustled through the sliding doors. In response to his request for directions to Eric's room, the nurse advised him that ongoing pandemic restrictions prevented visitations by anyone other than family members. Jake wandered to a blue sofa in the waiting room on the main floor where he sat, pulled his phone from his pocket, and dialed the cellular number Eric's wife had given him. He scanned the room as he waited. A few other people, obviously in a similar situation, waited for word on their loved ones. A woman answered just as his finger hovered over the disconnect icon.

Lyla's low, shaky voice belonged to someone in distress. He recalled meeting her at a backyard barbecue and remembered her as being short, with curly red hair and a bubbly personality. She sounded nothing like that today.

"I'm downstairs in the waiting room on the main floor," Jake said. "They won't let me come up because of the Covid protocols." He was almost afraid to ask, but he eventually did. "How's he doing?"

"Can you wait a few minutes? I'll come down and see you. I need to leave for a few minutes. We're just waiting for someone to tell us what's going on, but it's going to take time. I can tell you what I know. I know you and Eric are good friends."

"Sure, I'll be happy to wait. Can I get you a coffee?"

"I would appreciate that. If you don't mind, please get two with sugar."

When they disconnected, Jake hustled to the Tim Hortons around the corner and stood in line behind five others. He didn't know who she wanted the second cup for, but he had noted the phrase, "*We're waiting…*" Hopefully, Eric is well enough to drink coffee, he thought.

The line took longer to move than he expected, and, when he returned, he immediately spotted Lyla sitting on the same blue sofa he had occupied minutes earlier. Her pale, drawn face told Jake everything he didn't want to know about the stress she felt. A young man whom he had never met sat close to Lyla, holding her hand in his lap. The man was a younger version of Eric.

They noticed him approaching, and Lyla released the man's hand and got up, clutching a tissue to her chest. Her mouth turned down, and her eyes glistened. Before Jake said anything or handed her the coffee, she mumbled, "The doctor spoke to us a few minutes ago. The shock treatment in the ambulance didn't work. They injected him with clot-busting drugs, and worked on him for an hour until they eventually got some vital signs. They're hoping he'll stabilize, so they can transfer him to the Heart Institute. It's still touch and go."

Jake's heart sank as he set the coffees on the table and took the distraught woman into his arms. He offered the empty promises people do at times like these. "I'm sure he'll be fine. He'll be better than ever when they release him from the hospital." He noticed the young man, who had been sitting beside her, now stood watching. Jake let go of Lyla and introduced himself.

"Hi, my name's Jake Scott. I'm a friend of Eric's. We meet with some other friends every week for coffee."

The young man shook Jake's hand. "Thanks for coming, Jake. I'm Eric's son, John. Dad has mentioned you and the others. You seem to be a highly supportive little group. Dad says you share a lot of laughs. As

Mom said, we're in waiting mode. There's nothing worse than waiting. No news is good news, I guess."

"Well, I'm sure your dad will be just fine." Jake silently acknowledged he wasn't very good at this. They chatted a few minutes longer before everyone fell silent. Jake reached for the coffees and handed them each one. "I don't know if you're fond of apple fritters, but there are two in the bag." They both devoured the fritters and sipped on their coffees. As silence fell over the threesome, John glanced at his mom and said, "We need to get back upstairs, Mom. The doctor could look for us." He turned to Jake. "Thank you so much for coming. We genuinely appreciate it. One of us will call when we know something."

Jake nodded, acknowledging how little he could do. He wasn't contributing anything, and he suspected John and his mom would prefer to hear any bad news alone if it came to that, so he might as well go. He shook John's hand and touched Lyla's shoulder.

"I'll pass any information from you or John along to the others." He said his goodbyes and made his way down the hall and into the sunshine.

As he sadly approached his Subaru, he wondered if anybody had told Dani what had happened. Had it been another member of the group this happened to, Eric, ever the organizer, would have contacted her, but Jake suspected no one else would think of it. He unlocked his car, got in, and dialed her cell phone. No answer, so he left a message for her to call when she had a chance.

Jumbled thoughts raced through his head as he drove home. His first concern was for Eric. He willed his friend to pull through. Again, his mind drifted to Robert Weatherby, the owner of the same initials as someone who had evidently been in a dispute with Cassie Wright just before her disappearance. Something told him he needed to pursue the lead, even if Dani wouldn't like it.

He pulled into a space in front of a convenience store on Somerset Street, where he had purchased the same item twice a week for the last three years. Bells tinkled as he opened the door. The tiny sound reminded Jake of Tinker Bell every time he walked in. A faint, female voice shouted a greeting from the store's depths.

"Ah, Mr. Jake, you here to win loads of cash?"

Jake couldn't see the diminutive woman, but he answered. "It hasn't worked yet, Jing Wei, but I have a feeling in my bones that these tickets will be the ones."

The sweet scent of incense reached his nostrils as he closed the door. The old shop seemed to sag under the weight of traditional Chinese knickknacks, including toys, lanterns, and ubiquitous waving cats. Silk gowns embroidered with dragons hung from racks, and ceramic buddhas of various sizes occupied shelves. Jake thought there would be very little someone couldn't buy in the tiny shop, as the walls seemed ready to burst in a colorful explosion. It would be so easy for someone to grab something and race to the exit, but he didn't doubt that one of the many strategically placed cameras would catch the offender through its lens. The many cats in the store swung their arms rhythmically. As Jake wove his way through the crowded aisle, he recalled with a smile learning from Jing Wei that the cats weren't waving at all but beckoning good fortune into the store. She had also told him they weren't of Chinese origin, but Japanese.

When he reached the counter, he asked, "So, which one of your many cats is going to bring me good fortune today, Jing Wei?"

The Asian proprietor of indeterminate age peered over her thick glasses at him, an enormous grin widening her face. The tiny woman, her graying hair severely pulled back from a face full of story-telling lines, laughed and pointed to a large white ceramic version while offering her familiar response. "I always tell you to pat the belly of a Buddha, Mr. Jake, but if you insist on patting a cat, you choose that one," she said decisively. She added, "But don't blame me if it doesn't help. Your usual tickets, I assume?" Her smile broadened even wider as she watched Jake patting the white ceramic cat's head as she withdrew a plastic sheet from under the glass countertop.

Jake scrunched his eyes together, pretending as he always did to consider his choice among the myriad of colorful scratch-and-win tickets before randomly selecting three. He scratched the backs as the woman hunched over the machine printing off the weekly lottery tickets. Somehow, she remembered the numbers he played every time, a combination of his late wife's, Avery's, and his birth dates. As usual, he won absolutely nothing on the scratch-and-win. He paid for the tickets and thanked the woman.

She put her withered hand on Jake's arm and said in her soft voice, "I know it's selfish, Mr. Jake, but I always hope you don't win. I would never see you in here. You would retire in some warm place with some young honey." She cackled at her little joke.

Jake laughed along with her. "You don't have to worry about that, Jing Wei. I'll always come back and visit my favorite girl. No one can replace you. Maybe you and I will escape together."

"Yes, my husband wouldn't notice." Jing Wei giggled before putting her hand over her mouth as if she had just uttered a swear word she would never normally use. She referred to her husband's battle with dementia, and Jake knew she visited him in a long-term care facility every evening after the store closed and sometimes used humor to face the cruel disease.

After more laughter, Jake pocketed the folded lottery tickets and left. Visiting the store and sparring with Jing Wei always invigorated him. He had been going to the store since he was a kid. Tossing his money in the wind might produce the same result as buying lottery tickets, but as they say, you can't win if you don't play. Besides, it gave him an excuse to see how the old lady was doing. She couldn't possibly maintain the store by herself much longer. Just moving about obviously caused her great discomfort, and managing that inventory in a crowded space, especially with the pandemic's starts and stops, must have taken its toll. He wished he could win a lottery just so he could give her money to help her retire comfortably.

Jake parked his car in the garage and trudged up the steps to the front door. Despite the lift in his spirits from visiting with Jing Wei, his concern for Eric and Cassie Wright soon settled over him again. The oppressive humid air suited his mood. When he entered the house,

Oliver glanced over from his perch and meowed a greeting before climbing down and winding himself through Jake's legs. Even though his relationship with Oliver remained strained, right now, in his lonely house, he welcomed the cat's attention.

CHAPTER TWENTY-THREE

SHADOWS LENGTHENED IN the backyard as the evening closed in. The lamp in the darkening sunroom switched on automatically while the news anchor's mouth moved silently on TV. Jake had muted it just before falling into a deep sleep in his recliner. He had spoken briefly about Eric's condition to all the members of the breakfast group, except Dani, before he dozed off. All agreed to wait to contact Lyla, and they worked out a plan to take turns calling, so as not to overwhelm the distraught woman. A plate sat on the table next to Jake's chair, the greasy remnants of bacon and eggs visible on its surface. Oliver had long ago finished his meal and wandered off to another part of the house.

Jake jumped as his cell phone vibrated noisily on the table beside him. He pried his eyes open and shook his head to clear the cobwebs. The number on the display didn't register. He thumbed the icon to answer, but his mouth refused to cooperate. A strangled version of "hello" was all he could muster.

Eric's wife, Lyla, said, "Jake, I hope I'm not catching you at a bad time."

Jake's head immediately cleared as he marveled at how she asked that when she had more important things on her mind. He tried to measure her subdued voice for a sign of the state of Eric's health, but he couldn't draw any conclusions.

"No, of course not, Lyla." He waited for the woman to tell him, not daring to ask.

"Eric stabilized enough; they will transfer him to the Heart Institute. They injected him with a drug to induce a hypothermic coma to minimize brain damage. I don't know how long that will continue." She sniffled, and Jake waited while she blew her nose. "Jake, they almost called it. He had no vital signs and just before they declared him dead, his heart began beating again. An angel is watching over us. Eric isn't in the best shape, as you know. When he gets through this, he's going to have to exercise and watch his diet. He has a long way to go. Unfortunately, John and I are the only ones who can see him, because of the pandemic restrictions and the possibility of infection. I wanted you to know since you were so wonderful to come over."

It relieved Jake to hear the woman speak positively.

"He may be out of shape like the rest of us, but he's strong. When he gets through this, we'll monitor his cinnamon roll intake at Brew and Buns as a group. He'll be back to playing his bass in the band in no time. I'm sure he's working on a few chords in his dreams."

Lyla laughed quietly before saying, "Thank you so much for your concern. Yes, maybe he *is* working on his chords. I wanted to let you know the situation. Please let his other friends know, too."

Jake promised he would and hung up. Another call to Dani would be futile, as she would return his call the minute she became available. He called Pierre and Ryan and explained Eric's situation. Both men expressed dismay at Eric's condition and said they would call Lyla in a day, according to the schedule. They asked Jake to update them on any further developments as they happened.

After completing the calls, Jake flipped through the pages of a senior's magazine before grunting and tossing it back on the pile. The giant clock reminded him it was too early to go to bed. He prepared to shower, knowing full well the water wouldn't wash away his loneliness.

Jake had just wrapped a towel around his waist when his phone vibrated on the counter. His heart skipped a beat when Dani's number popped up on the screen. Stopping to visit Jing Wei had temporarily lifted his spirits, but seeing Dani's number brought a rush of warmth he hadn't experienced all day. Hearing her voice was just what he needed.

CHAPTER TWENTY-FOUR

JAKE ANSWERED WITH all the excitement he could muster, but his voice sounded flat and unenthusiastic to him. He hoped it didn't sound the same to Dani, but her response confirmed he was wrong.

"Wow, you sound like you've lost your best friend."

"We almost all did, Dani. Eric had a heart attack at breakfast this morning."

"Oh my gosh, Jake, that's horrible. Is he okay?"

"We don't know yet. They've placed him in an induced coma to ward off damage to his brain. His wife, Lyla, said she didn't know how long he'll be in the coma. It's a waiting game for everyone right now. We just have to hope for the best and pray he's strong enough to pull through."

"Okay, the next question is, are you okay? You sound down."

"I feel the weight of the day. With Cassie still missing, and now Eric's health problems, it got me down a bit. I'll be fine. I have Oliver to keep me company, and it's great to hear from you."

Jake grimaced as soon as the statement came out of his mouth. The cat had still not returned from wherever he had roamed to in the house.

"Oh yes, Oliver the wonder cat and constant companion," said Dani sarcastically. "I'll bet you don't even know where he is right now. Anyhow, I'm sure Eric will pull through. He's strong. I think Cassie's case will break soon too. It's a matter of time until Maria turns something up. I suspect all of this sounds kind of hollow right now, but things will improve. It's tough when we can't do anything but wait. Believe me, I know. I spend half my life waiting for something to happen with the cases I work on."

If Jake had taken a minute to think about what Dani said, he would have realized her words were not much different from what he told Lyla and John, yet they somehow made him feel better. The person delivering the words made the difference.

He said, "We have to take it day by day and see what happens. So, tell me about your day."

"We're still investigating the gang-related death from a couple of weeks ago. No one is talking for fear of reprisal. It makes it difficult, and the tensions just keep escalating among the rival gangs. There'll be another shooting soon. Mark my words. They have easy access to guns, which doesn't help, and they have too much time on their hands. What's that old saying? Idle hands are the devil's workshop? I think that's it. These kids need meaningful things to do, so they don't have time to pick fights and find trouble. In the meantime, every few days, there's another dead kid, and a family's life changed forever."

Jake agreed. "It's a difficult problem, for sure, with no simple solution. I'm all for allocating resources to helping our youth and mentally challenged."

"I think it's something that needs to be done," said Dani. "Meanwhile, we're also investigating the murder at Mer Bleu. It's like Jane Doe didn't exist when she lived. She had no identification on her, and Maria can't find anyone in the missing persons database that matches. She entered the details in CPIC and contacted NCMPUR to see if anything turned up, but so far, nothing."

Jake said with a laugh, "Whoa, back up. My head is spinning. Were you speaking English just now?" Although the first acronym was familiar from his reporting days, the meaning of the second eluded him. He had been absent from reporting long enough that the acronyms needed some serious dusting off, not unlike the coffee table in his living room.

"Oh, sorry. I just consider you to be one of my colleagues, only much more attractive and with a better personality. CPIC is the Canadian Police Information Centre. It's the infrastructure we use for sharing information across police agencies. You likely remember that from your reporting days. NCMPUR is not that recent, either. Don't tell me you're losing your memory." A short, joyful snort drifted over the line that made Jake laugh.

Dani continued, "NCMPUR rolls off the tongue, doesn't it? It's the National Centre for Missing Persons and Unidentified Remains. It's an entire infrastructure, but it includes a database of missing persons. Maria's team will publish the information about Jane Doe and solicit tips through the website. Hopefully, we'll get a hit soon."

"Do you still think there is a connection between Cassie and Jane Doe?"

"Other than their striking physical resemblance, it's hard to say."

Overwhelming tiredness crept over Jake as he considered the possibilities. If something connected the two women, it may not bode well for Cassie. He shuddered at the thought. Dani interrupted him, as if she could read his mind.

"I hope I haven't depressed you further with all this talk about murder and missing people. There is something else I want to share with you, and now is as good a time as any."

Jake's heart skipped a beat. *What now?* Could this day get any worse?

"What is it?"

The hesitation on the other end of the line was practically unbearable. Finally, Dani said, "I miss you when we don't have time to communicate. I enjoy our conversations so much, no matter what we talk about, and I look forward to having dinner, or lunch, or even coffee with you. But right now, I need to spend all my free time with Emilie. She's having a tough time with Haley's mom's disappearance. She's struggling to be a supportive friend, but it's an adult thing to do. I'm trying to offer Emilie support in my available time while she's trying to comfort Haley. It's complicated. Anyway, all that to say, I miss you, Mr. Jake Scott. But don't let it go to your head."

A sudden flare of joy raced from Jake's toes to the top of his head, as if the sun had just come up, brightening his day. At that moment, he couldn't have cared less what they had been talking about as the seriousness of the day's events lifted off him like a curtain on the opening night of a play.

He stammered, "I… I've been missing you, too, and you just, uh, you just made my day. Let me know when you're free, and we'll do breakfast, lunch, or dinner, or all three on the same day."

They talked for a few more minutes, until Dani had to go. Jake suggested that if Emilie needed a break, or just to talk, she should call him. Then he decided he would take the initiative and call the teenager the next day.

Dani hesitated, as if about to hang up, when she said, "Oh, there's something I didn't tell you about the Cassie Wright case. They tried to ping her phone, but received no response. Same for Jane Doe. Someone removed the batteries, or destroyed their phones, or something. Also, your instinct was correct in linking Cassie to Weatherby. A check of the phone records revealed that Cassie's last call went to a number belonging to Robert Weatherby. Don't let that go to your head, either. Maria will question him as a person of interest. Now, I really must go. I'll talk to you soon."

They hung up, both feeling happier than they had fifteen minutes earlier.

When Jake finished his nightly routine and climbed into bed, he briefly contemplated his plan to further investigate Cassie's disappearance. The revelation that she made her last known phone call to Robert Weatherby deepened his resolve. He hadn't shared his plan with Dani, because she would not approve. The fact Cassie's and Jane Doe's phones were missing made the situation more alarming.

Then he turned his mind to Dani's admission that she missed him and fell into a deep, satisfying sleep.

CHAPTER TWENTY-FIVE

JAKE WOKE THE next morning to the sound of thunder rolling overhead. A flash of lightning lit up the bedroom as another thunderclap rattled the windows. The storm rumbled nearby, judging by the seconds between the thunder and lightning. A blast of wind pattered the window with raindrops. He rolled out of bed and pulled the cord to raise the blind. The dark gloom of the sky suggested about three a.m., while the giant digital numbers on the bedside clock ticked over to seven forty-seven in the morning. The sight of the clock Avery had given him as a gift for his fiftieth birthday always brought a smile. A note informing him it had extra-large numbers for seniors had accompanied it. She had punctuated the note with a hand-drawn smiley face.

Jake seldom slept in these days. He threw on his robe and wandered into the kitchen, where he left the light off and lifted the blind. The tree in his front yard strained against the outburst as the bird feeder rocked back and forth in the wind. The birds that would ordinarily flit about fighting off the squirrel had taken refuge. Oliver didn't come running when he poured food into the cat's bowl. Perhaps the storm had unnerved him. Jake listened to the wind howl as he sauntered into the bathroom.

By the time he had finished and dressed, an uncanny silence filled the room. As many storms had done this summer, this one brought a lot of noise and threatened to do immeasurable damage before moving off someplace else. Another check through the window told Jake that the storm left only a few burly drops of rain in its wake. The clouds seemed ladened with rain, but not quite ready to let it go. It wouldn't help the grass that cried for moisture, despite Monday's rain, but maybe it was a prelude to something more significant next time.

This time, when he returned to the kitchen, he found Oliver wolfing down his food. The cat usually greeted Jake on the bed, or at the bedroom door in the morning, but perhaps he had hunkered down somewhere in the house to wait out the noise. Jake patted the cat on the head. "Time for a grocery run, Oliver," he said as he tossed the empty cat food bag into the recycling bin in the garage. Lightning forks still slashed across the sky in the distance, but the accompanying rumble of thunder took longer to reach the house. Mother Nature had dropped by, flexed her enormous muscles, and left.

Jake set the lawn sprinkler in the middle of the parched backyard so that it arched both ways, covering most of the yard's width. The grass took a beating every summer recently as the sun, which seemed more intense each year, beat down from sunrise until around two in the afternoon. Digging up the yard and replacing the grass with river rock and low-maintenance shrubs appealed to him more each year.

He set the timer on his phone for twenty minutes, so he would remember to shut off the sprinkler. The backyard would be a soggy mess without a timer. The grass might appreciate the extra moisture, and the City of Ottawa would readily reflect a bloated charge on his water bill, but his wallet would take a hit, and he would kick himself for being stupid. Better to set the timer.

Not that hungry yet, Jake returned to the house and dialed Emilie's number.

"Hi, Jake," she said as soon as she picked up the phone.

"Hi, Emilie, I hope I didn't wake you."

"No, I have a driving lesson this morning. I'm just getting ready to take the bus to my instructor's place."

"Do you want me to drive you to your lesson? I can pick you up in about five minutes."

"No, that's okay, thanks. The bus is two blocks away from the stop." Her voice sounded muffled through the mask required to ride on public transportation.

"Okay, well, I just wanted to see how you're holding up. It's a rough time for everyone right now, and specifically you and Haley, so I just wanted to make certain you're okay."

"I'm okay, thanks. Driver training helps keep my mind off things. I'm trying to support Haley, but she's pretty upset. I don't think I'm doing a great job. We talk every day, though. I have to go. My bus is here."

"I'm sure Haley appreciates any support you can provide, even though it may not seem like it. Remember, you can call me anytime. You have my number."

Jake tapped on the icon to end the call, then searched for Robert Weatherby, the psychologist. Within seconds, he had dialed and was waiting for someone to answer. As the phone rang, he considered how much trouble he would be in with Dani, if she knew his intentions. A woman answered with, "Dr. Weatherby's office. How may I help you?"

"My name is Jake Scott, and I found Dr. Weatherby through an online search. I checked his references, and it seems like he's the one to help me with my anxiety. I'd like to book an appointment."

"Sure thing, Mr. Scott. Do you have a referral to see a psychologist from your family physician?"

Jake realized he hadn't thought this through. With no referral, the Ontario government would not pick up the tab. Since he planned to see the doctor under fraudulent pretenses, billing the province didn't seem like the ideal thing to do, anyway.

"Uh, no, my doctor doesn't believe in psychologists. He calls them 'feel-good practitioners,' but I need help. My wife died three years ago, and I haven't recovered from it. I'm sure another doctor will give me a referral if you insist." He lowered his voice to sound more desperate. "I really need help with this. I can pay."

The woman said cheerfully, "I'm sure Dr. Weatherby will help. You're in luck. He has time in his schedule for consultation this afternoon." She lowered her voice as if conspiring with her caller. "Don't worry, Dr. Weatherby will give you his preferred rate. How about three o'clock?"

"That's perfect," said Jake. "Thank you so much."

He hung up and pushed back in his recliner. Under normal circumstances, the call might have seemed typical, but with his dusted-off investigative reporter's hat on, a couple of things made him suspicious. Recent reports showed a rising mental health crisis, because of the pandemic lockdowns, and yet, Dr. Robert Weatherby's calendar had an opening as early as today. Trying not to overthink the situation, Jake reminded himself there might have been a cancellation, or, perhaps, the doctor set aside certain times for consultations. Both were logical explanations.

Then, he thought of the receptionist's reference to the special rate and the implication that the doctor used two-tiered charging: one for those with insurance and a second for those without. Jake remembered from his reporting days that the practice was not uncommon, but it raised a question about the man's ethics.

He considered Dani's potential reaction to his plan. At the least, he expected a volcanic eruption from the Venezuelan, unlike any he had experienced before. His daughter, Avery, wouldn't be too happy either, but he had to do it. And what could one consultation hurt? He made a promise to himself to tell Dani, Maria, and Avery his observations after the consultation. Then he would be out of it.

CHAPTER TWENTY-SIX

JAKE SHUT OFF the lawn sprinkler and thought about the owner at Brew and Buns as he returned to the house. Presumably, no one had spoken to Amanda since Eric's heart attack. He wanted to check in on the young woman. The morning sun that had chased away the clouds suggested that a leisurely breakfast on the patio wouldn't hurt, either.

He put on his sunglasses and a gray linen Panama hat and wandered outside to a gorgeous morning. The storm had dragged the humidity off, leaving behind a day everyone could relish… no wind and perfect temperatures. Jake thought this kind of day could make him want to play golf again.

He arrived at the patio, just as a young man exited the restaurant, coffee pot and breakfast order in hand. Must be a new hire, thought Jake. The young server delivered the plate and poured coffee for a man dressed in business casual attire, then hustled to the next table where Jake sat. The tall, thin server had curly black hair and glasses. His white shirt and black pants gave him a professional appearance. He was very nervous and looked to be about eighteen. He managed, "Good morning, sir. Welcome to Brew and Buns. Would you like to see the breakfast menu?"

The young man's politeness momentarily took Jake aback. Not that it was a bad thing. He just wasn't used to being addressed formally in this restaurant and didn't recall the last time he had seen a menu. Good-natured ribbing usually accompanied food orders. He had been coming so long, it became like a second home, complete with the banter that goes with it. But, good for Amanda for turning things up a notch.

"No need for a menu, thanks. I'll have eggs over easy with tomatoes instead of potatoes, crispy bacon, and rye toast. And I'll have a large glass of orange juice, please."

"Any coffee with that, sir?"

"No, thank you. Just the orange juice will be fine." Before the server left, Jake asked, "Is Amanda in today?"

"Do you mean Ms. Abbott, sir? The owner? She's working in the back."

Jake realized with a start he had never heard Amanda's last name before. She had been simply "Amanda" as long as he had been frequenting the restaurant.

"Please mention to her that Jake Scott is on the patio and tell her I would like to speak to her if she has a minute. It's nothing urgent and, if she's busy, tell her not to worry about it. I can come back another time."

A confused look overtook the young man's features. "Uh… do you still want your breakfast if Ms. Abbott is too busy to come out?"

Jake laughed. "Yes, please."

The young man scurried off without taking a note. Jake passed the time watching people rush by on the sidewalk until his meal arrived. Most undoubtably had jobs within walking distance, and nearly all had their noses buried in their phones. He had nearly eaten half his breakfast and had just picked up a piece of crispy bacon with his fingers when Amanda showed up, wiping her hands on her apron. She had an overworked, harried appearance as she blew a wayward strand of hair away from her face. She plunked down in the chair opposite Jake with a heavy sigh.

"Good morning, Jake. It's good to see you, and don't you look dapper in your linen hat. You're lucky Jeff told me the order was for you. You almost had potatoes and barely cooked bacon. I think he confused your order with someone else's. He just started today. I think he'll get the hang of it. He just needs to remember to write the orders down."

The man who had received his order when Jake walked in, leaned forward from the table behind. "Did I hear you say the young man confused some orders? He messed mine up. I asked for my eggs over easy." He stabbed the two eggs on his plate with his fork. No yoke ran out. "Does this look over easy to you? I'm eating it, but it's not what I ordered."

Amanda agreed with the patron that, indeed, they did not look over easy and offered to redo his plate, or give him the meal free. The customer said he would let it go, but never again. Amanda rubbed her face with her hands, as if washing without water. She left one hand beside her face to shield the grimace she gave Jake and asked, "How's Eric doing?"

"That's why I wanted to see you, Amanda." He explained Eric's condition as concern swept across the owner's face. "I also wanted to see how you're doing. That episode shocked everyone. I admire the way you stayed calm and made sure everyone in the restaurant remained comfortable. You showed some tremendous leadership, and I wanted to thank you on behalf of our usual group and Eric's family. Are *you* okay?"

"Thank you! I had experienced nothing like that before, but I guess it can be part of the business. I hope I will never see it again. A stiff drink and a hot bath helped when I got home. It took a while to fall asleep, but I'm fine now. I just pray Eric pulls through."

Jake mopped up the egg yolk with his toast. "Eric's strong. I'm sure he'll pull through and be better than ever, although he may not be one of your best customers for cinnamon rolls from now on." Jake chuckled and, as he did so, he noticed the unhappy patron at the next table glaring in their direction. He leaned toward Amanda and whispered, "I shouldn't hold you up any longer. I think there's a customer you need to take care of."

Amanda pursed her lips and nodded. "Thank you for stopping by,

Jake. Enjoy the rest of your day." She got up and headed to the disgruntled customer's table.

Jake finished his meal and wiped his mouth with his napkin. He took the last sip of his orange juice and returned to watching humanity rushing back and forth on the sidewalk. Everyone hurried on their way somewhere, which made him grateful those days lay in his rear-view mirror. A few minutes later, Jeff showed up with the debit machine.

"How was your breakfast, sir?"

"Everything was great, Jeff. Thank you. You're doing a great job. Just listen to everything Amanda… uh… Ms. Abbott says, and you'll be fine. She's been in this business for a long time, and she's a wonderful person. You can learn a lot from her."

Jake applied a large tip to his payment to encourage the young man and headed along the sidewalk toward his house. Even though his life had become less frantic than the people rushing around on the street, he still had commitments. He had to meet Dr. Robert Weatherby.

CHAPTER TWENTY-SEVEN

ROBERT WEATHERBY'S OFFICE turned out to be in a refurbished, brown brick, three-story former apartment block on Metcalfe Street. Based on the white-lettered, black plaque beside the front door, professionals now filled the building. An ophthalmologist occupied one side of the main floor, and patients could conveniently walk across the hall to be fitted for eyewear by an optician on the other side. A dentist and an accountant tenanted offices on the second floor, while the esteemed Dr. Weatherby seemed to occupy the entire top floor.

Jake arrived early for his three o'clock appointment, so he dropped into the optician's office to kill time. A woman, who appeared to be in her fifties, approached as Jake gasped at the prices marked on the frames. She wore a brown blazer over a cream-colored top and hip-hugging white pants. Interestingly, she didn't wear glasses. Contacts perhaps. The slightest whiff of perfume preceded her arrival. She smiled as Jake picked up one spectacularly priced frame and tried it on.

The woman gushed, "They suit you so well. You have great taste. This is one of our most popular designers, and we have more of his compositions. Would you like to try some others on for comparison?"

Jake glanced at his watch. He still had a few minutes, so he agreed.

Everything about this store was pretentious, including the word composition. He decided to play a role.

"To be honest, I have an appointment with Dr. Weatherby upstairs in a few minutes, but I'm interested in a pair of sunglasses. The ones available off the shelf are boring. Something with a little more style would be ideal. I have a new girlfriend, and she dresses like a model, so I need to look half decent, know what I mean?" He raised his eyebrows at the woman, who smiled knowingly.

When she returned with five different frames, Jake noticed the attention she paid to a young couple who entered the building and wandered past the door to the optical center. It occurred to him that there could be a lot of downtime in the store. Many nearby office buildings remained vacant since the pandemic forced government workers to work from home.

He tried on a gaudy red frame that he wouldn't be caught dead in, although if Emilie had been there, she would certainly think they were wonderful. As he examined himself in the mirror, he said, "I noticed the noisy young couple come in. It must be a distraction when people wander by. This seems to be a high-traffic area."

"Yes, it can be distracting. However, some people, like yourself, who are early for an appointment with someone else in the building, drop in and buy a pair of frames on the way by. The location has its advantages and disadvantages. How do you like those frames? I think your lady friend would find you pretty appealing in those."

"They're certainly spectacular." Jake gestured to an equally gaudy blue pair. "I'd like to try those, too."

As he tried them on, he said, "I'd like to ask you a question." Jake chuckled as he added, "I don't know if there is a doctor/patient privilege with your customers, but a friend of mine has the most amazing sunglasses, and I'm sure she must buy them here. She raves about the place where she buys them, but I don't recall the name. She says the service is exemplary." The woman's face turned a pale shade of crimson.

He continued, "If she buys them here, that's good enough for me. A photo of her appeared in the newspaper recently, so I scanned the picture to give to her. I haven't seen her, so I have it in my wallet. Would you mind having a look and letting me know if she's one of your customers?" Jake quickly reached for his wallet and withdrew Cassie's photo before she answered.

He had her attention. She inspected the photo as he tried on the blue frames. "No," she answered slowly, "but I've definitely seen her. She was in the building. Maybe she had a dentist appointment, or the accountant does her taxes. She has been here a few times, but she must buy her glasses somewhere else." She sidled closer, brushed his arm, and said quietly, "I hope that won't change your mind about buying your frames here."

The perfume scent lingered as Jake took the picture back from the woman, folded it, and returned it to his wallet. He wanted to know when she had last seen Cassie, but it was difficult to ask without raising suspicion.

"Well, it's all about the quality, design, and service, right? I don't think I could go wrong here." He glanced at his watch. "Ah, but I still haven't found the right match, and I've run out of time. I'll have to try on more frames another day. I'll bring my prescription next time. Thank you so much for your help. I think I'm getting very close to the right frame for me, and one that will make my girlfriend thrilled. I'll see you again soon."

"Why don't you drop in after you finish with Dr. Weatherby?"

"I'd love to, but I have another appointment right after. I'm sure I'll have more appointments with the doctor, so I can do it then. Thank you."

"Wait, let me give you my card. There are two of us working here, and since we work on commission, I'd like to make sure that you buy them from me." She smiled with a wry wink and hurried to the counter. She returned with her business card, which she held out to Jake.

Jake glanced at the card and said, "Thank you, Sally. I enjoyed meeting you. I'll tell my friend she should buy her frames from you next time."

When he finally extracted himself from the shop and rode the elevator to Dr. Weatherby's office, he thought about the conversation with Sally. She had indeed been extremely helpful, but not for the reasons she expected.

CHAPTER TWENTY-EIGHT

WEATHERBY'S ACCOMMODATIONS APPEARED to stretch from one end of the floor to the other. A large wooden door faced the elevator, featuring a plaque with the name Dr. Robert Weatherby, followed by the initials R.P. Jake supposed the initials stood for Registered Psychotherapist. That only Weatherby's name appeared on the door seemed odd.

A large desk in front of a row of offices greeted him when he entered. The doors to all the offices, except one were ajar, revealing they were vacant. The common area's decor might impress the casual observer, but Jake recalled researching wood paneling for an article he wrote on finishing basements for the newspaper, and he instantly recognized that these wall coverings fell on the cheaper side. Dr. Weatherby was trying to appear to be something he was not.

A voice piped up from behind the desk, and he recognized it as belonging to the woman he had talked to on the phone. Only the top of her head was visible as he approached the desk, but when he neared, a stubby woman in her fifties peered sternly at him over rectangular-shaped glasses. Her cropped hair glimmered as white as snow. She reminded Jake of someone he couldn't place. When he announced his name, she flashed a brief smile and advised him that the doctor would be a little late. She asked him to take a seat and fill out a form. He sat in one of the two faux leather armchairs placed around an oblong wooden table. A selection of magazines lay scattered across the table.

The form attached to a clipboard required that he fill in details of his home address, health insurance, the name of the doctor who referred him, if applicable, and information about the reason for his visit. Jake used the pen the receptionist gave him to fill it in as completely and honestly as possible. He didn't have to exaggerate the depression he experienced off and on since his wife died. The doctor didn't need to know about Dani helping to pull him back from the brink of a full-blown meltdown.

He sauntered to the counter to hand in his completed form. He noticed the receptionist had one piece of paper beside the keyboard on her desk that she stared at intently. A stack of papers sat on a two-drawer filing cabinet beside her desk. She hesitated when he asked if there were many doctors in the office. "Uh, Dr. Weatherby is the only one working right now. We lost some doctors because of stress related to the pandemic."

When she said 'lost,' he guessed she meant they were gone for good. Psychologists succumbing to the very thing they were supposed to treat struck him as strange. Possibly his attempt to find something, anything, that would help locate Cassie caused him to jump to conclusions. He sat and waited, examining the framed floral paintings on the walls. They were all in soothing pastels. Jake didn't consider himself to be an art expert, but he suspected the paintings fell into the same dollar category as the paneling.

The phone on the receptionist's desk chirped, and she stood to announce that Dr. Weatherby could see him now. She pointed to the closed door. He followed the receptionist as the door slowly opened. She handed Jake's form to an impressive figure, standing about six feet, three inches tall. The man wore his dark hair short on the sides, but long and swept up on the top, giving him a sophisticated appearance. His pale blue eyes pierced Jake like lasers. He wore a white shirt and red tie, with no jacket over a pair of gray slacks. The man had chiseled good looks that Jake thought would be attractive to the ladies, but intimidating if someone allowed him to enter their space.

He greeted Jake with a calm, reassuring voice.

"Come in. Come in. It's nice to meet you, Mr. Scott. I would shake hands, but... you know... the pandemic and all." He gestured to a chair that looked like the ones in the lobby. "Please, have a seat. Can I call you Jake?"

Jake nodded as he glanced at a sofa along one wall of the large office. As he did so, he scanned the framed documents on the wall above it. They boasted of a man eminently qualified to do this job.

"I've never done this before. I assumed I would lie down while I spill my troubles on you. At least, that's the image I get from TV."

The doctor laughed. "That may come later. The choice will be yours. The idea of lying down for therapy came from Sigmund Freud. Did you know that?" Weatherby didn't wait for an answer. "Carl Jung, Freud's friend and supporter, let his patients sit. He theorized a therapist established a better relationship with a patient, if they sat opposite. Both were geniuses in their field, so I opt to give my patients the choice. But today, we are simply establishing a baseline to determine the best course to follow, so no need for you to lie down." He glanced at the form Jake had filled in. "I understand your wife died suddenly a few years ago. Tell me about that, please."

Jake related the story about Mia's sudden death, his sleepless nights, and nightmares ever since. He stated he expected to feel better by now. Weatherby interjected to pry more information from Jake as the story unfolded. Telling the story left Jake drained, but surprised that the doctor had skillfully extracted details about his feelings that he hadn't even divulged to Dani. He even told the doctor about the loud, oversized ticking clock in the sunroom. He came very close to divulging his relationship with Dani, but kept that part private.

Weatherby sat thoughtfully, with lips pursed and hands pressed together in a teepee shape in front of his face. He moved his hands away from his mouth and said, "Overcoming loss is difficult to do. I like to use a multi-point plan to help people through their loss. It sounds daunting, but it works. Today, I would like to tell you about the first four steps in the plan so you can start thinking about them before our next session. If you are to remember one thing from today, it should be that if the past is still present for you, it will be difficult to have a future."

While Jake pondered that, Weatherby outlined the four parts. "Number one, there is no schedule to recover from what happened. Two is that you should not put expectations on yourself, nor let others do it for you, and three, you need to accept what you cannot change. We'll work on these three ideas in the coming sessions. The plan's fourth part is finding strength in others. Have you been able to do that, Jake?"

Jake did not divulge information about the breakfast group. An alarm bell sounded in his head. *Why go directly to number four in the first of many sessions?* He wondered what Cassie might have told the doctor. He disclosed that he had no friends, that the negativity on social media disillusioned him, and that he had tried and given up on a dating app. Weatherby nodded his head knowingly, as if Jake's story sounded like most of the others he treated.

When Jake finished, Weatherby said, "We only have a couple of minutes left. I see that your family doctor has something against therapy and isn't willing to provide a referral. That isn't a problem. Therapy sessions can be expensive, but we can use some discretion in our billing for people not covered by insurance. Does this make sense to you, and are you prepared to see it through?"

"I'm willing to pay whatever it takes. I'm desperate at this point."

The doctor absorbed the information. He had a hint of a smile on his face. He said, "Okay, well, I can save you some money. Number four in the plan would be the most beneficial to you at this stage, and I can help with that. We will touch on the first three, of course, but we'll focus on number four. He touched the mouse on his desk and the computer screen came to life, illuminating his face.

"You're in luck. I have a cancellation tomorrow at three o'clock, if you can make it."

Jake agreed and thanked the doctor profusely, hoping he didn't spread it on too thick. He confirmed the time with the receptionist and headed through the door to the elevator. On the ride down, he pondered the charismatic doctor's skillful extraction and dissection of information. He could imagine Cassie being drawn into the web of someone like that. He didn't know if he was on the right track, but something seemed to be amiss.

One thing was for sure. Weatherby didn't discuss the first three points in the multi-point plan to recovery in any detail, and Jake had the uneasy feeling he never would.

CHAPTER TWENTY-NINE

HALEY SPRANG TO Jake's mind as he navigated the traffic and bounced through construction zones on the way home. Emilie had told him her friend was having a tough time, and it's no wonder. He resolved to call Haley soon, but once he cleared the downtown obstacles, he took the long way home along the Sir John A. Macdonald Parkway, just south of the Ottawa River. It provided a time to clear his head. Cyclists, rollerbladers, and walkers enjoyed the bike path, while he caught glimpses through the trees of sailboats tacking on the river. He mused it would take a skillful captain to capture an elusive breeze on this gorgeous day. The sun disappeared momentarily behind a puffy cloud before it re-emerged, seemingly brighter than ever. An idyllic day for most, but not for those worrying about the whereabouts of a family member or whether their spouse would live or die in the hospital. He tried to shove the negative impressions aside.

While it should have been rush hour, most of the government workers who normally occupied many of the office towers downtown now worked from home, so the traffic moved effortlessly. Jake didn't care. He had the windows down, his sunglasses on, the radio blaring classic rock, and for the first time in a few days, he relaxed. His linen hat sat on the passenger seat, his arm rested on the windowsill, his hair blew in the breeze, and he planned to enjoy the ride as long as it lasted.

He eventually wound his way to Island Park Drive, which took him to his home in Westboro. That uncomfortable space between expectation and reality hit him when he arrived home. The drive hadn't seemed to take as long as he expected, and the reality of Cassie's disappearance and Eric's illness hit him when he pulled into the driveway. It occurred to him to back out again and keep driving, but he would still have to come home eventually. He pulled into the garage and entered the house to find Oliver waiting for him. Despite the cat's irritability, he seemed to sense when Jake was low.

Jake knelt and paid attention to the cat until Oliver had enough and lumbered off. Jake realized he fed the cat too much and reminded himself for the umpteenth time not to do it again. Oliver had Jake's sympathies, since he should also diet, so, after he refreshed the water in Oliver's bowl, he prepared a snack of crackers, Boursin cheese, and pickles for himself.

He carried his plate to the sunroom, sat in his recliner, and pushed the handle to raise the footrest. The conversation with the doctor rattled around in his head as he munched on the crackers. The doctor's multi-point plan to deal with grief made sense. At least the first four parts Weatherby had introduced him to. He wondered about the over-emphasis on part four.

He dialed Haley when he finished his snack. She picked up on the second ring.

"Mr. Scott, I'm so glad you called. The police aren't telling us much. I'm hoping you can."

"I know they're doing their best, Haley. They're looking at your mom's bank accounts and her social media for clues. I'm sure as soon as they find something, they'll let you know. How're you holding up?"

A deep sigh came over the phone. "I'm doing okay. I'm having trouble sleeping. My aunt gave me some pills, and that helped."

Jake frowned at that. "I assume your aunt buys the pills over the counter?"

Haley chuckled despite her worry. "Oh yes, I've seen them advertised on TV. Nothing serious. I'm going to try sleeping without them tonight. I don't like pills."

"Well, do whatever you need to do, sweetie, okay? Can I interest you in going for lunch sometime? We'll see when Emilie's available, and we'll all go. It would give you a bit of a break."

"I would like that. Can I call Em and set it up for tomorrow? We can all go together if Mom comes home."

Jake hoped she was right. "That would be amazing, Haley. We have time to get together for lunch before my appointment at three o'clock. I'm definitely looking forward to it."

When they disconnected, Jake realized that if Haley's mom did return, he would have all afternoon since there wouldn't be a meeting. The subterfuge with Dr. Robert Weatherby would be over, and everyone could get back to their lives. He genuinely hoped that would be the case.

Jake's thoughts turned to Kevin Hall, Cassie's boss. He pushed the lever to set his chair upright and sauntered into his office. The computer hummed, coming to life when he pressed the space bar. A search of the manager's social media pages rewarded Jake with new posts. They all related to removing the pandemic lockdowns, and Hall had recently reposted a message from somebody with the couldn't-possibly-be-fake name of Johnny Doom. The post referred to the end coming soon, and underneath, Hall had posted a "wow" emoji. Just cryptic enough that no one could tell if his response ridiculed or agreed with the original post.

As if she read his mind, Jake's phone rang, and Dani's name popped up on the screen. Jake answered before it rang again.

"Hi! How are you? I'm happy you called."

"Hi, Jake. I only have a few minutes. I'm just driving home now. Em sounds a little down, so I want to take her out for a milkshake or something, but I also wanted to check in and see how you're doing."

"I'm doing great, thanks. Looking forward to seeing you when everything settles down."

"Yes, me too." The sentence trailed off as if something bothered her.

"Is everything okay, Dani?

"Yes, of course. I'm just missing my life right now. I don't feel like I'm spending enough time with the people I care about. What have you been doing? I know you're nosing around Cassie's disappearance. Have you come up with anything I should know about?"

The question disappointed Jake. He'd hoped she had just called to chat, but the conversation had abruptly veered to the case. He revealed part of what he had been doing.

"I met with Cassie's co-worker and her boss and talked to her fitness instructor. I wanted to understand what they're like." He grimaced, hunching his shoulders, as if about to be hit for doing something he shouldn't have. He waited for the reaction from the woman he cared about. An audible sigh drifted through the phone.

"You know that's what my colleagues and I do for a living, right, Jake? Okay, I know your instincts are good. What do you think?"

Pleasantly surprised by Dani's response, Jake continued. "Her colleague, Noah Kirkland, got pretty defensive when he mentioned they regularly had coffee together. He clarified he wasn't interested in women. Apparently, Cassie's attitude had changed recently. Something bothered her. Cassie had missed out on a promotion, and Kirkland said that disturbed her. He couldn't or wouldn't elaborate.

Dani interrupted. "Wait, you said Cassie missed out on a promotion."

"Yes, why?"

"I distinctly remember Maria saying Cassie beat Kirkland out for a promotion. That's odd. I'll pass the contradiction along to Maria, if you're sure you have the facts right."

Jake cocked an eyebrow at the phone before Dani said, "Never mind. Continue."

"Cassie's boss, Kevin Hall, didn't want to meet with me at all. He said he'd already told the police everything. I did some digging into his social media, and the guy seems to have some extremist views, although he's not vocal enough to incriminate himself. I imagine he wants to keep his job. You already know about my conversation with Jessica Davis, the friend. I also visited with Stephanie Taylor, Cassie's fitness instructor. She also mentioned that Cassie seemed despondent lately. She didn't fully take part in the fitness classes, which struck Stephanie as unusual. Not that it means anything. We all blow off our fitness regime from time to time. "

Jake stopped, waiting to hear what Dani had to say. When she remained quiet, he continued. "I also met with another person on Haley's list. Conrad Smythe."

"You mean the city councillor? I haven't seen the list since Maria is looking into it."

"Yes, he dated Cassie a few months ago. He divulged little about their relationship, but Stephanie Taylor told me Cassie said Smythe didn't like it when she broke it off. Her words were something to the effect that he doesn't handle rejection well."

Finally, Dani said, "You know Maria has covered all this ground, right? Or she will if she hasn't already. Besides, if you uncovered something, it should be Maria you talk to. I'm in homicide. She's responsible for missing persons. I know you're just trying to help, and I appreciate it. I know you have Spiderman senses. Are they tingling right now?"

Jake hesitated. Robert Weatherby might somehow be involved, but he didn't want to divulge that until he visited the doctor again. Not yet. He wanted to wait for the second meeting. He didn't like Kevin Hall's right-leaning choices, but there are many people like that. Then there was the contradiction between what Kirkland told Jake and what he told the Missing Person Unit. Now that he thought about it, he had nothing concrete, but there were a lot of little things that could add up to something.

"No, I can't draw any conclusions. There's a bizarre coincidence though. The three men all have identifying marks on their wrists. Kirkland has a birthmark, Hall has a scar, and Smythe has a Canadian flag tattoo. All on the same wrist. How's that for weird? I just wanted you to know."

Dani laughed. "Only someone as observant as you would even notice. It might be helpful later, though. Who knows?" They chatted for a few more minutes about life. Jake told Dani he promised to take her daughter and Haley out for lunch in the morning, to which she replied that Emilie had told her and was thrilled. After about fifteen minutes, Dani revealed she had arrived at her condo long ago but hadn't wanted to hang up. Jake had mixed feelings when they disconnected. Dani always left him with an afterglow when he talked to her, but he admitted to some regret for not having told her the whole truth. He promised himself he would tell her right after his next meeting with Weatherby.

CHAPTER THIRTY

THE MORNING SUNSHINE streaming around the window shade's edges and Oliver's intense stare from the top of the dresser contributed to waking Jake. He cocked one eyebrow at the cat.

"How did you get up there, Oliver? You shouldn't be up there."

The cat responded by nudging a small sample bottle of Tia Maria precariously close to the edge with his paw. He looked to ensure he had an audience. Apparently satisfied he had Jake's attention, he leaped awkwardly from the dresser to the bed before thumping onto the floor and wandering through the door and around the corner toward the kitchen. Everything would have been okay, had his tail not caught the Tia Maria bottle in mid-leap, knocking it off the dresser's edge.

It was one of a handful of sample bottles Jake had picked up at the liquor store to hand out as gifts to his breakfast buddies. He purchased an extra to enjoy with his coffee one day, but hadn't used it yet. He sat up hastily, expecting to see the bottle shattered on the floor, but miraculously, it had simply bounced and rolled under the bed. Fortunately, the lid stayed on, but Jake's sudden movement sent the room spinning, so he lay back on his pillow with a deep sigh. He gathered his senses for a few minutes before throwing on his ragged blue bathrobe and tracing

Oliver's route into the kitchen, where he poured a diet portion for the constantly hungry cat, along with some water.

A few minutes afterward, freshly showered and dressed in a tee-shirt, shorts, socks, and sandals, Jake enjoyed his own breakfast of bacon, eggs, and rye toast and had started to wash his plate when his phone blipped, announcing a text had arrived. Texting would never be his preferred option, but he soon realized after Avery gifted him the smartphone that he would need to learn to text to talk to Dani's daughter, so he gradually picked up some of the vernacular. The text read, *Hi! Haley said lunch is on you. LMAO Let's go to the food court at the mall. YOLO, am I right? I can walk to your place. LMK!* followed by a smiley face.

Jake knew Em threw in the acronyms to tease him. The first time she did it, he had no clue what she meant to say in the text, but he had become used to it. He translated it as, *Hi! Haley said lunch is on you. Laugh my ass off. Let's go to the food court at the mall. You only live once, am I right? I can walk to your place. Let me know.*

He smiled and shook his head as he typed.

Sure, swlmha 11:30?

He got the response he hoped for.

What does that mean?

Hey. You're the texter. I thought you would know. LOL! I said, sure, shall we leave my house at 11:30?

The response bounced back practically before he finished typing.

You can't just make stuff up lol, but k to your question.

There hadn't been a word from Dani or anyone else about Cassie, so, sadly, it would just be the three of them for lunch.

Jake had time to clean up and read his paper before Emilie bounded up the steps at the front door. The giant clock had just ticked emphatically to 11:29 when Emilie arrived. He rose to his feet to greet her as she burst through the door, all smiles, her face red, as if she had been running. He walked down the hall toward her and, as she glanced at him, a look of horror crossed her face.

"Uh-uh. No way, Jake. That doesn't work."

Jake's brow furrowed in concern.

She rushed toward him. "Socks and sandals? Have mom and I taught you nothing?" She leaned down and yanked his socks down to his ankles. Standing up again with a lopsided grin, she mumbled, "Better."

Of course. He had committed a fashion faux pas that apparently needed to be corrected immediately. He just nodded, turned down the hall, and, with a sigh, removed his sandals, pulled his socks off the rest of the way, and dropped them onto the floor in the bedroom. Sockless in his sandals just seemed wrong, but he received a thumbs up from the fashion-conscious Emilie.

The two of them drove quietly in the sunshine to Cassie's sister's place. Posters with Cassie's picture dotted the poles leading to the neighborhood, and Jake understood Haley had been busy doing something positive and staying busy. Tear away phone numbers hung untouched at the bottom of the posters. The sight of the posters settled in the pit of Jake's stomach with a dull thud, a reminder that Cassie remained unaccounted for.

They found Haley sitting on the step, her elbows resting on her knees and her fingers tugging at the corners of her eyes. Jake recognized the pose as a reaction to a tension headache, something he had done many times himself after Mia's death. When they rolled to a stop in front of the house, Haley's youthful, grim face clearly showed her anxiety. She climbed into the car with a muted greeting. Stilted conversation followed on the way to the mall.

While the fast-food court in the shopping complex wouldn't have been Jake's choice for lunch, he didn't want to object. They all ordered from A & W and took their food to the table. Haley barely touched hers, noting that she didn't feel hungry. Jake and Emilie tried to keep the discussion light while Haley quizzed Jake again about anything he might know. He wished he knew more, but offered little. He chose not to divulge what he found out about Robert Weatherby or his suspicions about Kevin Hall. Conrad Smythe might even factor into the equation.

The girls decided they wanted to shop for a few minutes, so despite

Emilie's suggestion that Jake might want to "hit up the men's shops," he gave the teenagers a time limit and sat people-watching. Anything to distract Haley from her thoughts.

The girls returned on time and empty-handed, except for the Styrofoam container Haley held with her mostly uneaten lunch. The threesome drove back to drop Haley off at her aunt's before continuing to Dani's condo, where Emilie got out of the car. She thanked Jake for helping Haley set things aside for a few minutes.

After changing into gray dress slacks and a blue sports shirt at his house, Jake set off for Robert Weatherby's office. He found a rare vacant parking spot on Metcalfe Street and hurried past the optician's door, relieved to see someone other than the ebullient, if not annoying, Sally behind the counter. He arrived at precisely the scheduled time, and the receptionist told him to wait again in the plastic-leather chair, suggesting the doctor kept extremely busy.

After fifteen minutes, the phone on the receptionist's desk chirped, and she gestured to the closed office door with an apology for the delay. "Dr. Weatherby is an extremely busy man. He's one of the most prominent psychologists in the city, you know. You are fortunate that he will look after you."

Jake nodded, doubting the comment about the busy Dr. Weatherby, and entered the office to find the psychologist sitting behind his desk. The doctor rose to greet him and asked how he was doing. Even though fewer than 24 hours had passed since his last visit, Jake didn't have to exaggerate to express his feelings of despondency. The doctor quickly addressed stages one to three of his multi-point plan before jumping to the fourth.

"As part of the healing process, Jake, we must find strength in others. That will be our focus today. You mentioned you don't have any friends, and you have joined no support groups. Please elaborate."

Time to put on a performance.

"I haven't made any new friends. The ones that Mia and I socialized with when she was alive hung around for me at the beginning, but they kind of drifted away. They all have their own lives, so I understand. I have made no new friends. I never considered a support group."

"We need to work on that. Also, people who are grieving regularly stop watching the news because the state of the world contributes to their depression. Do you think that is the case?"

The transition to the news surprised Jake. He recalled Kevin Hall's ambiguous conspiracy theories about the news.

"I quit watching the news or reading the papers shortly after Mia passed away. Too many opinions and not enough news. The internet directs us whichever way we lean, whether it's right or left. There's no room for differences of opinion, and I think the government is trying to control us with their pandemic lockdowns. There are many theories out there that could be true, but we don't hear them through mainstream news because they like to keep the truth from us." Back in his reporting days, he tried so desperately to make sure the reader saw both sides of a story. That wasn't the picture he wanted to paint now. He elaborated. "I even think it's probable the CIA was involved in 9-11. Why weren't there more photos of the plane that hit the Pentagon, for example?" Jake hoped he hadn't gone too far.

The doctor seemed to perk up.

"I can help you with this. There are organizations that would benefit you. You will meet new friends who share your interests. There's one I recommend for people like yourself, called the Guardians of Truth, and I think it's just what you're looking for. Some of my clients attend, and they all claim it's valuable for them." The doctor clicked on his mouse to check. "I don't have time on my calendar until next Wednesday, but I see the group is meeting tomorrow night. Typically, meetings are held on Mondays, but there is a special one on Sunday. I must inform you, though, there are strict requirements for joining the group. Because of my status as a psychologist, my patients don't have to go through as many admittance procedures, but you must sign a non-disclosure agreement. I can send it home with you to read over, and you can let me know if you're still interested. I can pick you up if that works for you. The location is difficult to find." Weatherby reached into his drawer and pulled out a five-page document, which he handed to Jake. He glanced at a clock on the wall. "I see our time is up. Let me know what you think."

Warning bells chimed in Jake's head. *A non-disclosure agreement. Really?* He looked at the document. "I don't know if I need this organization."

Weatherby assured him it fit with phase four of the recovery plan. He handed Jake a card. "Here's my private number."

Not wanting to appear too eager, Jake told the doctor he would consider it and call him. He thanked Weatherby and hurried from the office, again thinking the doctor did his job thoroughly, but something was going on here, and the Sunday meeting might be key. He wondered if Weatherby had something to do with Cassie's disappearance. Jake didn't think he had enough to bother Dani with it.

It could have been the biggest mistake of his life.

CHAPTER THIRTY-ONE

JAKE READ THE non-disclosure agreement deliberately. It raised many red flags that should concern anyone, but Jake suspected the people who signed it were desperate enough to believe anything. It prevented the person signing from divulging the meeting location, anything that transpired at the meetings, or anything pertaining to some guy named Julian. Severe consequences awaited anyone who did so.

There would be no need for anyone to reveal anything about the organization if it turned out to be legit. The document would be worthless as a Canadian penny if the organization proved illegal. Jake found a pen underneath the edge of a plate among the dishes on the kitchen table, shrugged, and signed.

He called Weatherby on his private number. When the doctor answered, Jake tried to sound enthusiastic.

"I wanted you to know I signed the document. This could be what I need. It's exciting that it's such a closed group. The secrecy makes me curious. It must be something special."

"Julian doesn't want everyone in there. It's for people who can relate to each other's problems. He's concerned that non-believers will dilute the message by spreading misinformation about its purpose. You know how people are. I'm glad you're planning to join us. Of course, if you find out it isn't for you, you can leave. I'll pick you up at six tomorrow."

Jake would have a day to wonder if he made the right decision. He could be totally wrong. As he stood under the showerhead the next morning, a little remorse settled over him for not telling Dani, Maria, or Avery where he planned to go. There would be time for that when he got back from the meeting. They would all try to talk him out of it if he told them, so he opted to ask for forgiveness rather than permission. He had to satisfy himself.

His phone rang as he emerged from the shower. He wrapped the large towel around his waist, tied an ugly knot at his hip, and checked the phone's display. Dani. He answered before it rang a third time.

"Hi, Dani. How are you?"

"Hi, handsome. I'm doing great, thanks. I wanted to thank you for taking the girls to lunch. Emilie raved about it when I got home. She said you helped Haley, too."

Jake examined his distorted image in the steam-coated mirror. He thought his chest and stomach were not horribly out of shape for an old guy. "Thanks, but I'm not sure I did that much. Haley is truly upset, as you can imagine. I don't know what we can do until your colleagues locate her mom. How's your investigation going?"

"If you can fit me in, I'll tell you over brunch. I need a break and would love to see you."

"Of course, I have time, and I would love that. What time and where?"

As Dani would have to drive from the police station, they agreed to meet at Brew and Buns and chose 11:30. Jake couldn't be happier, but he pondered how to keep his plans to attend the Guardians of Truth meeting from the astute detective.

The morning dragged on. Jake shone a laser light on the floor for Oliver to chase for a few minutes until the cat decided he had enough of his human's foolishness. In Oliver's cat mind, he probably wished Jake would learn how to slow down the laser pointer. Jake enjoyed two cups of coffee with his morning paper and was about to pour a third before realizing that his ever-shrinking bladder may not handle another cup or two at brunch. He set the pot back in its place. He caught up on the sports scores on TV. Ultimately, the loud, obnoxious clock ticked over to the time to wander to Brew and Buns.

Low, threatening clouds greeted Jake when he stepped outside. His mind had evidently been some place else when he read the day's forecast in the paper, as he assumed it would still be sunny and warm. He returned to the house to change from his shorts into long pants and grab a summer-weight jacket to ward off the chill. *What happened to summer?*

His arrival at the restaurant coincided perfectly with Dani's. She sauntered down the street in white jeans, a black blouse, and a light jacket. Smiles lit their faces when they noticed each other, and they hugged when they simultaneously arrived at the entrance to the patio. Dani said, "What do you think? Shall we risk it and sit on the patio? The clouds haven't produced much rain lately."

Jake hesitated for a moment. He enjoyed being outside as much as anyone during the summer, since winters were so long, but the chill in the air convinced him.

"I think it's a little cool. Let's see if there's room inside."

Amanda waved from behind the counter and, Jeff, the young server who waited on Jake the last time he had visited, nodded as they found a seat in the crowded restaurant. Jeff hurried to them with a coffee pot, which he set on the table after filling their cups without spilling a drop. He efficiently removed a notepad and pencil from his apron, ready to take their orders. Jake noted that the young man had learned since his last visit and was far less nervous.

Dani ordered a fruit cup with oatmeal, while the pancakes were irresistible for Jake. They talked about Jake's lunch with Emilie and Haley while they waited for their order. Jeff arrived with the orders about ten minutes later.

Jake drowned his pancakes with a generous helping of maple syrup. As he sliced them into bite-sized chunks, he asked, "How is your investigation going?"

"I assume you mean the Jane Doe investigation. It's beyond slow.

As you know, it's the victim that gives us the most clues. We can check their lifestyle, habits, relationships, employment records, etc., but we still don't know who Jane Doe is. The forensics people discovered little at the scene. They found a footprint, which will be useful for convicting the perp when we find him. I say 'him,' because it would take a strong person to carry the body into the marsh. Possibly two people.

"Of course, we have DNA, fingerprints, and hair samples, and we know that an overdose of a sedative caused her death, but until we figure out who she is, we're in limbo. We're trying to track down where the sedative was purchased. It's not that common, so it narrows the possibilities. I have one of my investigators showing Jane Doe's picture to Cupid's Choice, on the off chance she registered there. That's just following up on my gut instinct. We posted her picture on our social media pages, and it will be on the news tonight. Someone knows her."

Jake jerked his head back at the mention of Cupid's Choice. *What were the odds of a connection?* He credited Dani for even thinking of that. "I'm sure you're doing everything you can. Nothing new on Cassie's disappearance that you know of?"

Dani's eyes crinkled in a smile as she concentrated on reaching to the bottom of her fruit cup with her spoon to fish out a remaining half strawberry covered in a dollop of yogurt. "Well, Mr. Scott, I think you should date Maria Allard since you keep prying for information about that case," she teased. "I wouldn't have to be the middleman. It just so happens that Maria is looking into the relationship between Cassie and Dr. Robert Weatherby, but there's client-patient privilege involved."

"Do you know if Maria has spoken to the councillor, Conrad Smythe? I suppose it's politically sensitive, but Smythe said he and Cassie dated."

"If she hasn't, she will if it's necessary. She'll be working in the background and following up quietly before she determines how necessary it is. Politics has nothing to do with it. It's a routine investigation. Tell me what you've been doing. I assume you're still nosing around."

Jake gulped while chasing a last bit of pancake through the golden-brown syrup pond lying on his plate. He took his time, chewing deliberately, as if to savor every morsel. "Not really," he lied, without looking up from his plate. "I'm just checking into the social media of the people on Haley's list. I'm sure Maria has developed another list expanding on the one Haley and her aunt provided." When Jake eventually glanced at Dani, her eyes locked on his like a hawk's on a doomed rodent.

"Can I trust you, Jake Scott?"

Jake gulped repeatedly and thought fast. *What can one meeting with the Guardians of Truth hurt? I'll report everything to Maria and Dani if anything comes of it.*

He evaded the question.

"I'm sure Maria is doing everything she can. I just hope and pray Cassie shows up unharmed and soon."

Dani observed him quizzically, but said nothing more. Jake grabbed the bill when it came and paid with his card. As they sauntered arm in arm toward Dani's car, she asked what his plans were for the day. Jake told a half-truth and shrunk under the burden of guilt.

"I'm going to call Eric's wife to see how he's doing. I'll let you know. And your plans?"

"Em and I are going shopping and to a movie. I would invite you, but I think I need a little her-and-me time. I hope you understand."

They reached the car as Jake assured her that he did. When they climbed into the car, she put the keys in the ignition, but didn't start it. She said, "There's something I've been meaning to do for a long time."

She leaned across the seat and pulled Jake's head toward hers with her hands. Jake's eyes flew open in surprise as his heart started pounding. In that split second before their lips met, he understood that what was about to happen had started when he first laid eyes on Dani. It took a long time to get to this point. He struggled to draw a breath. Her warm breath brushed his cheeks an instant before his eyes fluttered closed, and their lips met in a long, lingering kiss. He tasted her soft, warm lips with his, not wanting it to stop.

They pulled apart after a few minutes, both short of breath and neither knowing exactly what to say. A couple in their early twenties sauntered by frowning at the scene in Dani's car, even though they had undoubtedly done the same thing in their young lives. Jake still tasted Dani on his lips. They held hands and gazed into each other's eyes until finally, Dani broke the silence.

"I've wanted to kiss you for a long time. I get it that you're still healing after your wife's death, and I have my issues with work and my past relationship, but it's time we took the step, don't you think?"

Jake's mouth broke into a wide smile. "I couldn't agree more, Dani. I just didn't know how to talk to you about it. If you had waited for me, we might be old and gray. That kiss tasted like more."

"Okay, but then I have to go home," Dani said.

It lasted longer and tasted even sweeter the second time. It brought with it an invitation of more to come. Jake thought he could probably float back to his house without his feet touching the ground.

CHAPTER THIRTY-TWO

J AKE STILL BASKED in the kiss's afterglow, and he realized if he didn't fill the time in the afternoon, he'd go crazy. He called Eric's wife, Lyla, to check on her husband's condition. When her worried voice came on the line, he sensed she needed company, so he asked if she would meet. While he offered to meet anywhere, she preferred staying close to the hospital, so they agreed on the medical center's coffee shop at 2 o'clock.

As Jake drove to the hospital, he licked his lips, still mindful of the taste of Dani's mouth. The concerns about their relationship seemed to melt away with that single, incredible moment. He contemplated how things can abruptly change. Sometimes for the better and sometimes for the worse, but they can change quickly. One moment his wife was alive and vibrant, the next moment she wasn't. Something happened to Haley's mom, suddenly disrupting their daily routine, with no assurance that life would ever be the same again. Eric's health changed in a microsecond. Jake tried to shove the negative ideas aside to focus on his slow-to-develop, yet quick-to-change relationship with Dani.

Jake circled the streets, looking for parking, hoping to avoid the exorbitant rates in the lot. He realized finding a spot would be like winning the lottery, which he hadn't done despite the good luck he was supposed to receive by rubbing Jing Wei's ceramic waving cat. He reminded himself to check his freshly bought ticket. Suddenly, the intermittent flash of a turning signal caught his eye, and a driver pulled out of a space on Ruskin Street. The cat had brought him good luck after all.

He pulled into the spot and, as he got out of the car, drew his jacket tighter to ward off the chill in the air. The wind whistled through the trees, bringing with it darkening clouds. He leaned into the breeze until he reached the entrance to the hospital. Lyla waited at a corner table in the coffee shop and stood to hug him when he arrived. He noticed her drawn face as her sad eyes, darkened by half-moon-shaped circles underneath, sought his.

Jake had already had too many cups of coffee, so he left his coat on the chair at the table and hustled to the bathroom while Lyla ordered tea for herself. When he returned, she stood second in line. She gestured for him to sit.

Her body language when she returned told Jake the news wasn't good. She held her hands on the paper cup as if to warm them but more likely, Jake surmised, to keep them from shaking. He waited for her to speak. She inhaled deeply, sucking the sides of her mask in as she did.

"Thank you for meeting me, Jake. It's so kind of you to keep us in your thoughts and to visit. I wish you could go to his room, but it's still not allowed."

Lyla continued, "He came out of the coma, but the doctors intubated him while he was under. He developed pneumonia. They might have to put him in an induced coma again." Lyla sniffled and blew her nose into a tissue. "It's so hard."

Jake put his hand on her shoulder. "I know it is, Lyla. Just remember you have lots of friends to turn to if you need anything. I'm sure there are many I don't even know, but Dani Perez, Pierre Chevrier, Ryan Cambridge, and I are all available should you need anything. They are all breakfast club members and good friends of Eric."

He pulled his phone from his pocket to call up his contact list. His contacts barely filled a page on his phone. He said, "I want to give you the phone numbers of Eric's friends. Each one, and especially Dani, will help you in any way possible. So, if you can't contact me, please reach out to them. They are great people, and they all like Eric. Do you have a pen?"

Lyla glanced quizzically at Jake with her head cocked to one side. "There is an easier way. Just tap on the name and then on 'share contact.' Then send it to me. It's easy."

Jake repeated her instructions out loud as he made his way through the steps. In less than a minute, he had forwarded the three contacts to Lyla's phone.

"Isn't technology wonderful?" he said.

They chatted for a few more minutes as Lyla finished her tea. She raved about the good work being done at the Heart Institute. Jake did his best to improve her mood, and she seemed somewhat more cheerful when they parted. Obviously, Eric had a long recovery ahead of him.

When Jake arrived home, he called his three friends to update them on Eric's condition. Ryan and Pierre answered, and he left a message for Dani. Neither Ryan nor Pierre had a problem with Jake giving their numbers to Lyla. The lack of response from Dani relieved him. He would have loved the opportunity to talk about their kiss, but it would have also meant evading any talk of his plans. He glanced at his watch. In a few minutes, Robert Weatherby would swing by to pick him up for his introduction to the Guardians of Truth. His introduction and his indoctrination.

A guilty feeling rushed through him when he thought of hiding his plans from Dani. How would she ever trust him if he couldn't share even this with her? He picked up his phone to dial just as Weatherby pulled into the driveway.

CHAPTER THIRTY-THREE

ROBERT WEATHERBY ARRIVED in a bright blue BMW five minutes early, at 5:55. Jake put his phone back into his pocket and headed for Weatherby's car. A robin's cheerful song washed over him as he strode toward the waiting vehicle. He strained to see the source of the chirping through the green leafy canopy on the front yard, hoping the folklore about the sight of a robin bringing good luck held true. The happy warbler hid out of sight in the branches, and that somehow added to Jake's anxiety. At least the sky had cleared, so he shook off his jacket in the warming air.

The unmistakable, yet undefinable scent of a new car greeted Jake as he sat on the pillowy leather seats and cast a brief glance at the gleaming mahogany dash. Weatherby said the drive would take around 50 minutes, so they would arrive in plenty of time for the session. "Julian's words are meaningful, and you'll understand why you came. Being around other people will be uplifting. You're doing the right thing, Jake."

Jake handed him the signed document while commenting on the amount of detail required. Weatherby nodded as he flipped to the signature page. "We need to be careful with people who join. Some don't agree with our doctrine and will try to bring us down with their fake news. We only want true believers and people who want Julian's help."

Weatherby drove the car west along Highway 417. They rode mostly quietly, with Jake posing occasional questions and receiving monosyllabic answers. Golden grain and tall corn stalks waved in the breeze in fields by the highway as they passed. A dust cloud trailed behind a green tractor tilling the small field with a 10-foot cultivator. On the other side of the highway, cars rolled by one after the other, with, Jake assumed, families returning from cottage country. Weatherby turned off the road and drove south of the town of Almonte, passed a densely wooded area, and arrived at a long gravel laneway. Jake wondered if he could find the isolated farm on his own.

They snaked along the rutted laneway through the woods until it opened to a yard with a neglected white house, but well-kept granaries and a shed. Vehicles sat scattered in a field opposite the woods and next to a large red barn. The variety of parked cars and trucks resembled a used car lot with every make, model, and color from modern and expensive to older and barely functional. The barn appeared dilapidated from the outside. Worn, flaked paint and rotted boards led Jake to assume no one had used it for some time, yet it seemed to be Weatherby's focus.

On the barn's west side, a medium-sized excavating machine busily dug a large hole. The machine barked with every scoop. Jake idly wondered what they called those things today. A man sat in a cab operating a boom with a bucket with teeth on it. Jake recalled the cartoon version of the steam shovel named "Snort" in a book called *Are You My Mother?* He read the book to Avery 1,000 times when she was little. Jake suspected Mia had picked it up in a used book sale since it was published in the sixties, but Avery sure loved it. He turned away from the pile of dirt and the random thoughts about the machine doing the work.

Jake concluded the property appeared to be a working farm based on the machinery and buildings, but a serious-looking young couple walking together toward the barn and the collection of parked cars suggested something else. He peered at the clock on the dash, 6:45. Jake examined his feelings. Anticipation? Anxiety? Curiosity? He decided on a bit of all three. Weatherby edged into a spot between a half-ton truck and a small foreign car. Jake barely had enough room to squeeze through his open door without scraping the paint on the car opposite, but they got out of the BMW and walked towards the barn.

The building's interior left Jake speechless. It was ornate compared to the outside. Rows of occupied benches faced a raised stage. A red velvet curtain separated the stage from the area occupied by the attendees. A matching carpet covering natural stone tiles paved the way to the benches. Modern pendant-style lights hung on long cables from the vaulted ceiling. Jake only made out shapes of heads and the front of the stage in the dim light.

Two young women in their late teens offered pleasant greetings to Jake and Robert at the door and held out woven baskets. One brushed a strand of brown hair from her eyes, tossed there by the whirling ceiling fans. They wore colorful, tight, mid-thigh dresses, too much makeup, and broad smiles. Jake glanced at Weatherby, who greeted each by name.

Are they expecting donations already? Jake wondered.

Weatherby fished in his pocket but didn't pull out his money. Instead, he deposited his cell phone in the basket. Clearly, they wanted Jake to do the same, but when he did, the shortest girl asked him politely with a broad smile if he wouldn't mind turning it off before dropping it in the basket. He retrieved it and did as she asked.

"Julian doesn't want ringing cell phones interrupting the service," Weatherby offered as an explanation as they walked toward the benches.

Jake's anxiety level ticked up a notch. Talk about overkill. *Couldn't the almighty Julian just ask people to silence their phones like they do in any other public space? Seems pretentious to collect the phones.*

In the semi-dark room, Jake expected most attendees to be crammed into the back benches like any church congregation, but he followed Weatherby to the front, where they squeezed into a space that was barely large enough for two. Jake's heart rate sped up again. He didn't know what to expect. He glanced at the couple beside him, but both had their eyes closed.

Jake noticed a small clock by the stage. 6:55. The crowd's murmuring simmered down. Jake surveyed the attendees. Some spoke quietly to each other, but many stared at the stage or bowed their heads and closed their eyes like his neighbors. He turned to peer at the surroundings. It startled him to see someone had covered the few windows in the barn, which accounted for the faint artificial light illuminating the interior.

He turned to the man sitting beside him. "What brings you here?" he asked.

The man, who sat beside a much younger woman, said he had been coming for weeks. "Julian and his doctrine have been so good to us. I used to question everything, but I understand why now. I needed to leave the medical field that was strangling me to find true happiness. The decision made me nervous, but I was convinced it was the right one. Julian's going to save us all."

Jake mumbled, "Mmm," as he nodded thoughtfully at the man, who glanced at his companion before turning forward to gaze at the stage again. He risked annoying the man by asking, "Do you mind telling me what you did in the medical profession?"

The man replied from the corner of his mouth.

"Pediatric surgeon."

Jake sat back in his chair. *Seriously?* This guy gave up a career of saving kids on the advice of some guy named Julian to find internal peace and everlasting happiness? How many years had he studied? How many children's lives had he saved or enhanced with his skill, and how many could he save in the future? Was his career so bad, he had to give it up to find happiness? Julian must be something else.

Jake returned his attention to the stage. At precisely seven o'clock, the lights dimmed further, and the pulsating sound of heavy metal music pounded through two enormous speakers on either side of the stage. Most of the attendees closed their eyes now, absorbing the music's thumping bass. It reminded Jake of a rock concert or a wrestling match he had been to as a youth as the bass rhythms drilled into his chest and the bench shuddered beneath him. But he sensed this crowd being swept into something much larger—much more significant to them.

Even Robert closed his eyes, his head slowly bobbing to the music as the crowd waited for something to happen.

Just like a rock concert, theatrical fog rose in clouds from machines at the sides of the stage, and whirling fans shoved it toward the center, thick enough to obliterate the area where Julian would presumably enlighten the gathering. When the white fog completely shrouded the stage, the music stopped as suddenly as it began, and the crowd stilled. The raucous noise of seconds ago gave way to an unsettling murmur wafting through the throng like an electrical charge. Every pair of eyes tried to penetrate the cloud like they were waiting for a miracle. Jake marveled at the spectacle's choreography. Laser beams shot from the ceiling, creating an eerie effect in the fog until fans above the curtain kicked in, forcing most of the drifting cloud toward the crowd. A tickle formed in Jake's throat from the dry ice, forcing him to cough emphatically. Angry eyes turned toward him, and Robert shushed him.

The red velvet curtain parted. The front of the stage remained dark, save for a glow in the remaining fog at the center, created by one strategically placed brilliant spotlight shining from the ceiling. Through the fog, Jake observed something move at stage level. The crowd rose and clapped, rhythmically chanting Julian's name over and over. A hazy apparition rose on a platform from a hole in the floor. A man slowly ascended, his arms outstretched from his white-robed body. The platform stopped when it became level with the stage, and the standing crowd erupted into a cacophonous roar, paying homage to the man standing alone in front of them. The man's form shimmered in the glowing cloud. Jake rose and admitted to being caught up in the spectacle as anxiety turned to excitement. Robert yelled and clapped loudly beside him. Then, the man on stage held his hands up for quiet, and the crowd stilled and sat. Only the whirring fans interrupted the silence. The crowd seemed to stop breathing simultaneously.

Julian was about to speak.

CHAPTER THIRTY-FOUR

JULIAN RETRIEVED A mic from the stand in front of him and extended his arms again before bringing them toward his bosom, as if to embrace the entire crowd in a group hug. He talked into the mic with a soothing voice, like a seasoned veteran. "My flock, my flock, my flock. I am so pleased to receive you tonight. This is our most important gathering to date. There is one last chance for you to save yourselves, and you will be thankful you gave up your time to come. This is where you will hear the truth. You are the chosen ones because you have sacrificed to be here tonight. Why? Because you understand when you hear the truth, and you will benefit from it.

"God warned me of something that will affect us all. It is more important than ever that we heed His word. A spiritual awakening is upon us, and I can save only those among you who truly believe. The bunker's being built outside as we gather. You've seen it! It's because of you we can go on, and it will quickly become clear why it is necessary. It belongs to us because we truly believe." His voice picked up. "Some try to bring us down by denying the Word. No one can save them. Because you truly believe, you will be part of the spiritual awakening of which I speak."

The man's words implored the gathering to listen to him and him only. The combination of words and voice was irresistible. Julian raised his soothing voice to a thunderous roar when the script, as Jake thought of it, demanded it. The crowd hung on every word. They were largely quiet, but shouts of "amen" and "Julian saves" occasionally rang out.

Jake's brow furled as he focused. The voice sounded vaguely familiar. Jake concentrated on identifying the sense of familiarity niggling at the back of his brain. He tuned out to examine the man's face. Jake didn't recognize him. The familiar voice must be his imagination. Unfortunately, this was rapidly becoming a waste of time. It was unlikely that this group knew anything about Cassie's disappearance. He tuned back in as the voice became more urgent.

"… comet 12p Pons/Brooks. It has a strange name, but you can search for it. If you do, you will read about the scientists who discovered the comet in 1812. It moves past the earth every 71 years. The next scheduled pass, according to the internet, is in the coming year. But here's the problem that you won't read about." The voice rose. "I alluded to this at our last assembly, but I must tell you again because I know you believe, and God enlightened me with more detail. They won't tell you this because they don't want widespread panic. They want people to enjoy their remaining days."

Jake wondered who "they" were.

Julian continued, "It is indeed worse than we thought, and we must act immediately to finish the bunker. When God spoke to me last night, He warned me that the comet has broken into pieces and some of the larger ones have changed orbit."

The crowd sat glued to their seats, hanging on every word. The intensity of the room stunned Jake. *These people actually believe this shit.*

"The pieces could hit earth directly." He shouted, "SOME PIECES ARE 1,100 METRES ACROSS. THAT'S 3,600 FEET, LADIES AND GENTLEMEN." Julian paused for that to sink in. Then he pressed the mic to his lips and whispered with a hitch in his voice, suggesting tears would flow at any moment. "Do you understand what that means?

It means mass extinction." Gasps from the crowd. "MASS EXTINC-TION, LADIES AND GENTLEMEN."

Jake marveled at the command in the man's voice as it rose and fell, drawing the crowd in and setting them up for the finale.

"It is not possible to sugar-coat this. Don't believe anything you read. Don't believe social media. They won't tell you the truth. NASA is tracking the comet, but they won't tell you. *I* alone will tell you the truth, and *you* are the fortunate ones who will benefit from my knowledge."

A man shouted, "What if a piece hits near here? How will a bunker help? It looks like a hole in the ground."

Julian's eyebrows creased in a frown, as if challenges were foreign to him. When he recovered, he said, "God told me it will not hit that close. We will be safe in our bunker. Reinforced concrete walls have been poured below the surface. You'll be amazed. We'll stock it with food and other supplies and a generator. The extent to which we stock it will be up to you."

There it was. The beginning of the pitch for money.

A woman cried out, "When the pieces hit, what will happen to the earth? Will they be large enough to knock the earth out of orbit?"

Another frown. Jake sensed Julian feared he might lose control. It was becoming fun to watch. He had to admit, the man thought quickly on his feet as he recovered.

"There will be widespread devastation. Giant tsunamis will flood coastal cities. Water vapor will shoot into the atmosphere, creating del-uges of rain that will cause catastrophic flooding and mudslides. Dirt and ash will fly into the air, blocking the sun's rays, which means the earth will be cold for several years, killing plants and wildlife. Only those in bunkers like ours will survive."

Another panicked voice rose from the back. "What about our kids, and friends, and relatives? Can we bring them into the bunker?"

Julian spoke through tight lips. This was not going as expected.

"Of course, you can bring your children, but remember, the more people we have, the costlier it becomes. You can't tell anyone else about it. There will be nonbelievers among them who will try to stop us. Only those who contribute generously to building the bunker can enter. Space is limited and will only be available to the most generous. I will make sure you and your children get in. Call your friends and relatives and tell them you love them, but you mustn't tell them what you know. Unfortunately, we must block anyone who can't abide by these rules. Remember the agreement you signed. Don't stay behind. Watch your inboxes. We'll advise you by email when it is time to enter the bunker for a tour."

Jake noted the reference to the most generous among the congregation. Julian played his part well. It likely scared the people enough to give up their life savings. He made a mental note to read up on the comet when he got home. He noted Julian said the comet *could* hit the earth. That left a lot of wiggle room in space terms. Of course, if he really believed this guy, he wouldn't accept anything he read, anyway. Having been a reporter, he was aware the news was sometimes skewed, but no one worth his salt would keep something like this quiet for long. Not with everyone divulging everything they know about anything on social media. Mass panic be damned.

Julian tried to soothe the panicked group, his words lighter and more optimistic. Jake understood the next step in the scam. Julian set the table. Next would come the full course meal. To complete the charade, Julian would expect the followers to dig deep to save themselves. In the end, there would be no comet, no mass destruction, no bunker, and no Julian. Jake waited to see what would happen next.

He scanned the crowd again. They did not look like uneducated people. It seemed to be a mix of blue-collar and professional people. Most wore expensive clothing and, judging by some cars outside, many had well-paid jobs. The scam wouldn't be worthwhile unless the crowd had money. *Did Cassie have money?* Based on the apartment she shared with her daughter, it sure didn't look like it. Once again, Jake thought he was wasting his time listening to all this.

It amazed Jake that something like this attracted intelligent people, but inherently, he understood. Julian had a charismatic personality and obviously understood the psychology of acquiring followers. The crowd comprised individuals who had something in common. They sought something and probably allowed Weatherby to recruit them. A man like Julian with "inside information" would appeal to some. The social aspect of being around people of like mind would attract others. Regardless of the reason, they were about to be swindled. Julian's voice interrupted Jake's reverie.

"Now's the time, ladies, and gentlemen. We're the chosen ones, but we all must contribute generously to complete the bunker on time and stock it well. We won't be able to leave the bunker for a few months, or even a year or more. We need food, entertainment, medical supplies... We need to build a small city underground, and we need to do it collectively. Of course, the most generous will have better accommodations.

"TURN UP THE HOUSE LIGHTS! I want to see the faces of my beloved flock. I want to know my future friends and neighbors. God loves you all. He hears you when you give generously, and we will all be together in loving harmony inside our bunker." He lowered his voice. "Our young ladies will circulate now, giving you one last chance to be part of this wonderful adventure."

Now he's calling it an adventure! Jake thought. It had suddenly transformed from a nightmare to an adventure. The lights in the barn clicked on to reveal a large group of panicked people reaching for their wallets.

CHAPTER THIRTY-FIVE

JAKE BLINKED WHEN the house lights abruptly came on at Julian's beckon. He tried to find out who turned them on and saw a formidable blonde man close to the switch. Jake shifted in his seat as perspiration trickled from his armpits, and he wiped his forehead with his arm. *Why was it so hot?* The words and mission of the Guardians of Truth's leader caused his blood pressure to rise, but Jake didn't think that was the cause of his discomfort. He didn't accept a word of the crap Julian had sold so far. He was already mentally framing a freelance article he planned to write when he got home that would expose this charlatan.

Jake glanced at the ceiling fans. The steady, whirling blades that had cooled the place were as dead as the air in the barn. Jake peered over his shoulder at the door. Shut! Only one fan still operated at the front, cooling the "savior." On cue, a teenage girl he hadn't noticed before passed through the crowd lugging an insulated bag containing ice-cold bottled water. Her shoulder drooped as she struggled with the bag's weight. The girl finally arrived at the row where Jake and Robert sat. "Yes, please," Jake said as he wiped his brow again. He noticed the girl wore a short dress and heavy makeup like the two he'd met earlier. Damp circles darkened the armpits of the girl's dress, and beads of sweat popped on her forehead. "Seven dollars, please," she whispered. Jake gulped and pulled out his debit card.

Easy listening music designed to soothe the anxious crowd drifted from the speakers this time. Jake observed Julian eyeing the group from the stage, no doubt calculating his riches and noting the most generous as the credit card machines whirred. He suddenly realized Weatherby was talking to him.

"What do you think, Jake? It's pretty scary. I'm scared to death, but I know Julian personally, and I can vouch for his credibility. He knows of what he speaks. He speaks with God faithfully. You can be part of the awakening and join us. If you remain outside the bunker, there's a good chance you will die a slow and painful death when the comet hits. We don't know what we'll face when we emerge from the bunker, but we know we'll be part of something wonderful.

"All these people have similar issues. They have trouble living in a material world without truth. These people are the cream of the crop, handpicked by Julian and me. You will be compatible with them, and we already have a relationship. I knew you would want to be a part of the awakening. This is the first time Julian has been specific about the coming doomsday, but there have been hints. We have the chance to be saved. Normally, you have time to attend more sessions, but we are out of time. Julian says the comet is getting closer every day.

"It's going to be expensive, so we all must do our part. I've put everything I have into the bunker. I assume you paid your house off, and you have retirement savings you can give. My understanding from Julian is that, just like in an apartment building, the more you contribute, the more comfortable you'll be in the bunker. I think you agree that it just stands to reason."

Jake played along for now. Weatherby's sales pitch sounded practically as good as Julian's. Like they were reading the same book. He had learned at the knee of a master.

"It's scary, indeed. Of course, I have savings, but I have a small limit on my credit card. I don't know what others are giving, but I'm sure I can come up with enough to be absolutely comfortable in the bunker. How do I do that?" He recognized a brief flicker in Weatherby's eyes.

Weatherby said, "I have authority to collect on behalf of the organization. All money goes to the Guardians of Truth. We can meet in my office tomorrow, and you can sign over whatever you feel comfortable contributing. I'll remind you, though, that there will be no need for your money when the comet pieces hit. The survivors will have to create a new form of currency. Money will mean nothing then."

Jake nodded, as if in agreement. "Yes, let's meet tomorrow. I have a line of credit against my house, so I can write a check. I also have retirement savings that I can contribute. Do I make the cheque out to the Guardians of Truth?"

"Yes, that would be best. Perhaps to save time, have it certified by the bank. We can meet at my office at noon if that works for you."

Jake continued to test the water with Weatherby. "I think that will create a problem. My bank is pretty concerned about scams. They will need to report an extraordinarily large, certified cheque to FINTRAC, Canada's financial intelligence unit. It stands for Financial Transactions and Reports Analysis Centre. Something like that. They track large transactions for money laundering. I wrote an article about it once and interviewed some people from the organization. They're thorough, and a large transaction will just raise unnecessary suspicion."

Weatherby considered for a few seconds. Eventually, he said, "Okay, you're right, but the organization has been registered by the tax department as a non-profit, so it shouldn't be a problem. Others who have been here a long time have been donating a series of small, but still substantial amounts. Let's discuss this in the car on the way home. We'll figure out a way."

The man nearly salivated at the prospect of getting his hands on Jake's life savings. Jake wondered how anyone could do that as one of the teenage girls arrived at their row. She handed the credit card machine to an elderly couple at the end of the row. Jake didn't see the exact amount the gentleman punched into the machine, but the card reflected a platinum color, indicating a high dollar limit. He hit the number keys seven times. The potential size of the contribution made Jake's stomach lurch.

When the machine came to him, Jake shook his head at the surprised girl and handed it to Weatherby.

"Don't you want to be saved?" she asked. When Jake shook his head again, the girl said, "Would you like to sign up for Julian's newsletter? It's only $600 a year."

Jake pondered why he would need a newsletter if they were all in a bunker. Weatherby handed the machine to the next person in line and held his hand up before Jake challenged the girl. "It's okay, Mindy. Jake and I will work it out on our way home."

While the girl moved to the next row, an unsettling prickle danced on the back of Jake's neck. It was an extra sensory perception that something was wrong without being able to pinpoint it. Of course, the thought of signing his money over to someone else could do it, even though he had no intention of following through. Something else bothered him. Jake sat perfectly still, letting it wash over him, ignoring Weatherby, who was still selling the doomsday theory.

Jake focused on the girl who carried the machine, watching as more people contributed. He recognized Weatherby's receptionist among the crowd when the girl arrived in front of her. The receptionist made eye contact with Jake, a thin smile crossing her lips as she waved. She didn't seem bothered by the doomsday scenario painted by Julian. It seemed odd to Jake, but something else made him feel uneasy. He regarded the rest of the crowd. Many had their heads bowed and their eyes closed. Some chatted worriedly. The whole spectacle brought the fiery sensation of acid reflux to his chest, but that still didn't account for his unsettled feeling.

Finally, he looked back at the stage where he found the source of his discomfort. Julian stared right at him. He might have been silently admonishing Jake for not using the credit card machine, but even from a distance, Jake perceived more in the dead eyes. Julian seemed to stare straight into Jake's soul. Worse still, there seemed to be recognition.

CHAPTER THIRTY-SIX

JULIAN TURNED AND stormed off the stage when Jake returned the stare. He didn't do his usual dramatic departure, dropping back into the hole in the stage on the platform he had risen on. He had no time for that. The crowd's murmuring followed him as he left. In his agitated state, he fumbled with the bottom of his robe to reach into his pocket for his phone. He texted his bodyguard, Luke Erickson, poking fiercely at the screen until his finger eventually found the right keys.

"*Where are you?*" he demanded. "*I want you here. NOW!*"

Julian stalked around the concrete floor of the spacious room backstage. He glanced toward the closed door leading to the room where Cassie Wright was being held. No sound came from the room. His head vibrated like it could explode. He muttered a curse as rage tore through him. The restless sound of the crowd filtered from the front of the stage as Weatherby opened and closed the door beside the platform and rounded the corner.

The second Julian laid eyes on him, he screamed, "WHAT THE HELL ARE YOU DOING?"

Weatherby stopped in his tracks, as if he had dropped an anchor. "What do you mean what am *I* doing? What are *you* doing? The crowd doesn't know what's happening. They think their savior has abandoned them. That story about the comet breaking into pieces was genius. You have them in the palm of your hand. Get out there and close the deal. If you don't, they're going to think you're a fake." Weatherby chuckled as he attempted to defuse whatever bothered Julian. The man was volatile, but Weatherby had no clue what set him off this time.

Julian whirled on Weatherby and got right into his face. "You want to know what's bothering me? Do you know who the guy you brought here is? He's a goddamned former reporter, that's who. He's been poking around since Cassie Wright went missing, asking a bunch of questions, like he's a police officer or something. He could upend this whole thing. What were you thinking?"

Weatherby lifted his brows skeptically. "Are you sure? He sounded pretty convincing. He says he's ready to sign over his entire life savings, including a line of credit on his house, tomorrow."

"Don't be so stupid, Weatherby. He won't sign over anything. Did he even use his credit card, other than to buy a bottle of water? The only reason he's here is to investigate Cassie's disappearance. You've screwed up."

"Well, he won't recognize you. The prosthetics are too good. There's nothing that can lead him to you."

Julian stalked in circles around the floor, gesturing wildly with both hands as he walked. "How can you be so sure?" he shouted. "Cassie Wright recognized me. There's a chance this guy will, too. I remember now. His name is Scott something. No, that's not it. His last name's Scott. John? No, Jake. That's it. Jake Scott."

Weatherby tried to control the situation, gesturing with both hands for Julian to lower his voice. "Stop shouting. The crowd is going to hear you. Return and finish what you started. Tell them how important they are. Reinforce your story about the comet. They've just given us a boatload of money, so remind them why they did it. You can't just leave them hanging. Go back out."

As Weatherby finished encouraging Julian, Luke Erickson wandered in, his brow moist from apparent exertion, and his gigantic hands thrust deep into his pockets. "What's up, boss?" he asked. "It sounded urgent."

"You're damned right it's urgent." He gestured to Weatherby. "This genius brought a former reporter here who knows me. The guy needs to be eliminated. I have to return to the stage. When I'm done, Weatherby, get Scott back here. Luke, I want you to give him the same treatment as Cassie. Throw him in the room with her. We'll deal with both in a couple of days."

The two men glanced at each other but nodded in silent agreement. Weatherby reluctantly returned to his seat beside Jake, but Julian gestured to his bodyguard to hang back. When Weatherby turned the corner, Julian said quietly to Erickson, "We can't trust Weatherby. This is an unforgivable mistake on his part. After you deal with the reporter, take care of Weatherby. You'll get his share of the cash. Bury him in the woods or in the hole you dug out there. I don't care. Make sure he won't be found for a long time. I don't want to see him again. Understand?"

"Of course, boss, as long as you're sure."

"I'm sure. I have to go."

Julian didn't bother using the mechanical platform this time, choosing to return the same way he left. He returned to the stage to muted applause from the concerned crowd, and, in his best soothing voice, he assured them everything would be fine. He reminded them that God loved them, and they were the few chosen to survive the apocalypse. As he surveyed the crowd, he observed concerned, but relieved faces. He avoided the curious stare of Jake Scott.

CHAPTER THIRTY-SEVEN

BASED ON THE crowd's reaction, they sensed something amiss when Julian stormed off the stage. Palpable relief filled the room when he returned. Julian's arrival back on stage coincided with Weatherby rejoining Jake. Even in the gloomy light, Jake noticed the crimson color on Weatherby's face. Despite Julian's soothing voice, Jake saw he too was agitated by the way he stomped onto the stage and his rapid hand movements. Julian's chest rose and fell as he drew a deep breath to compose himself before he began speaking.

Many in the crowd clutched each other with tears streaming down their faces. Jake wasn't sure if they were tears of worry for their loved ones, or tears of joy at having the good fortune to know the savior in front of them. Perhaps a little of each. Julian had pulled himself together, artfully speaking of the awakening and how wonderful it would be to be part of the new world and to shape things to their liking. There would be other survivors, but there would be no way to connect without telecommunications systems. Julian assured the crowd the world would be a better place without social media and fake news. He pointed out simple advantages to the new world that brought muted murmurings of "amen."

Jake listened intently to the man again. Something about the voice reminded him of someone he had met recently. He recalled the people he had encountered as part of his investigation. There was Cassie's colleague, Noah Kirkland, the man who made a point of telling Jake he had no interest in women, and who apparently lied about the promotion. There was Kevin Hall, the conspiracy theorist and Cassie's boss, who didn't want to spend any time talking to Jake. Then there was the city councillor, Conrad Smythe, who dated Cassie for a short time and didn't like being rejected. Jake identified the one among the three who the voice sounded like, but the face didn't match.

Julian evidently concluded he had soothed the crowd enough, so he wound up his presentation. Jake noticed the big man at the side of the room flipping a switch. The theatrical fog machines kicked in and the strobe lights came on to recreate the shimmering effect. Julian reassured the attendees they would hear from him via email when the time came to tour the bunker. He offered one last opportunity to contribute to the cause. As the girls swept through the crowd with their credit card machines again, Jake leaned toward Weatherby. "What was that all about?" he asked. "Julian seemed upset."

Weatherby had clearly had time to think about an answer and immediately pointed out that Julian became overwhelmed by the awful burden of sharing news about impending doom. He added. "Julian loves his flock as he likes to call them. He is grateful to have the gift to converse with God and share his knowledge with his flock. It frequently overwhelms him. By the way, I told him about you when we were backstage, and he would like to meet you. He has met everyone here personally, and he thinks it is important to know every member of his flock who will share the bunker with him. All who have met him consider it an immense honor to have an audience with the great man."

Jake hesitated for a moment. He recalled almost wilting under Julian's stare merely moments before, and how that seemed to coincide with the man's abrupt departure from the stage. Jake sensed that Julian somehow recognized him. At the same time, the familiarity of Julian's voice still unsettled Jake. It couldn't be, though. Jake didn't recognize the man's face. They had never met.

Jake's curiosity, training, and years as an investigative reporter got the better of him. He thought of the old saying, in for a penny, in for a pound. It would give him something more substantial to tell Dani when he returned home. He said, "It would be an honor to meet such a great man," deliberately using Weatherby's words.

"Great, but I don't want anyone seeing us go backstage to meet Julian," said Weatherby. "They would all want another personal audience with him, and he just doesn't have the time right now. We'll wait until the crowd is gone."

Jake and Weatherby waited as the crowd rose and filed toward the front door. Many held hands while some still cried.

The pair sat silently, watching the crowd disperse.

CHAPTER THIRTY-EIGHT

NONE OF THE normal chatter and laughter of a congregation leaving church accompanied the crowd as they filtered toward the back. A collective sadness and apprehension hung suspended over the shuffling group. They would be much sadder when they realize Julian had duped them. Jake realized he had to stop this madman before the money disappeared into the wind to some offshore account, where no one could recover it. He glanced over his shoulder as the imposing Scandinavian-looking man appeared to lock the door behind the last person to leave. A lump of discomfort knotted in Jake's stomach.

Weatherby seemed to hesitate as he, too, watched the large man hurry from the back of the room to disappear through the door beside the stage. The man practically loped, moving incredibly smoothly for his size. After the door shut, Weatherby said to Jake, "Let's meet the great man."

Every fiber of Jake's being screamed, "Don't do this," but his investigative side told him he had to. He wanted to stand eye to eye with the man perpetrating this scam. He wondered what kind of man would hurt people the way Julian had. "Let's do it," he said.

The pair walked toward the door beside the stage. Weatherby

opened it and stepped aside to allow Jake to enter. They walked into an area devoid of any furnishings. Various props lay scattered across the concrete floor and leaned against the walls, and two doors led to separate rooms. Exposed wooden beams supported the roof. It contrasted starkly with the opulent area they had just come from, more in keeping with the outside of the building.

A closed door separated one room from the open area. A different door opened to what appeared to be a luxurious office. A machine roared inside. Jake presumed the office belonged to the "great man." Julian confirmed his suspicions as he appeared in the office's doorway with the large man behind him. Julian had removed the white robe and stood in the doorway staring at Jake, wearing a blue, open-necked shirt and black pants. He didn't look like a savior without the bombast and white robe. In fact, he could have easily fit in with the congregation that had occupied the seats moments earlier.

Julian spoke as he leaned against the doorway to the office. "Thank you for joining us back here. I'm glad Robert convinced you to meet me. This is the inner sanctum. Few see this area. I generally greet members of my flock out front. I think you can see why." He laughed as he remained in place, while the larger man edged past him, circling around Weatherby and stopping closer to Jake.

The big man's proximity made Jake intensely uncomfortable, but he said, "I can't honestly say I blame people for not wanting to come back here. There isn't much to see."

Julian pushed off from the doorframe and sauntered toward Jake. "I'm curious to know why you're here, Mr. Scott. I'm certain you're not here to be saved, although you have stumbled across a wonderful opportunity to join us in the bunker to avoid the impending apocalypse."

"I wanted to meet you to see what kind of man you are, Julian."

Julian stopped two feet in front of Jake and laughed. "I'm the chosen one. Weren't you listening? I'm saving these people from a doomsday scenario. They're embarrassingly grateful and understand nothing comes for free. They reach into their wallets and use their cash and credit cards to secure their space in the bunker. I didn't see you contribute, though, and that concerns me deeply. Don't you want to be saved?"

Jake wanted to say, "Oh, I want to be saved, Julian. I want to be saved from losing my life savings to a fraud." He realized that if Julian knew why he was there, he might not leave. He wondered if Cassie had figured out the scam, and if they held her captive behind the closed door. At least if that was the case, she would still be alive. Instead, he said, "Of course, I want to be saved. Robert and I worked out an arrangement. We're going to meet tomorrow, so I can make my payment. I understand the larger the payment, the better the accommodation in the bunker. I think my contribution will establish me nicely down there." He laughed nervously, so fixated on his lie that he failed to see Luke edging behind him. He said, "I understand Robert mentioned my name."

Julian nodded. "He did, yes, but I recognized you the minute I laid eyes on you. I know why you're here, though. I just want to hear it from you."

The comment stunned Jake, but now he knew the reason for the recognition in Julian's eyes from the stage. Jake still had no clue about the man's identity. Aside from the familiar voice, there were no meaningful signs. The face was not familiar.

Sweat trickled down Jake's back, partly from anxiety, but also from the stifling heat in the room. The sultriness from the front of the stage had filtered back to this area, and Jake recognized the sound coming from the office now as that of an air conditioner. Jake wasn't sure if he imagined the slight air movement coming from the office door. If there was any, it had little effect on the area they stood in. His shirt clung to him like cling wrap as he realized he may not leave the farm. If Julian really knew the true reason he was here, he wouldn't let him go. How did Julian recognize him? He studied the face again but saw no telltale signs.

Or were there? Jake was not the only one suffering from the heat. Sweat shone on Julian's brow and dampened his blue shirt. More than just ordinary sweat. A drop of colored moisture wriggled down Julian's brow and plopped on his shirt. It momentarily mesmerized Jake. *What would account for the color?* Then he understood. Makeup! The man wore stage makeup. And a lot of it. *Is the face behind the mask recognizable?* Jake realized Julian was still talking.

"… the minute I saw you're still nosing around about Cassie Wright. You're not here to be saved. You're sticking your nose where it doesn't belong."

Jake dropped all pretenses. "That's right, Julian, or whatever your name is. I'm going to expose you for the fraud you are, and if you had anything to do with Cassie Wright's disappearance, the police are going to find out. They know where I am, and they're just waiting to hear from me."

Julian, plainly agitated, pulled at his face, peeling off the special effects makeup that hid his identity. As the silicone and latex pieces rained down on the floor, Jake glanced at Weatherby, who appeared shaken by Jake's assertion that the police knew of his whereabouts. Jake understood that unless they bought his story, they would never let him go. He had to get out of there.

Weatherby turned to Julian. "Do you think that's true? Do you think they know?"

Julian still faced the floor as he removed the makeup, so Jake was still unable to identify him. He said, "I don't give credence to a word of it. This guy's an investigative reporter. Or he was. He's going to want to find out the truth and run to the police. It's an ego thing. The police don't know he's here. He's lying to protect himself."

Jake wondered if he would recognize the man once the makeup was gone. He was certain he already knew because of the voice. *Did he really want to know?* He didn't have to wait. Another telltale sign gave away Julian's identity before the makeup disappeared. Shock waves rattled Jake to the core. The shirt sleeve came up on Julian's arm when he pulled at his makeup, and any lingering doubt was removed. He had talked to this man recently. In that instant, his fears that he was doomed if he didn't escape became a certainty. He tried to suppress a feeling of rising panic.

He turned to run, but the two steps he managed carried him straight into a brick wall by the name of Luke Erickson. Struggling was futile as the gigantic man's muscular arms closed securely around him. The fresh, angry red scratch that crossed the big man's eye and down his cheek made him even more menacing.

Erickson spun Jake around to face the man who called himself Julian. Jake stared into the dead eyes of a man he had interviewed.

Julian said, "It's really too bad you didn't let this go, Scott." He nodded to Erickson and a sharp pain exploded through Jake's neck. The face of the fraudster, kidnapper, and probable murderer dimmed and faded into the distance as Jake collapsed on the concrete floor.

CHAPTER THIRTY-NINE

WEATHERBY COULDN'T CONCEAL his uneasiness at what just happened. Even though he knew it was coming, his ashen face failed to hide his feelings. The sickening smack of Jake's head hitting the concrete floor was too much. He didn't like this part of the job. Erickson didn't support Jake as he fell, and a pool of blood accumulated around the fallen man's head. Weatherby collected himself enough to help Erickson by grabbing Jake under the arms to carry his limp body toward the closed door.

Drips of blood trailed behind as they struggled to hold Jake while Erickson flicked on the light switch and unlocked the door. Once inside, they dumped Jake on a mattress and left. When they closed the door and shut off the lights, the room reverted to its silent, oppressive darkness.

They came back to the center of the floor, where Julian was even more agitated than before. Chunks of latex theatrical makeup lay strewn around the floor at his feet. Angry red blotches covered his face where he had peeled off the latex. His hair stuck out in multiple directions, and he glared at a spot on the floor. His narrowed eyes searched for something that wasn't there.

Weatherby continued walking toward him while Erickson veered toward the office. "Everything okay, Julian?" he asked as he cautiously approached.

"HOW CAN EVERYTHING BE OKAY?" Julian roared, his voice echoing off the wall and rafters. "*You're* the problem. *You* brought that other woman here who challenged my teachings. Then you brought Cassie Wright, and she figured out who I am. Next, you brought that former reporter here. He would expose us in a second. We have to eliminate them because of you. That's three murders that *you're* responsible for."

While Julian ranted, Weatherby, with his back to the office doorway, failed to see Erickson emerge with his hand tucked behind his back. The big man silently closed on the pair, moving with the stealth of a cat.

As Weatherby made a bid to explain himself to Julian, Erickson plunged the syringe into his neck. He dropped just like Cassie and Scott, but rather than his eyes simply closing, they rolled back in his head. He twitched and foamed at the mouth for about fifteen seconds until he grew still.

"Make sure he's dead," Julian said.

"He should be, Boss. I tripled the dosage I gave Cassie." He snickered as he bent to feel for a pulse at Weatherby's neck. "Yup, definitely dead. I'll dispose of the body."

"You're going to have to deal with his car, too. I don't want that around here."

"It'll be like they never existed, Boss."

"Okay, good. You're a loyal man, Luke. Take the cash from the collection baskets. Much of the collections will be credit and debit card slips but take the cash for yourself. I'll give you more tomorrow. Let's meet back here briefly, and then you'll never see me again. I don't think anyone in the assembly would recognize you but move to another city just in case. A man with your experience can get a job anywhere. As soon as you're done with Weatherby's body, get rid of Wright and Scott."

Erickson thanked Julian for his generosity, then they shook hands and parted ways. Julian returned to his office while Erickson grabbed

Weatherby's shoulders and dragged the body through the door, past the stage, and to the barn's front. Unlike with Jake, no blood trail complicated the process. He would clean the drag marks left behind by Weatherby's feet later. He made sure there were no stragglers left in the yard. All the cars had disappeared except three, so he hauled the body to the one belonging to Weatherby. He put the body into the seat after opening the passenger door. He found the keys for the vehicle in Weatherby's pants pocket and deposited them in his own.

Julian's Mercedes raced down the lane in a cloud of dust. Erickson thought he would be happy enough not to see the man again after tomorrow. He paid adequately, but he was becoming irrational, and Luke hadn't planned on murdering anybody. Since everything had unraveled so quickly, he assumed Julian would leave town as soon as possible. He planned to hightail it too, as soon as the bodies were gone.

The so-called bunker was a sham, of course, so it took time to enlarge the hole enough to accommodate a car. The concrete walls beneath the surface that Julian alluded to didn't exist. Erickson used the excavator to build a smooth slope into the hole. The hours ticked by as he fashioned the last resting place for Weatherby and his car. The machine's lights were all he had to go by as the clouds obscured the moon. He wondered if the machine's noise would carry to neighboring yards. No matter, he had to finish the job.

Once the hole appeared sufficiently deep and the slope adequate, he shut off the excavator and wandered to Weatherby's car. He glanced at Weatherby, who appeared to be sleeping in the passenger seat, except for his head lolling against the window. Only the eerie sight of his open eyes in the dim overhead light revealed the fact he was dead.

Erickson steered the car down the ramp and into the hole. He fished in his pocket for the syringe he had used on Scott and Weatherby. He hadn't told Julian that he hadn't emptied the whole dosage into Scott. When the former reporter sagged from the shot, the needle withdrew before he emptied it. He told himself the dosage he administered would be enough to keep Scott slumbering until morning. Besides, Julian would have freaked out with the state he was in. Erickson didn't want to have to deal with that. He tossed the syringe into the hole.

It took much more time to cover the car with Robert Weatherby inside. This had been an exhausting day. In the morning, he would dig up some trees behind the barn and plant them in the loose dirt covering the hole. He patted himself on the back for thinking of it. No one directed him to do it. He thought of it himself. Right now, though, the adrenaline had stopped pumping, and fatigue gripped him as if he suddenly carried bags of rocks. It had been a long day. He wanted to count his cash before he returned to the city. He could fall asleep dreaming about the many destinations he could visit and the final locale where he would settle with a bevy of beautiful women to surround him. Erickson planned to deal with Cassie and Jake the next day before he flew out of town permanently.

He dragged his aching body to the barn and opened the door to an eerie silence. A jolt of fear shot through him until he flicked on the light. Despite his size, he didn't like large, quiet spaces, especially in the dark. That's why he planned to drive home. He hurried to the door by the stage and passed through, stopping at the entrance to the enclosed room. No sound. Precisely what he wanted to hear, even if he didn't like the quiet.

Next, he stopped at Julian's office, where the collection baskets were kept. The anticipation of the cash waiting for him excited him. He opened the office door, flicked on the light, and hurried to Julian's desk where the collection baskets regularly sat when not in use. A sinking feeling overcame him as he drew near. He couldn't see any cash in the top basket. Even the debit and credit card slips were gone. A feeling of dread settled over him like a wet blanket. He peered into the basket and removed the top one from inside the second. Then the next. They were totally empty. Erickson picked them up and hurled them across the room with a curse. As he did so, as if to add insult to injury, a loonie, one Canadian dollar left at the bottom of one basket, rattled off a filing cabinet.

Julian had cleaned them out, leaving nothing but empty baskets for Luke Erickson.

CHAPTER FORTY

LUKE STALKED BACK through the barn, muttering obscenities and things he planned to do to Julian. He locked up the barn and climbed into the vintage red Mustang he had purchased with the extra money earned from working for the man he was furious with right now. He slammed the door and started the vehicle. The exhaust's throaty rumble always gave him chills, and the idling car's vibration normally soothed him. The car's name and growling exhaust conjured images in Luke's mind of stallions straining at their bits under the hood, eager to get going. Luke let them loose, slamming the accelerator down and spraying stones and dirt everywhere. The car fishtailed down the laneway as Luke's anger controlled the gas pedal.

Julian initially hired him to discourage anyone from snooping around the property. His boss was always paranoid, as Luke had seen no one other than Weatherby or Julian and his adherents. It was easy money, supplementing his income from the construction job that had been off and on during the pandemic. He enjoyed firing up the excavator and digging the hole intended to convince the attendees they would have a home while the rest of the world died a slow, miserable death. The machine was a smaller version of the one he used on his construction job, but he loved the smell of the overturned earth and the satisfaction of working on a project. He loved getting his hands dirty.

Luke didn't give a damn about the people who attended the assemblies. In his mind, if they were stupid enough to believe Julian's wild conspiracy theories, they probably deserved to be swindled. Things got out of hand when the blond woman challenged Julian's money quest, and later, Cassie Wright questioned his identity. Still, what did the man expect? Not everyone would be foolish enough to continue to fall for his stories.

His anger subsided when he realized there must be some mistake. Julian probably forgot his promise to leave the cash in the collection baskets. After all, he was pretty agitated with Weatherby for bringing that reporter guy to the meeting. Although he had little to do with Julian, Luke liked him. On some level, Luke even admired him for his accomplishments. As his mind slowed and his body relaxed, he decided he would carry out the rest of the assignment with the assumption that he would receive payment, as Julian promised. Julian had never let him down before, so why would he start now? Cassie Wright and Jake Scott knew too much, so they had to be taken care of no matter what. He had no problem with killing people if he didn't have to look them in the eye.

Another thought wormed its way into his brain. *What if Scott was telling the truth about the police? Maybe I should turn around and take care of Wright and Scott right now.* Then he remembered Julian was adamant that Jake lied about the police and continued driving.

The Mustang's powerful engine protested as he tapped the brake to slow at the stop sign before hammering the accelerator to leave an erratic trail of burned rubber on the highway leading back to Ottawa. He imagined the stallions' frustration at having to slow down. As he roared along the highway, he recalled Julian saying he would see him tomorrow, so as his thoughts cleared, Luke made a plan.

Julian told him if things went wrong, he was to return and "take care of everything." Those were his exact words. He would drive back to the farm in the morning and burn down the building with Cassie

Wright and Jake Scott inside. The fire would have to start behind the stage close to the room that held Wright and Scott in case the smoke attracted a neighbor's attention, and the fire department arrived too quickly. If everything went according to plan, he would watch the barn burn until Julian showed up. He mentally congratulated himself on his plan. It was foolproof, and at this stage, as long as he got his money, he didn't care what Julian thought. He would move to Barbados, or the Bahamas, or somewhere warm with the money Julian would give him. And if Julian didn't show up to pay him, he might have to delay his plan somewhat. He would need to track Julian down first to collect his money. And then he would have to repay the man for reneging on his promise.

***

Jake gradually regained consciousness, but he couldn't be sure if his eyes were open or closed. His brain urged him to wake up, but his eyes gave nothing away. The darkness seemed supernatural. He blinked over and over as he tried hopelessly to penetrate the dark. *Where am I?* he asked himself. He moved his fingers and toes. Everything seemed to work. He touched the thin, lumpy mattress beneath him. He reached out his right hand but yanked it back when he touched the cold concrete floor beyond the mattress. A mildewed odor of dampness fattened the air, but a coppery aroma fought for attention as well. He recognized that smell. Blood!

A pain stabbed at the back of his head. He lifted his head enough to feel a lump on the back, surrounded by a crusty substance that glued strands of his hair together. The scent of blood grew stronger when he pulled his fingers away. Someone must have hit him on the head before dumping him. He wondered how much blood he had lost. Judging by the size of the sticky spot on the mattress, it was a lot.

A chill scraped along Jake's spine, accompanied by an overwhelming urge to vomit. He squeezed his eyes shut and held his breath, willing his stomach to settle down. He gulped multiple times to keep it under control. Eventually, the nausea eased, and the cobwebs slowly began to clear from his brain. He remembered things that happened before he arrived here.

He recalled the meeting he attended. The recollection of palpable fear just before he lost consciousness roared back to him. Julian! That's what this was about. His threat to expose Julian's scam led to this, and they must have knocked him unconscious. He concluded he might have a concussion based on the lump on his head, the headache, and the fog that wouldn't clear.

He needed to relax, so he took slow, deep breaths, hoping to disperse the fog faster. His eyes adjusted, but darkness still obscured his vision. The quietness in the enclosed space could drive him mad, if he had to stay long. It made him think of Mia's ticking clock at home, and he decided he would give anything for that right now. Still, as he listened, he sensed he wasn't alone. A strange, eerie feeling of an unseen presence raised the hair on the back of his neck. *Was someone in a corner observing him? Was it a hidden infrared camera with a lens piercing the dark?*

He tried to see the corners of the room, but complete, unforgiving blackness met his eyes. He turned his head to the left. Wait. There was something there. A large shape between him and the wall. Jake tried to sit, but nausea overtook him again, and he had to lie down. He lay on his back, listening. A sound like shallow breathing broke the silence in the room. Jake's muscles tightened as he strained to listen. *Could it be his imagination? Dreaming?* Then absolute silence. *Did it stop?* He tried to focus, concentrating as hard as he could. He heard it again. It sounded like slow, but steady breathing. He imagined the air in the room being sucked in, and then expelled. The walls seemed to close in and expand in the pervasive darkness.

Close in and expand.

Close in and expand.

Jake's stomach tightened into an unrelenting knot. An irrational fear overtook him. He had to get out of there. Now! Then he realized it would not be that easy. He shook his head to shake the image of the walls contracting and expanding. He wasn't alone in this confined space. Someone else shared the room with him. He was sure of it.

His heart skipped a beat. It had to be Cassie Wright. He bolted upright, but his head spun like a ride at the fair. This time, he overdid it. He collapsed on the thin mattress, as his body gave up, and he fell unconscious for a second time.

CHAPTER FORTY-ONE

JAKE DIDN'T KNOW how long he had been out when he woke up to the oppressive, disorienting darkness the second time. It might have been minutes, or even hours. He had no way of knowing. Avery had encouraged him to use his phone as his timepiece. He wished he hadn't listened as his phone now lay in a basket somewhere. He had to gather his thoughts further. Depending on the time he had been here, Avery and Dani could be in panic mode by now. He mentally kicked himself for not telling Dani his plans. How stupid could he be? It was foolhardy, but too late now. He got his ass into this mess. He had to get his ass out.

He recalled passing out when he tried to rise too hastily, so he lay on his back for a few minutes. The last thing he remembered before he passed out was the shape on his left side, so he reached to touch it, but it lay too far away. He called out in a thin, ragged voice that surprised him. "Is someone there?"

No response.

He remembered the goose egg on the back of his head and the blood surrounding it. Now, he realized his neck hurt too. He touched the spot and grimaced. Stiffness radiated from it, exactly like the heaviness in his arm when he received the vaccines for the pandemic, but more pronounced. Not painful. More of a dull ache. He needed to put all that aside and force himself to focus. He listened for any sign of life in the room. He heard the soft noise again, slowly, in and out. It had to be labored breathing.

Jake tested the waters by pushing himself up on an elbow. His head swam, and bile rocketed to his throat, but nothing he couldn't handle. After a few seconds, he shoved himself more upright and rested again to let his stomach settle. He glanced to his left and verified the shape he had seen earlier. Even the slightest movement sent his head into freefall, but he had to know. *Take it slow.* Someone or something lay on the floor, and he had to find out who or what.

He called out again with no response. He needed to know if it was a person. It had to be Cassie Wright. He tried to stand, but his brain rolled like waves on the ocean, forcing him back onto the mattress. After a few more minutes, he rolled off the mattress onto the damp, cool concrete. It worked better than trying to stand. He shoved over on his side until he hit something soft. He recognized the texture of another thin mattress, like the one he had been on. The shape lay within arm's reach now.

He reached and touched a bare, female leg. A shudder went through him. "Cassie? Cassie Wright?" No response. "Are you okay?" Still nothing.

The thought of moving slowly became a distant memory now as he pulled himself onto the mattress. He touched the person's hair to find it was shoulder length and stringy, like it hadn't been washed in a while. Jake nudged the woman's hip, confirming she wore a dress or shorts. Positivity replaced apprehension, as he had surely found Cassie Wright. Her features were impossible to see in the dark, but it had to be her.

He shook the woman's shoulder, but she didn't wake up. He shook more vigorously, rocking her back and forth. Still no response. He rolled her onto her back, shook both shoulders, and slapped her cheeks lightly. Her head lolled to one side, but this time she mumbled something. He leaned his ear closer to her mouth to make out her indistinct words.

"Le… uh, leave me a… a… lone."

The statement sent a chill racing through Jake. Had they touched her? Jake remembered the large man named Luke. Had *he* touched her?

Jake shook her again. He said, "My name is Jake Scott. Is your name Cassie Wright?"

An unintelligible mumble.

Jake leaned forward, tapping her cheeks again. "Can you hear me? Can you tell me if your name is Cassie Wright? Nod your head if you're Cassie Wright."

Jake peered at the woman, trying to make out her face in the dark. He nearly missed it, but his hand resting on her cheek detected a slight up and down movement.

Elation ran through him. She just confirmed she was Cassie Wright! *But what's wrong with her?* he wondered. *Why won't she wake up? They must have drugged her.*

"Cassie, we must find a way out. Can you wake up?"

Jake's thumb rested lightly on her mouth. Her lips quivered, but the sound was unintelligible. He pressed his ear against her lips and said, "Cassie, repeat that. I'm not sure what you said."

"D… daughter?"

Her words came from her lips so soft, he almost missed it, but Cassie asked about her daughter. It was encouraging.

"Haley is fine, Cassie. I talked to her yesterday, and she's doing fine." Jake didn't know how long he had been held captive, or when he talked to her, but the idea of seeing Haley recently could comfort Cassie. "She is eager to see you, so you have to wake up, so we can plan our escape. It will take two of us, Cassie. You need to force yourself to wake up."

He sensed Cassie tried, but she just couldn't will herself into consciousness. Her eyes fluttered, but immediately closed. Then her lips moved again, and he sensed, rather than heard, soft words. The most she had spoken. He said, "I'm sorry, Cassie. Repeat that. I didn't catch what you said. He leaned closer again, his ear practically resting on her lips.

"B… bucket. Handle." Her last word was no louder than a whisper. "W… indow."

The words made absolutely no sense to him.

And Cassie lost consciousness again. This time, when he shook her, she didn't wake up.

CHAPTER FORTY-TWO

OR A MOMENT, Jake wondered if he'd lost her. A chill raced through him as he prepared to do the same chest compressions he had started on Eric in what seemed like ages ago now. Guilt washed over him. He should be offering comfort to Eric's wife right now, not locked in some dank room, wondering what fate awaited him. Thankfully, a gradual rise and fall greeted Jake's hands when he placed them on Cassie's chest. He pondered what on earth she meant as he listened to her breathe. Had he heard correctly? Was she delirious? Jake shook her repeatedly, but her body remained still. At least her breathing had returned to normal. She mentioned a pail and handle. And a *window*? He had no perception of a window in the place. He couldn't even see the walls in the inescapable darkness, let alone a window. Still, he had to believe she knew something and had tried to tell him.

His head throbbed less now, and his stomach had settled down considerably. Progress. He sat up, and the motion brought less nausea. Cassie could not help right now, and Jake decided he had to move. He had to get them out. The big guy might return anytime, and Jake feared when he arrived, his and Cassie's lives wouldn't last much longer.

He pushed himself to his feet, wobbling on rubbery legs, nearly losing his balance. Even though he didn't have far to fall, he might as well have been 100 feet off the ground in a howling wind on a tight-rope. He bent his knees and held his hands in front of him like a surfer until the latest wave subsided. A hesitant step nearly caused him to lose his balance as his foot left the mattress and landed on the floor.

He had trouble believing the window Cassie mentioned existed in this darkness. He shuffled around Cassie and straight forward with his hands out for a few feet until he bumped into a wall. Little did he know his route followed the identical path Cassie had pursued days earlier. Sound-deadening material softened the wall, which somehow sent more dread cascading over him. Jake moved quicker now, forgetting about the pain in his head and the nausea in his stomach. It was life or death for them both. He just wished Cassie would wake up to save time by telling him what she meant.

He took a cautious step and felt the wall's surface as far as he could reach in all directions, poking and prodding. Then he repeated the process. Another step. More poking and prodding. Each step brought more depressing results. Suddenly, he reached a spot with some give in the surface material. *Was this it?* Could this be the window Cassie talked about? Maybe he hadn't been hearing things.

Jake tested the material, finding where the solid edge stopped and the part with some give began. He dug his nails into the section that seemed to cover an opening, but the material's thickness prevented him from getting a grip. He tried to find a gap where the tiles joined, but when he did, there wasn't enough room to force his fingers in to allow him to dig a hole. Cassie had mentioned something about a bucket, and she'd said it in the same breath as the window. *Was there a bucket in the room?* It's possible, Jake thought. He recalled she also mentioned a handle. He realized she may have been talking about a makeshift tool to pry through the material to reach the window. Jake didn't want to waste more time trying to break through the material until he found that bucket.

The pain in his head and his wooziness had vanished, thankfully, although he still realized his movements were slower than they would be ordinarily. He continued his slow march around the room's walls, feeling the surface and shuffling his feet, hoping to stumble over the bucket. It didn't take long before he kicked something plastic and sent it rattling across the concrete floor. The reason for it being there became apparent, as he realized he would need to use it eventually. At least their captors must empty it since no contents spilled from it as it bounced across the floor.

He reached around until he retrieved it. It had a metal handle. It had to be what Cassie referred to. Like a blind man reading braille, he determined that the bucket was of standard design with a metal handle with the ends bent at an angle and inserted into holes on either side. Cassie was talking about using the ends of the handle as a tool to make a hole in the tiles covering the window. He could have kissed her.

He thought pulling the handle out of the pail would be easy, but his weakness and the metal handle's strength surprised him. Finally, he dislodged the handle by setting the pail on its side and kicking at it. Cassie was right. The angles of the ends of the handle made an ideal tool to jam into the tiny gap where the tiles at the side of the window joined. He gingerly felt his way back to the spot where he thought he would find his target and got to work with the handle.

Jake dug and pulled at the sound-deadening tile. He furiously jabbed at the material because he didn't know when the big guy would be back. He made steady progress until the handle flew from his hands and clattered to the floor. *Dammit!* Jake sank to his knees and crawled around the space, wasting precious minutes. It seemed to take forever for a sweep of his hand to connect with the handle. He picked it up and got back to work. When he inserted his fingers, the size of the widening gap gave him hope.

It troubled him that the expected light didn't come in as the ragged hole widened. In fact, the room had not brightened one bit. It remained as depressingly bleak as when he'd started. Finally, when he'd diligently widened the gap enough, he stuck his hand inside and met with more resistance. *Had all this been for nothing?* He yanked at the material covering the window and pulled off three-quarters of a tile.

Sweat dripped from his face, leaving dark splotches on the concrete that he couldn't see.

The room remained dark as a cave, even as he separated the tile from the window, as dark as it had been before. He knocked on a different material that still covered the window. His heart sank. He might as well have been knocking on patio stones. He had removed the tile only to uncover another barrier. They had covered the opening with plywood.

CHAPTER FORTY-THREE

OVERWHELMING EXHAUSTION OVERCAME Jake as he sunk to his knees. The sweat, effort, and raw fingers had accomplished nothing. There seemed to be no way out. Nausea and dizziness returned as he crawled back to the mattress. A kaleidoscope of thoughts ran through his mind when he lay down. He wondered about Avery, and if she was worried sick about him. The recollection of kissing Dani followed, bringing with it a simultaneous sense of hope for their future and despair at being locked up in this room. Then the thought of Eric, attached to several machines in a hospital room, came next. At least, Jake hoped he was still alive. He thought of Dani's daughter, Emilie, and the promising art she produced. Cassie's daughter, Haley, came to mind along with the fear and anxiety she must be facing. Then there was Oliver. He and the cat didn't always get along, but he missed the temperamental feline. Mia loved the cat, so Jake did, too. He had so many reasons to escape.

He shook Cassie again.

"Cassie, you have to wake up. We need to discover a way out."

She did not react. Even though her breathing had returned to normal, she couldn't seem to pull herself from her sleep. It was like she was in a coma. Jake sighed and rolled back to his own mattress where he let the exhaustion settle over him, and he joined Cassie in a deep sleep.

***

Luke Erickson drove to the farm after his own fitful night's sleep. He had spent the night questioning whether Julian would honor his commitment to pay for the extra work. If Julian didn't pay him, he resolved to doggedly track the man down, even if it was the last thing he ever did. He pulled into the yard, not truly surprised that he didn't see Julian's car. Okay, if that's the way he wanted to play it.

Erickson drove his Mustang to within a few feet of the barn door. Julian didn't like anyone parking that close, but to hell with him. He lifted an object from the back seat before striding to the entrance where he unlocked the door. He moved through the common area and past the silent stage after flicking on the light. There was no sound at the door of the room holding Cassie and Jake. He set the object down, turned on the light, and unlocked the door. Both of his captives lay passed out on their mattresses. Clearly, they hadn't moved since the night before. Scott's wound had stopped bleeding as he lay on the dried blood.

Then Erickson noticed the gouged pieces of acoustical tile lying on the floor. He immediately figured out what had happened. One of them had awakened sometime during the night and cleverly used the bucket's handle to break through the tile. Clever, but not clever enough. Erickson snickered at the plywood covering the window. When they put the other woman in the room, Julian's insistence that he cover the window opening as an extra layer of protection seemed like overkill. The man had proven right once again. How disappointed Scott or Wright must have been when they discovered the plywood.

Erickson sauntered over to Jake's mattress and savagely kicked him in the ribs. There was no response. Perhaps the former reporter was dead. Oh well, it would save him from dying of smoke inhalation. Erickson thought of administering another dose of drugs, but why bother? There would be no escaping the room if they woke up. He left and locked the door, pulling on it a few times to make sure it was solid. He turned off the light. *Good riddance to you both*, he thought.

He picked up the object he had set down before and wandered to Julian's office. The collection baskets lay on the floor where he had hurled them last night. The loonie that had rattled off the filing cabinet lay on the carpet, taunting him. Obviously, Julian had not returned. Erickson placed the object he had been carrying beside the desk. He had grown up with the noisy old space heater all through his time at his parents' house. His grandparents may have even used it before that. Paint had flaked off the gunmetal gray heater, and the front grill was dented from people tripping over it. It had none of the modern-day safety features if it tipped over. He didn't know why he salvaged it, but it had remained in his basement for a few years after his parents passed. He just couldn't bring himself to get rid of it.

Now, it would be used again. The frayed cord lay twisted across the carpet. Bare wires protruded from the covering in several places. He'd tested it at home, and it would work beautifully for the purpose he had in mind. He lifted the carpet to lay the frayed cord underneath and threw Julian's robes over top. The cord remained unplugged for the moment.

The converted barn had a colorful and enhanced interior, and a few coats of paint freshened its exterior appearance, but old rotting wood made up its infrastructure. If someone truly wanted to improve it, other than cosmetically, they would have torn it down and started over. That had not been the case, and the structure would burn beautifully. Some of the props in the open area outside the office would provide the necessary accelerant, and pressurized cans of sealant and adhesive removers lying about would even explode. The place would be engulfed in flames by the time anyone noticed. The two captives would die in the flames. He expected the blaze would be so complete, that the inspectors would never know the door had been locked to keep them inside.

Erickson had gone over the plan countless times in his mind and convinced himself of its reliability. He had never done the planning before and wished he could run it by Julian, but certainly that would not be possible.

Before he plugged in the heater, he wanted to plant the trees where the car and Weatherby lay buried under feet of dirt. If Julian hadn't shown up by the time he finished, he would put his plan to burn down the barn in motion. And later he would hunt Julian down, extract the money he was owed, and kill him.

CHAPTER FORTY-FOUR

JAKE COULDN'T BELIEVE he hadn't cried out when Erickson kicked him in the ribs. He had been sleeping until the bodyguard turned on the light. He'd opened his eyes to the sudden brightness and promptly closed them again. The realization that Erickson would see the shredded tile immediately sprang to his mind. He pretended to sleep until he figured out what the man planned to do next. Jake readied himself to fight, even though he realized that without a weapon, he couldn't do much against the much larger and younger man.

Jake listened as the man prowled around the room after he spied the pieces of tile. He braced himself as Erickson grunted and approached, but he didn't expect the kick in the ribs. An involuntary whoosh escaped his lips, but he hoped it was quiet enough that Erickson didn't notice.

Fortunately, Erickson left the room immediately after, giving Jake time to recover. The room went dark again. The sudden brightness followed by sudden darkness meant Jake had to wait until his eyes adjusted again. He gingerly felt his side where he'd absorbed the toe of Erickson's boot. The probing sent a jolt of pain to Jake's brain, but he didn't think the kick broke a rib. He had to set it aside and worry about it afterward.

The immediate goal was to get out of this prison. But how? They had evidently drugged Cassie, and Jake suspected they'd done the same to him. It might account for the stiffness in his neck. Right now, he had so many places on his body that ached that he couldn't decide which hurt the worst. He had to forget them all and concentrate on waking Cassie.

He wondered how long it had been since he ate. The other aches and pains masked the hunger. Despite that, he wished he had more energy. He rolled to his side with a groan, pushing himself over until he lay beside Cassie. He grabbed her shoulder and shook her as vigorously as he could. No response. He tried again. This time, she stirred.

"Cassie, can you hear me? Wake up."

Cassie rewarded him with an unintelligible mumble. At least, it was something.

Jake slapped her cheek again. It had worked last time. "CASSIE, YOU HAVE TO FORCE YOURSELF AWAKE. We need to find a way out of here. I can't do it alone, and I'm not leaving you here."

He leaned closer to Cassie, and he thought her eyes fluttered. He persisted, slapping her cheeks and calling her until she mumbled, "Who… who are you?"

"I'm Jake Scott, remember? I know your daughter, Haley. She's doing really well, but she needs you at home. You and I have to find a way out." Cassie's eyes drooped shut. He slapped her cheek again. His words were urgent. "Cassie, stay with me. I need you awake. We need to find a way out."

Her words came out clearer this time, giving Jake hope she was regaining consciousness.

"Mmm… try the window? So dark."

Thank God. "I did as you suggested. I used the handle from the bucket and pried out pieces of the tile covering the window. You were so smart to think of that, but there is a piece of plywood under it. It's impossible to budge. I can't see a thing in here. Are you hurt in any way? Did anybody touch you?"

"Uh, no, I don't think so. I can't remember anything after a meeting. Bathroom?"

"We don't have a bathroom. All we have is that bucket you told me about. I can lead you to it."

"I remember now. Okay."

Jake stood with a groan as his side protested at the movement. At least his brain had cleared, and he hoped Cassie's would soon. He put his hands under her arms to hoist her to her feet. Her body weight pulled at his sore ribcage, eliciting another groan.

"It sounds like you're not okay," she mumbled.

"The big guy kicked me in the ribs, but I'm fine. Let's find the pail, so you can do what you have to do, and then we'll figure out a plan."

The pair wobbled toward the center of the room until the shape of the bucket emerged before them. Jake set it upright for Cassie.

"This is so embarrassing," she said.

"I know. I have to use it too when you're done. Are you okay to sit?"

"I'll be okay. Just so weak and tired. I'll need to lie down again."

"You can't, Cassie. We need to be alert so we can deal with the man. I'll return to the mattress and turn around. Let me know when you're finished, and I'll help you back to the mattress." He wanted to give her space, even though he couldn't see anything.

When Cassie finished, Jake helped her back to the mattress. He used the bucket and made his way back to his mattress. He insisted Cassie remain sitting with her back against the wall, so he didn't lose her again. He did the same.

Cassie wanted to know everything about Haley. He patiently told her everything he could. He had more important things on his mind, but he needed Cassie alert and calm. When she seemed satisfied, she told him the big man brought sandwiches and water sometimes. Then he changed the subject to their escape. The conversation didn't last long. They took inventory of potential weapons. None, really. It was impossible to see much, and they had to deal with their adversary's enormous size. The element of surprise was what they had to count on.

They had to jump the man using their hands, feet, and teeth. Cassie told Jake about scratching Erickson's eyes with her nails. She confirmed she would do it again in a heartbeat if given the chance. They would even throw the bucket's contents at him. They discussed whether they would hear him coming in the sound-deadened room. Cassie told Jake about hearing the indiscernible, mumbled words when she had first awakened. They agreed their only hope was to lie in wait and listen, then ambush him. They would pretend to sleep and jump up from their mattresses when he approached. They would attack anything. His eyes, ears, balls, instep—whatever presented itself as a target. They would fight like animals, hoping to disable him, and then run like hell for the front door. And if that didn't work, they concluded, they were doomed.

CHAPTER FORTY-FIVE

LUKE ERICKSON'S ANGER grew into a blind rage as the hours passed, and Julian didn't arrive. He concluded Julian had no intention of paying him for the latest work he had done, or the bonus for the work he was about to do. He glanced at his car, tempted to drive off and forget the whole thing. He didn't care anymore about Julian, and with Weatherby dead, he could just walk away. The Wright woman and the former reporter would starve to death in the room. But something told him he needed to wipe out any evidence that might tie him to the Guardians of Truth, and the best way to do it would be to destroy the building and everything inside. If it held some special meaning for Julian, all the better. It would be fun to see Julian's face just before he killed him when he told him he had burned the barn to the ground.

The time passed rapidly, and when he checked his watch, it surprised him to see mid-afternoon had arrived. He bitterly ground the gears of the tractor he had driven from behind the barn. Finally, he shut off the machine and climbed down to examine his handiwork. A nice row of young birch trees that he dug up behind the barn lined the area over the top of the hole where the car lay buried. Perfect. No one would suspect that a car lay underneath the trees. What a surprise it would be if someone ever unearthed the car! It had been a lot of work, but it satisfied him completely as the sweat dripped down his face from the afternoon sun. Keeping busy took away some of the edge from Julian's betrayal. He knew it wouldn't last.

Luke started the tractor again and drove it back behind the barn. He left it close enough that the fire he planned would likely consume it. He had to hurry. The sun set around 8:30, and he wanted the barn gone by then. The smoke from the fire would be less visible to neighbors than flames burning in the night. He repeated his earlier activities, striding to the front of the barn, unlocking the door and turning on the lights. He glanced around the room, realizing he wouldn't miss this place.

Luke stopped at the door to the room holding Wright and Scott. He contemplated checking on them. Maybe he should give them each another dose. The dosages he had needed to give the pair continued to be a guessing game for him. He told Weatherby and Julian he knew what he was doing, but he had no clue.

He put his hand on the door handle and tried to turn it. It remained securely locked. He took the key from his pocket and inserted it in the lock, but when he rested his ear against the door, nothing but silence greeted him. Precisely what he wanted to hear. They must both be completely out of it, so he'd probably administered the right amount. Or they were dead. If not, they soon would be. He would earmark all the chemicals left in the bottle for Julian.

Rattling the door against its frame reconfirmed no one would get out without a sledgehammer. He pulled the key from the lock and dropped it back into his pocket.

Luke hurried to the office. Everything remained as he'd left it. He pulled on the drawer to the desk where Julian kept the syringes and dosage bottles. Locked. *Dammit!* He searched for something to pry it open, but saw nothing that might work. He reared back and kicked at it. His kick missed the mark, but the result turned out nicely. His work boot connected with the desktop enough to lift it an inch above the top of the drawer. He smugly awarded himself a zero for style and a ten for results. Not enough to get his hand inside yet, though. He savagely kicked at it again with all the force he could muster. This time, the entire desk moved, and the top separated from the frame, exposing everything inside. Luke hoped a stash of money might spill out, but no such luck. He did, however, find the chemicals and syringes he was looking for.

He stuffed them in his pocket and plugged in the heater, turning it to full blast. The fan whirred to life, and heat poured from it. Luke sat in Julian's luxurious chair, his feet propped on the shattered desk. He anxiously waited as the old fan ran as designed, albeit noisily, heating the room as if it were brand new.

Luke waited. A wisp of smoke tickled his nostrils, or it might have been wishful thinking. He decided he would have to use gasoline as an accelerant if this didn't work. He wanted the fire to look natural, but the desire to burn the place to the ground trumped everything else. He would do what was necessary.

Abruptly, the lights in the office flickered and went out. The heater's fan blades stopped turning. Luke didn't enjoy being left in the dark in the building, but he tolerated it because he associated it with success. Light still filtered in the open door from the large area outside the office, so the heater must have shorted out the circuit he'd plugged it into.

A thrill rose in Luke's body as he stared at the carpet, watching smoldering embers chew a hole in it. No flame still, but an acrid smell filled the room as vivid red and orange edges grew in the carpet over the top of the wire. Thin wisps of smoke drifted into the air. Luke sat, mesmerized, as the carpet smoldered. This was working beyond his wildest dreams, but would it be enough to start the inferno he needed?

It didn't take long to answer his question. Within a minute, the smoke turned into a flame. Julian's robes ignited. Luke tossed some of Julian's books onto the fledging blaze, and soon fire licked up the wall and at the desk. Everything escalated quickly. The unaltered, old infrastructure would be consumed swiftly by the fire. Luke decided he better get the hell out of there as the dry, old building was about to go up like a box full of old wooden matches. The fire would be uncontrollable when it reached the material in the outer area.

The thickening smoke made it extremely hard to breathe as he hurried through the office door. He chuckled as he ran past the door to the room holding Wright and Scott. Wouldn't want to be them, he thought as he hustled through the building. When he arrived outside, he turned to see the smoke rolling into the area in front of the stage.

In Luke's haste to reach his car, he didn't notice a second vehicle parked a few feet away. So used to seeing cars in the lot, the fact that it was there didn't immediately register. Nor did he notice a shadowy figure emerging from around the corner. The figure silently crept behind him as he bent to unlock the door to his prized Mustang. This time, he didn't get to enjoy the throaty rumble of the car's engine as something solid nearly split his head open.

CHAPTER FORTY-SIX

JAKE AND CASSIE lay quietly on their mattresses, listening intently for any sound in the outer area. They had no concept of time. It could have been the middle of the night or mid-afternoon. They had to stay alert in case someone showed up. It would be their one and only chance.

They had dragged the bucket to within reach between the mattresses. An overpowering odor rose from the bucket, dominating the enclosed room, but it had to be part of their arsenal, whether they liked it or not. They had to think they had a chance, or they'd lose all hope.

The seconds ticked by achingly slow, but they eventually turned into minutes and then hours. The room reeked of sweat and human waste, but worst of all, despair. Jake's muscles tightened with tension with each passing second. Before lying down, he had stepped on the curve in the bucket handle to straighten it, and now he held it like a knife. He flexed the hand holding it. His muscles had grown stiff from gripping the handle too tight. He planned to strike at the big man's eyes when Cassie heaved the contents of the bucket. They just had to stun him enough to get around him and run for the door.

Neither counted on the plan to be foolproof. Cassie had described her failed attempt to run, and to Jake, it sounded uncomfortably like their new plan. It was the best solution they could come up with in the dark prison.

Jake's voice grew hoarse from trying to keep Cassie awake. She kept drifting off, and he couldn't allow that to happen. She had fallen asleep again when a thump sounded at their door.

"Cassie, wake up!" Jake insisted urgently.

"What is it?" her voice sounded weak.

Jake whispered, "He's here. Wake up. He's at the door. Grab the bucket. Remember, the lights will blind us when they come on. Just squint long enough to see roughly where he is and throw the contents of the bucket. Got it?"

They had practiced getting up from the mattresses and stepping hurriedly straight forward, so they would be directly in front of the door. They were aware of the number of paces it took and where to stand. Jake's only concern now was whether Cassie would be awake enough to handle her part of the task. He knew she was ready when she leaped up and picked up the bucket. She involuntarily moaned in disgust as the contents sloshed. The missing handle made gripping the bucket more difficult, but Cassie had practiced that too.

The door rattled again, and they assumed their positions. Jake held the handle with about three inches protruding from his fist. He ignored his sore side and the other aches and pains and coiled his body like a spring. He had to do his part. Their lives depended on it. They heard a key inserted into the lock. The door rattled again, harder this time. Suddenly, everything fell quiet. They heard absolutely no sound from beyond the door.

They waited for minutes until Jake whispered, "He must have left."

"I can't hold this bucket much longer. What do we do?"

Jake said dejectedly. "It sounds like he's gone. Let's relax and listen for a few minutes. We have to be in the best shape possible when he returns."

Cassie sighed as they headed back to their mattresses. They lay back down, waiting and listening as before.

Time crawled along for what seemed like hours.

Suddenly, Jake's body bristled as he caught a whiff of an unfamiliar smell invading the room. He turned to face Cassie. "Do you smell that?"

"Mm… what?" Cassie had dozed off.

"I think I smell smoke. Can you smell it?"

Cassie said sleepily, "All I can smell is the stench of that damned bucket."

Jake sniffed the air again. The odor had grown stronger.

"No, there's definitely smoke in the air." His words tumbled out. "It must be coming through the vent. I hope it's coming in from outside." He honestly didn't believe that.

Cassie was wide awake now. "I smell it now, too. What's going on?"

"I don't know, but it's getting thicker." Jake pulled his shirt up over his nose. "Cover your nose with anything you can." He got up from the mattress and raced toward where the door should be without counting his steps. He thudded headlong into the door and grabbed the handle. It wouldn't budge. He heaved his body weight against it, but it stood unmoving, as solid as the wall. He felt along the edge of the room, coughing as he went. His eyes watered, which made his vision even worse. He found the window opening and pounded on it with his fists, but he wouldn't be dislodging the plywood that covered it.

They were going to die from smoke inhalation if they didn't leave. Jake's lungs burned from the searing smoke. If he could locate the vent, he might be able to stuff his shirt into it, *if* he could figure out a way to reach it. He dropped to his knees, trying to find fresher air. He told himself he just needed a second to gather himself, but he started to lose consciousness and leaned against the wall for support. A voice was calling him just as his eyes closed. The voice sounded far away, like it had traveled across the universe as it penetrated the smoke and cobwebs forming again in his brain.

It was Cassie.

"Jake, someone's at the door again. I have the bucket and the handle. GET OVER HERE! We need to be ready."

CHAPTER FORTY-SEVEN

JAKE SHOOK HIS head to revive himself. He peered through the haze in the direction Cassie's voice had seemed to come from, but it was beyond dark in the room now. The smoke had obliterated any visibility they once had when their eyes adjusted. He pushed himself to his feet and stumbled forward with his arms outstretched.

"Cassie, say something, so I can find you," Jake uttered.

Cassie retched a deep cough. "I'm over here. Reach for my hand."

Jake fumbled in the dark until he found her outstretched hand.

The doorknob turned.

"Remember, the light will be blinding," he mumbled, his voice sounding hoarse and soft. "Let fly with the contents of the bucket as soon as you spot him in the doorway."

A crack appeared in the doorway and smoky light filtered into the room. The terrifying sound of flames crackled outside the door. As the crack in the doorway widened, heavy pungent smoke poured into the room, and Cassie coughed forcefully, her lungs trying to jettison the acrid air. Jake squinted at the doorway as a figure appeared. He shouted, "Wait," to Cassie, who desperately tried to stifle her cough so she could drench the person with the contents of the bucket.

It wasn't the giant man who showed up. In fact, the person who entered looked as far removed from the giant man as anyone could. Jake wondered if his squinting eyes deceived him. *Had the smoke overcome him?*

Robert Weatherby's short, white-haired assistant hurried into the room.

What the hell? Jake wondered. Whose side is *she* on? He held the bucket handle securely between the fingers of his right hand, ready to strike if she came close.

Cassie's coughing subsided enough for her to whisper, "Do I throw it or not? I can't see who it is."

Jake ignored Cassie. The stocky woman in the doorway appeared to be assessing the situation. He recalled that the receptionist reminded him of someone when he first met her. Framed in the light and flames behind her, to Jake at this moment, she resembled a younger version of Queen Elizabeth II.

The woman approached while coughing and gesturing wildly with both hands.

"C'mon. We have to go. The whole place is going to go up."

Jake found his voice. "Why are *you* here? Where's the big guy?"

The woman said through a cloth she now held over her nose, "Believe me, you would sooner have me here. We have a few seconds to get out. I'll fill you in later, but I suppose you won't trust me unless I tell you something." Her words tumbled from her mouth. "The big guy you're talking about, Luke Erickson, is lying unconscious by his car. I needed his keys to the room to get you out, so I hit him with a tire iron. I figured something was wrong when Julian stormed off the stage, so I snuck back and witnessed Erickson giving Robert an injection. Robert collapsed, and I nearly screamed. Robert hasn't surfaced since." She barked a hoarse cough. "I followed Erickson back here and suddenly the barn caught on fire, so I went outside and waited for him. I figured you two must be in here and would have no way out. Now, let's *go!*"

She pried the bucket from Cassie's stiff fingers and set it down.

Cassie had listened quietly, stifling her coughing fit. Tears streamed from her clenched eyes. When the woman stopped talking and turned to go, Cassie said incredulously, "Grace?"

The woman said impatiently, "Yes, it's me, Grace. This fire will fry us all if we don't go."

When neither moved immediately, she shouted, "NOW."

Jake thought quickly. Either they go with this woman, or they stay and die of smoke inhalation or worse. There were so many questions, but he grabbed Cassie's hand and rushed to the door.

Jake couldn't believe his eyes when they left the room. Flames licked at the walls and devoured the supplies around the room like a chainsaw chewing through a sapling. They dodged sections of the ceiling crashing to the floor. A section of smoldering insulation wafted lazily downward on the currents generated by the inferno. They had just stepped through the gates of hell.

Flames reached for the ceiling on the route leading to the front of the stage, but Grace didn't hesitate, charging straight for the doorway. She ran breathlessly on her short legs, her white hair brightened by the red and orange fire and hazy blue smoke. As they ran, Jake realized there was no other way, and he understood now that she wanted to save them.

They arrived at the wall of flame blocking the doorway, and Grace slid to a stop. She said, "Okay, look, I don't know what's on the other side, but we have no choice. You need to run through these flames and get into the main hall area. Then run for the front door as fast as you can."

Jake said, "What about you?"

"Don't worry about me. I'll be right behind you."

Jake barely heard her over the crackling flames. He saw through the fire that the other side was untouched so far. The narrow doorway meant they had to go through one at a time. He turned to Cassie. He hadn't realized she had pulled her skirt up to cover her mouth and nose. "Are you okay? Can you do this?"

The heat from the flames became more intense, the fire's roar growing progressively louder. The monster crackled and popped as it flexed its muscles, placating its insatiable appetite by devouring everything in its midst.

Cassie's muffled voice came through the cloth. "Like Grace said, we have no choice." Without another word, she gathered her remaining strength, let her skirt fall away from her face, and with her arms covering her head, sprinted headlong toward the wall of flames in the doorway. She leaped like a hurdler when she arrived at the flames. The wind from her movement fanned the flames even harder, and they became thicker and more intense. Silence followed for a few seconds until a voice rose from the other side.

"It's okay. I'm a little singed, but okay. The fire hasn't reached here yet, but it's coming. *Hurry.*"

Jake followed suit, copying Cassie's approach with his arms covering his face and head. The severe heat hit him like a hammer, but his momentum carried him through to the other side. The fresher, but still smoky air instantly soothed his lungs, and as Cassie said, the fire had not yet reached this part of the barn. He agreed with her, though. It wouldn't be long.

He glanced at Cassie. The fire had blackened her face with soot and frayed the tips of her hair on one side. She swatted at the smoldering hem of her skirt. Jake checked for any hot spots on his clothes and slapped them with his hand to put them out. His right cheek screamed like he had lain in the sun for far too long.

They waited for Grace to come through the flames, but a crash on the other side startled them. The thin wall of flames they came through swiftly became opaque and the fierce heat drove them further into the common area. Jake instantly guessed what had happened. Additional ceiling tiles had fallen, feeding more oxygen to the beast. Part of the roof might have caved in.

Jake and Cassie simultaneously shouted for Grace, but they heard no answer. A jolt of fear shot through Jake as they shouted Grace's name over and over. The unstoppable roaring flames swallowed their words. Jake started toward the burning doorway, but Cassie grabbed his arm.

"You can't do it, Jake. She's gone. We have to go." Her words were barely out of her mouth when another enormous crash from the back shook the building. It sounded like the whole back part of the barn caved in. Jake thought he saw the roof over his head shimmy. The velvet curtain at the front of the stage suddenly caught fire and bright orange flames snaked along the timbers at the ceiling, sucking up the oxygen as they slithered toward the open front door.

Jake felt like he was sitting inside a barbecue with the lid closed. As he and Cassie rounded the benches to run for the front door, Jake couldn't stop thinking about the woman who had risked her life to save them. He didn't know her well, at all, actually, but the woman had saved their lives. Hopefully, by some miracle, the fire burned a hole in the back wall through which Grace escaped. The chances were extremely slim. He would never forget the sacrifice she made for them. She deserved a better fate.

CHAPTER FORTY-EIGHT

T HEY REACHED THE door to the barn and peeked around the corner. There was no sign of the baskets holding the cell phones the young women had collected when they entered. A battered blue Ford Escort sat left of the door. Rust chewed at the fenders and the lower half of the crushed left quarter panel nearly rubbed against the tire. An older model Mustang, in much better condition, sat a few feet from the building with the driver's side door hanging wide open. Jake pointed to it and said Erickson's name in a loud whisper, but they saw no sign of the large man. They leaned down to look underneath the car, but seeing nothing, they realized he must have wakened. That meant he could be lurking anywhere.

Jake whispered, "Do you know how to hot-wire a car?"

Cassie snorted. "No, they didn't teach that sort of thing at the schools I attended. Why?"

"I noticed a key in the door lock when we left the room, and at least one more hung from the ring." Jake glanced anxiously over his shoulder as he spoke. "We were in such a hurry, I never thought to grab them, but Erickson's car key might have been on that ring. Grace likely had hers in her purse. Both cars are useless to us without keys, and Erickson is around here someplace."

"Well, we can't stay here." The crackling from the flames behind them grew louder as oxygen poured in the open door, feeding the ravenous fire. "The fire is getting closer and closer." Her voice rose to a nearly frantic pitch as she said, "The fire will engulf the whole barn soon. We can't get caught now after what Grace did for us. What're we going to do?"

"You run around the corner of the barn and wait for me. Possibly one of them left the keys in the ignition. I'll check. Watch for my signal. Run as fast as you can for the woods if I shake my head. I'll be right behind you. Keep watching your back. Erickson could be anywhere. If you spot him, run in the other direction."

Cassie nodded, but Jake noticed dark half moons of fatigue under her eyes. The soot on her face made it look like she had readied herself for guerilla warfare. It emboldened Jake. But he worried about her remaining strength following her ordeal cooped up in the cell with no light and barely enough food or air to survive. At least she seemed more lucid. He thought the adrenaline rush of fear had revived her, but he didn't know how long it would last. He wondered when she had eaten last. His rubbery limbs exposed his own weakness, and he hadn't been through anything like what Cassie had. They had to keep going.

As they agreed, Cassie ran to the corner of the flaming barn, but the heat forced her to keep her distance. Jake hoped she was out of Erickson's sightline, wherever he was. He headed for the driver's side of the Escort, hoping it belonged to Grace. She may have left her keys in her haste to deal with Erickson. His heart sank when he opened the driver's door and saw the ignition slot empty. He checked the dash and pulled down the visors. His search produced nothing. He rushed to the Mustang and peered through the open door. He leaned inside to the overpowering pine scent of a cheap Christmas tree air freshener dangling from the mirror. As he glanced at the ignition, a creaking noise followed by the slam of a screen door caught his attention. It came from the front of the house about 200 yards from the barn. Jake peered over the dash. The sun cast a shadow over the ramshackle house. The roof sagged, cracks spider-webbed through the windowpanes, and the paint on much of the siding had long since peeled away. Erickson stood at the top of the broken steps.

Jake hurriedly dropped his head to scan the dash, seats, and floor of the car for any sign of keys. They were nowhere to be seen. As Jake peered over the dash again, Erickson lifted something to his shoulder. The sun reflected off the barrel of a rifle.

CHAPTER FORTY-NINE

DANIELA PEREZ DRUMMED her fingers on the desk, listening to the phone ring for the third time. The unsettled feeling that had bothered her all night still rumbled in her stomach. She hoped she was wrong this time, but over the years as a homicide detective, she learned to trust her instinct, and she unwillingly leaned that way now. She felt relieved when Avery finally answered.

Avery's tone ticked up a notch, as she instantly thought the worst when she heard Dani's voice.

"Dani, it's great to hear from you. There's nothing wrong with my dad, is there?"

"That's what I'm calling about, Avery. I'm sure everything's okay, but have you heard from him lately? He hasn't called me, and I didn't get an answer when I tried to call him. I left messages, but he hasn't responded. Maybe he's mad at me, but for the life of me, I can't imagine why. We enjoyed ourselves the last time we were together."

"I haven't heard from him for a few days. Last I heard, he was looking into the disappearance of Emilie's friend's mom, but he didn't give me any specifics. You don't think something's happened to him, do you? I told him to stay out of it, but you know my dad. He just can't keep himself from using those investigative skills he seems to have been born with."

"I'm sure he's fine. The last time you talked, did he say he was going somewhere or planned to talk to somebody?"

"No, he asked me to help him investigate a dating site. I'm sure you already know about it. Cupid's Crush, or something like that."

"Cupid's Choice. Yes, he told me. I'm sure he'll show up with new theories on the disappearance that will turn out to be true."

Dani sensed hesitation on the other end before Avery plunged ahead. "Did he tell you we made up a profile on the site to track down someone with the initials R.W.? Since he thought R.W. was male and had dated Cassie, he needed a female to do it, so he enlisted me. His intuition turned out to be right since the initials belonged to a psychologist named Robert Weatherby."

Dani felt her face burn a little. *Why didn't he ask me to do it?* "He didn't tell me about setting up a profile, but he told me about Robert Weatherby. Listen, I don't want you to worry. Try calling him periodically. My colleague, Maria Allard, the Head of Missing Persons, will have already talked to Weatherby about Cassie Wright's disappearance, but I'm going to talk to him, too. If you hear from your dad, please let me know."

"I will. Thanks so much for calling. I'm sure he's not mad at you. He thinks the world of you and Emilie. I hope he's told you that."

Dani recalled with warmth the kisses she and Jake had shared, but she said simply, "Not in so many words, but I know. Let's reach out again soon. Take care, Avery, and don't worry."

Just before she hung up, Dani asked, "You wouldn't happen to know where your dad keeps a spare key to the house, would you? If Oliver hasn't been fed, I'm sure he's starving by now."

"Oh, that cat. He and Dad have a love/hate relationship, but they tolerate each other. He keeps a key in the bottom of the light fixture next to the door. Just unscrew it, and the key should be there."

Dani thanked Avery and told her again not to worry. She pondered the thought of Jake asking his daughter to help him set up a profile on

Cupid's Choice. He did it to track down the man with the initials R.W., but still… She decided to talk to him about it as soon as he resurfaced.

Dani edged the unmarked police issue Ford Fusion into the traffic on Elgin Street. As she drove one-handed into the sunshine, she nearly poked herself in the eye with the temple of her sunglasses. The list of potential suspects ticked through her mind like a To-Do list.

She pulled into Jake's driveway and unscrewed the decorative bottom of the lamp beside the door. The hollow plastic piece rattled and proved to be just large enough to hold the key. She had to admit that Jake chose a clever place to conceal it. Most people hid their key under the welcome mat or in a flowerpot, as if robbers wouldn't look there. The residents might as well leave it in the keyhole.

She slid the key into the lock and slowly opened the door with a feeling of dread. She knew Oliver would be hungry, but the real reason for asking Avery for the key was to satisfy herself that something hadn't happened to Jake.

She had entered houses where someone had died, and she immediately knew that was not the case here. The house just felt like it had been closed for a while. Like the owner was on vacation. She closed the door while blowing a breath of relief through her lips.

Oliver greeted her with a sharp meow, as if he held her responsible for the lack of food delivery to his bowl. "You'll have to wait, Oliver," she said. "I need to look around first. You can speed things up if you tell me where Jake is."

The cat responded by threading himself through her legs as she bent and scratched him under the chin.

"Jake, are you here?" she called.

No answer.

Dani walked through the house. Unwashed dishes lay in the sink, and a pile of plates and cutlery sat on the table. A few TV dinners, other sparse food, and a handful of bottles of beer were in the refrigerator. She pressed the power button on the computer in his office before continuing her search. He had made his bed, and his robe lay on the end where he had tossed it. Nothing looked out of the ordinary. When she returned to the office, the computer had fired up, but the password protection prevented her from accessing it. Handwritten notes on the desk referenced his discussions with the various players in Cassie Wright's disappearance.

As she turned to leave the office, her heart warmed at the sight of a picture tucked into the corner of a whiteboard on the wall. She recalled him clumsily taking the selfie with his phone when they had skated on the canal the previous winter. It showed the two of them cheerfully flaunting brown mustaches left by the hot chocolate Jake had bought them. Her heart flipped as she recalled the day. She'd understood then that Jake would be the man for her if he felt the same.

Her eyes left the photo, and she scanned the notes on the whiteboard. Jake had written several comments about his meetings with various people, most of whom he had told Dani about, but one stood out. It meant nothing to her, but it might be important, so she took out her phone and snapped a picture. Jake had circled the note three times as if it meant something significant to him. It read, "The Guardians of Truth."

Dani fed Oliver and scratched his head again while he ate. She said wistfully, "I guess I have to win your heart if I'm going to win Jake's."

All she heard was the clock in the sunroom as she pulled the door shut behind her.

CHAPTER FIFTY

DANI SAT IN her car and called the Head of Missing Persons. Maria Allard answered immediately.

"Hi Maria, it's Dani Perez. How are you?"

"I'm fine, Dani. What's up? How are your investigations going?"

Dani chuckled inwardly at the detective's no-nonsense approach. Maria's section had more work than they could manage, but she wanted to tread carefully to avoid any jurisdictional issues.

"We made an arrest on the gang shooting. A kid finally gave up the shooter. That's not why I called though. I hope I'm wrong, but I might have another missing person for you. My friend, Jake Scott, has been out of touch for over 48 hours, and it's really unlike him."

"Jake Scott. You mean your friend that called with some suggestions related to Cassie Wright's disappearance? I'm afraid I wasn't particularly nice to him. I appreciated his input, but he caught me at a bad time. Do you think this relates somehow to Cassie Wright?"

"Jake's a former reporter, and he wouldn't stop poking around until he found what he was looking for. It's possible he was getting close to something. I might be blowing the whole thing out of proportion, but I'm worried about him."

"Sounds like Jake is more than just a friend. I'll ask the same questions we ask everyone, except I'll be a little blunter. Are you sure he didn't run off for a 24-hour romance or go out of town to visit relatives? We don't have the resources to go on a wild goose chase."

Dani chuckled. She could almost see Maria using air quotes on the word "romance." "You don't know Jake. I can't see him running off for a 24-hour romance, as you so delicately put it. Her thought was *if he did, I'd kill him myself.* The only living relative I know is his daughter, Avery, and I just spoke to her. There's no need to launch an official investigation yet. I'll do more digging. He was looking into the psychologist, Robert Weatherby. Did you find out more about him?"

"Not much. His social media doesn't reveal much. We talked to his receptionist, and she gushed about how he had helped so many people find peace. *I* should make an appointment with him if he can do that. She said he focused on people who felt their friends and the pillars of society had let them down. People who were lost, no self-esteem. People who needed someone to guide them. He must be some kind of miracle worker."

Dani had a flashback as Maria spoke. She had investigated a cult that resulted in multiple deaths once, and those were the very words used by a psychologist on the witness stand to describe the reasons people join. *Could The Guardians of Truth be a cult?*

"Have you talked to any of the people he allegedly helped?"

"We haven't been able to track any down. The receptionist, Grace somebody, threw a cloak of secrecy over it so thick we couldn't penetrate it. We're getting a warrant. There's no doubt Weatherby and Cassie had a thing for each other, though. We have witnesses who saw them having a cozy dinner together. There were texts between them that started innocently but became more intimate. I don't know if there's much there, though. Your friend Scott mentioned a few other people that dated or knew Cassie, and we're running them down, too. What about your Jane Doe investigation?"

Dani sighed. "It's not going anywhere. We haven't been able to identify her. I wanted to show her picture to the dating site, Cupid's

Choice, but they don't actually have an office here. We sent her photo to their head office in New York City, but they said she wasn't in their system. It will certainly help when we find out who she is."

Maria hesitated several seconds, then said, "Since neither of us is getting anywhere, do you have time to brainstorm?" She continued before Dani answered, "Let's say one of the people on our list is responsible for Cassie's disappearance. Wait a minute."

Dani had the impression that Maria just needed to walk through the suspects aloud, so she was prepared to listen. She heard paper rustling in the background again before Maria spoke.

"I found it," Maria said. "You should see my desk. Actually, you shouldn't. It's an embarrassment. Okay, let me see. There's the city councillor, Conrad Smythe. The buddies of his that we talked to said he was pretty upset when Cassie dumped him. Smythe denies it, of course. He wouldn't want anything to affect his political aspirations, so if Cassie had something on him, it could give him a motive. There weren't any mean texts to Cassie or anything, but we're monitoring him.

"Her colleague, Noah Kirkland, noted there had been a change in Cassie's attitude recently. He thought something was bothering her, but he didn't know what. His colleagues told us it disturbed him that Cassie got the promotion he wanted. It seems unlikely that he would be so upset as to make Cassie disappear, but it's a possible motive, and people have killed for less. We also got a call from him complaining about your friend asking the same questions we did. He called it harassment, but I wouldn't go quite that far.

"Cassie's boss, Kevin Hall, is an interesting character who moved himself to the top of our list, along with Weatherby. He's a bit of an extremist. There are views on his social media that suggest his thoughts are out there in conspiracy land, so we followed up. He deleted some posts about his federal government employer that are of the tin hat variety. That doesn't mean he would have a reason to want Cassie to disappear, but what if she discovered he was a nutcase and spilled the beans? He could lose his job. It's a plausible motive, and something we're looking into."

Dani just listened.

"There's also Jessica Davis, a friend, and Stephanie Taylor, Cassie's fitness instructor, who both referred to Cassie as not being herself lately. In sum, the ones we are zeroing in on so far are Weatherby, Kirkland, and Hall. We're going to bring them all in to grill them more."

Dani said, "Jake mentioned a weird coincidence. Smythe, Hall, and Kirkland all had a distinguishing mark on their wrists." She described the marks as Jake had related them to her.

Maria said, "That is weird. All on the same wrist, too. If they were all the same, it would establish a link. Right now, it would just help us identify them in a plane crash or something."

"I agree, but it may come in handy for identification purposes later. Let me throw something else in the mix, Maria. Have you heard of the Guardians of Truth?"

Maria's voice raised slightly. "I remember that term in some of the social media we reviewed. I can't remember the context, or who referenced it. It will be in my notes. I assumed it was someone talking about speaking up for what they believed in or telling the authorities what to do. Why?"

"Jake's daughter told me where the house key was so I could make sure he hadn't fallen down the stairs or something. He had written the phrase on his whiteboard and circled it a few times, as if it meant something. He capitalized the beginning of each word like it was an organization or business of some kind."

"Okay, I'm going to find my notes on it. It sounds like it's worth looking into."

"Thanks, Maria. Would you have any problem with me showing Weatherby our Jane Doe's picture to gauge his reaction? I can wait until you bring him in if you like."

"No need to wait, Dani. Have at it. We can use all the help we can get. I know you'll let me know how it went when you're done."

CHAPTER FIFTY-ONE

THE DRIVE TO Weatherby's office didn't take long, and Dani lucked out with a parking spot on a side street around the corner. She removed her sunglasses and slid them into her purse as she strode to the office. An attractive, bored-looking blonde woman standing at the door of an optician's store on the main floor nodded with a smile as she passed. Dani continued walking to the elevator and rode to the third floor. She exited to see a sign announcing Weatherby's office. A faint light winked through the sidelight beside the door.

Dani tried the doorknob, and to her surprise, the door swung open unimpeded. The sight inside made her pause. It looked like a severe windstorm had hit the office. Dani listened for a sound but heard nothing. She snapped on the light switch beside the door and shouted, "Ottawa Police!" Only the hum of the flickering fluorescent light in the waiting area greeted her.

She pushed the door wide open and called out repeatedly, but the office was empty. She scanned the room as she entered, making sure not to touch anything that could provide evidence. Drawers to the filing cabinets at the reception area yawned open and were largely empty. Papers lay strewn across the floor. Dani drew a pair of latex gloves from her pocket and continued to Weatherby's office. There were more papers tossed on the carpeted floor. Scratches on the front of a desk drawer suggested someone had forced it open, and the contents lay scattered everywhere. Cables and electrical cords attached to the wall were now plugged into nothing, indicating a computer had been stolen. Even Weatherby's overturned leather chair spilled its insides from a jagged tear. Someone had done a thorough job of rifling the place.

Dani checked the bathroom in Weatherby's office and the empty rooms down the hall. Whoever had done this had vanished. She returned to the receptionist's area and flicked on a desk lamp. A rectangular spot sat dust free on the desk. Extension cords lay like coiled snakes across the floor. The thief had evidently stolen a laptop as well as Weatherby's computer. Empty file folders lay amongst the papers scattered across the floor. Dani lifted the file folders to read the tabs, but there were only numbers. She stood to read the nameplate on the desktop.

Grace Anderson.

Dani called in the break-and-enter. She stood outside Weatherby's door for a few minutes pondering what she'd just found as she waited for her colleagues to arrive to secure and document the scene. *This can't be a coincidence,* she thought. It must be related to Cassie's disappearance and potentially the Guardians of Truth. *But what? And where is Jake?*

Weatherby's office door showed no signs of damage. Either someone was remarkably good at their job, or they had a key. Dani heard footsteps in the stairwell and two young female police officers emerged through the door. After Dani explained to the officers what she'd observed, she rode the elevator back down, and walked into the optician's office.

The blond woman, who had been standing at the doorway when Dani went up to Weatherby's office, greeted her with a smile as she entered. The smile faded when Dani displayed her credentials.

In response to Dani's question, the woman introduced herself as Sally.

Dani said, "Someone broke into one of the upstairs offices. The police officers who just went up will formally interview you when they're finished, but I'd like to ask a few preliminary questions if you don't mind."

The woman perked up at the thought of excitement enlivening her day. "Of course not. Anything I can do to help. Was it the accountant's office?"

"No, why would you think it was the accountant's office?"

"I don't know. I just thought they might have something worth stealing. Quite a few people work there, so there must be a lot of computers and such."

"I suppose that's true, but I'm referring to the psychologist's office. Doctor Weatherby."

"Oh! I wonder what they wanted there."

"That's what we'd like to know. Did you see anyone that caught your attention or someone leaving with a large box recently?"

"I can't say I did. I see people when I'm not busy. It gives me something to do when I'm here by myself. I watch people come and go."

"Okay." Dani took her phone from her pocket. "I want to show you a few pictures from social media. Please tell me if you can identify anyone."

A woman walked into the store just as Dani was about to show Sally a picture of Cassie Wright. Dani said abruptly, "Sorry, this is police business. I'll have to ask you to come back."

After the offended woman turned on her heel and left, Dani showed Cassie's picture to Sally.

"Yes, I recognize that woman. She came into the building a few times. A man showed me her picture a few days ago. He said she was a friend who might need new frames, and he was going to recommend us to her."

"Can you describe the man?"

Sally described Jake perfectly.

Dani frowned as she warned Sally about the next photo she was about to show her.

Sally's eyes widened. "Oh my god. Is she dead? She sure looks dead. I've seen her go by, too. I'm sure of it."

"You wouldn't know her name, would you?"

"No, I just remember her walking by."

Dani continued showing Sally pictures from social media, throwing in some at random to ensure the woman didn't think she recognized everybody.

Sally stopped her. "Wait, I've seen that man. He's been in quite a few times over the last several months. In fact, I saw him just the other day. Come to think of it, I never saw him leave. I guess I was busy."

"Are you sure it's the same man?"

Sally pointed at the picture. "Yes, I'm sure. He wore a short-sleeved shirt, and I noticed *that* on his arm."

CHAPTER FIFTY-TWO

JAKE COULDN'T KNOW that Erickson had shot many deer in his days and considered himself an expert shooter. Nor could he know that his head was sighted in the rifle scope as Erickson pulled the trigger. Just as he did, the step Erickson stood on cracked and gave way, and his foot dropped into the gap. His aim veered off the mark just enough that the bullet shattered the windshield of his Mustang, ruining the leather driver's seat as it tore through.

Jake was leaning into the driver's side of the Mustang when a sound like the cracking of a whip, followed by the retort of the rifle echoed through the air. The bullet whizzed by his right ear. A puff of seat stuffing appeared as the bullet exited the driver's seat and lodged in the back seat.

He sat frozen for an instant, but his brain told him the next shot would not miss, so he dove into the dirt and scrambled behind the open driver's side door. The next bullet chewed the dirt by his feet. He glanced around the car's bumper to see Cassie's horrified face peering at him from the corner of the burning barn, her mouth agape. He motioned for her to stay back.

Jake popped his head up to see Erickson struggling. He couldn't tell what was going on at the house, but he raced for the corner of the barn. A bellow from Erickson followed him every step of the way. Jake turned to see Erickson free his foot and charge toward the barn.

Jake grabbed Cassie's hand as he ran past, dragging her with him. Her feet seemed frozen to the ground in fear, so Jake stopped to grab her by the shoulders to shake her.

"Cassie, we *have* to go! He's trying to kill us."

The words shook Cassie from her paralysis, and they sprinted for the woods behind the barn. Jake wondered as he ran why the neighbors couldn't see the blaze. Smoke billowed into the air, and the scent had to carry on the wind. He hoped the fire department had been called but realized it could take time for them to arrive in a rural area.

A bullet whizzed through the branches overhead, shearing off leaves. Cassie screamed and ducked. Jake hunched his shoulders and pulled her deeper into the woods, dodging and weaving to avoid fallen branches while other low-hanging limbs scratched their faces and legs and clawed at their clothing. The ground vegetation became thicker the deeper they went, making it more difficult to run. Jake expected bullets to cut them down any minute as a cramp stabbed him in the stomach. He found a large tree and pulled Cassie behind it with him as he leaned over and wretched.

Cassie rubbed his back while saying breathlessly, "Jake, I… I… want to tell you who Julian is in case you make it, and I don't."

Jake leaned over with both hands on his knees after wiping his mouth clean with his hand.

"I know who he is, Cassie," he breathed. "I saw his face. We'll find a way out. We must, for ourselves and for Grace. She may have died to save us."

Jake hastily peeked around the tree but saw no sign of Erickson. *He might circle around to attack us from the front*, he thought. He listened for any hint of their adversary approaching. The birds that the gunshot had silenced were in full throat again, possibly covering the sound of Erickson's approaching footsteps.

He scanned the woods, but all he saw were shadows. Any of them could have been the man determined to kill them. Cassie hung onto Jake's arm so tight it would leave a mark. They waited in absolute silence, but to Cassie and Jake, their terrified breaths sounded like thunder.

A thicket of small trees and shrubs lay about 40 feet in front of them. They could hide there until nightfall if they had to. Jake's breathing returned to normal, and he surveyed the area again. Everything seemed quiet. Had Erickson given up? He decided they should make a run for it. He grabbed Cassie's hand and pointed to the thicket. Cassie nodded, and they ran.

The bullet crashed into the tree beside Cassie's head, shearing off a piece of the trunk. The retort of the blast echoed through the trees. She cried out in pain as shrapnel struck her above the eye. A second shot dug into the dead leaves in front of them, missing Jake's leg by inches.

Erickson had them pinned with nowhere to go. Footsteps crashed through the woods on the left as the hunter tried to line up a better shot. Jake scanned the forest floor for a fallen branch to use as a weapon. The only useful one lay 12 feet beyond reach and would pull him away from the cover of the trees they hid behind. Jake looked anxiously at the trickle of blood dripping down Cassie's face. A branch would be no challenge to a gun. Their only chance was to dart out to grab the branch, and then he and Cassie would have to outsmart the hunter somehow. It seemed like an impossible task.

Jake turned to whisper his plan to a wide-eyed Cassie. He felt the sight of her tugging at his heart. The smoke and flames from the fire had blackened her face, and the bleeding had intensified as a rivulet plowed its way through the soot. Her skirt and blouse hung in tatters, singed by the fire, and ripped by the branches. Her eyes drooped from exhaustion.

"We can't stay here, Cassie. He'll circle around until he can pick us off like sitting ducks. We need to outsmart him. I'll grab the branch to use as a weapon, then we run back to the barn. Stay low. Hide in the old house until someone comes to rescue you, and I'll try to circle behind him."

He didn't wait for Cassie to object. He grabbed her hand and rushed for the dead branch. A bullet ripped through the leaves above his head as he leaned to grab the branch. Again, the gunshot echoed through the trees, but it sounded different this time. It seemed to come from further away… closer to the farmyard where he and Cassie wanted to go. Maybe he should change the plan and move deeper into the woods. Suddenly, he heard another sound bringing hope with it. Sirens rose and fell in the distance.

He looked over his shoulder at Cassie. "Someone must have called the fire department. The police will show up, too."

As they sat back in their hiding place, Jake noticed for the first time a swarm of bugs circling their heads. He glanced at the angry red welts dotting Cassie's neck. It just added to her miserable appearance, but he realized all of it added up to nothing a few days' rest wouldn't cure. Jake listened as the sirens grew closer, but another sound emboldened him. The throaty rumble of a car that had to be Erickson's Mustang, followed by tires spinning on the gravel. Obviously, he didn't want to be caught in the yard. They heard the car tires screeching at the end of the laneway as Erickson headed away. A few minutes later, the sirens' wail petered out as the trucks pulled into the yard. Cassie looked at Jake hopefully, and Jake nodded. Cassie lay her head against Jake's shoulder and cried.

They waited until they heard shouts in the yard. Blue and red lights bounced eerily off the trees around them as they rose painstakingly from their crouching positions. Dark had fallen, making it next to impossible to see in the dense bush. Jake held Cassie's hand as they gradually wound through the lush undergrowth and low-hanging branches until they reached the outskirts of the woods. Flashlights bobbed through the woods in the distance. *They must be looking for Erickson*, Jake thought. *But how would they know?*

They staggered from the edge of the woods to the sight of streams of water jetting from large, pressurized firehoses snaking across the yard as the firefighters doused the building's skeletal remains. Cassie and Jake passed unnoticed.

A police officer leaned against his car, watching the firefighters subdue the flames. He noticed the two ghost-like apparitions approaching from the corner of his eye. His cardboard coffee cup paused at his lips as he took in the sight.

He lowered the cup to chest level, and, with a slight grin, he said, "We've been looking for you two."

CHAPTER FIFTY-THREE

JAKE REALIZED THEY must be quite a sight. Cassie's appearance strongly hinted at her ordeal, from her pale, scorched, sunken cheeks and bug-bitten skin, to her tangled hair and torn clothing. For the first time, illuminated by the roof bar's light, he noticed a dark blue bruise on her cheek where Erickson had hit her when she'd tried to escape. Jake glanced down at himself and realized he hadn't fared better. His tattered pants and shirt and blistered hands suggested a story to be told. He didn't know what his face looked like, but he felt incredibly fatigued. He said wearily, "This is Cassie Wright. I believe you've been looking for her. My name's Jake Scott. What day is it?"

The officer immediately overcame his initial surprise. He shone a flashlight on their faces and retrieved a phone from a pocket with his other hand. After checking their photos on the screen, he nodded apologetically. "Sorry, I just had to confirm for the record. It's Thursday. Hop in the car."

Jake asked, "What's the date?" The police officer told him, and when he opened the car's rear door so they could lift their exhausted bodies into the vehicle, Jake realized Cassie had been captive for more than a week with little to eat or drink, and without the benefit of sunshine. He marveled at her strength. He had been missing for much less time, and he felt like crap. The odor of food in the car made his stomach growl.

The officer shut the door and hurried around the back of the car. He climbed in the driver's door and used his cell phone to tell someone, apparently more senior, that the two captives had emerged from the trees behind the burning barn alive and well. He used his radio to call off the search in the woods. Jake knew from his reporting days that the encrypted communication equipment would prevent anyone from monitoring the police frequency with a scanner.

The officer lifted a partially eaten pizza from the front seat and handed it to Jake.

"You two are probably starving. Sorry I don't have more to offer, but you can share this. I'll get you some water from the trunk."

He left the car and promptly returned to the front seat with two bottles that he passed to Jake.

Jake thanked the officer as he loosened the top of a bottle before passing it to Cassie, who was demolishing a piece of pizza. Jake turned to the officer. "I know you have a lot of questions, but would you mind if Cassie calls her daughter on your phone? She must be worried sick."

"Of course, but first we need to get you checked out." He called through his open window to a man standing beside a car behind the firetrucks and gestured to him to come over. The officer said, "Lloyd is a paramedic, and he'll look you over. While he's doing that, I need to take a statement. It will be quick, I promise. My name is Constable Bannister, and I'm with the Ontario Police. Please tell me what you were doing in the woods behind the barn." He flicked on the overhead light in the car to take notes.

Lloyd provided Jake and Cassie each with an energy drink to replace electrolytes and carbohydrates, which they gratefully accepted. Jake sighed, but patiently related the story of Julian, Weatherby, and the Guardians of Truth, and how it must have been Erickson who started the fire. While Lloyd checked Cassie's vitals and took a blood sample, Jake described Erickson chasing them into the woods and shooting at them. He told the officer about Grace, Weatherby's receptionist. The officer interrupted occasionally to ask for clarification. He was most concerned about Erickson's whereabouts, but all Jake could tell him was that he assumed the big man had turned south away from the approaching sirens. Bannister radioed to his superiors about the man who called himself Julian, Weatherby, and Erickson and the Mustang that Jake had described. The paramedic had finished applying salve to Cassie's various burns and abrasions, and she sat quietly with her arms wrapped around herself, staring out the window into the darkness, her haunted face reflected in the glass. As Jake continued to relate the details of his part of the story, her shoulders shook uncontrollably. The paramedic said, "I'll grab a blanket from the trunk."

A few minutes later, with the blanket snugly wrapped around her, Cassie told her story in terse sentences while Lloyd checked Jake's condition. Cassie's heart wasn't in it. Her fatigue and desire to talk to her daughter trumped the police officer's professional training to extract her statement, and plainly, she considered this additional torture to what she had already endured.

The paramedic applied the cream to Jake's wounds and checked his ribs to determine there was no break. When he suggested they should be transported to the hospital for observation, they both declined. All they wanted was a good night's sleep, so Lloyd agreed to arrange for them both to visit a clinic the next day for x-rays and further consultation.

Constable Bannister handed his cell phone to Cassie. "That's good for now. Thank you. Here's my personal phone." The officer continued to make notes while the firefighters, who had given up on saving the barn, nonchalantly poured water on the surrounding area, and occasionally stared into the car.

Cassie's shoulders sagged when Haley didn't pick up the call, but she left a message.

"Honey, it's Mommy. I'm safe. I'll be home soon. You can call back if you get this message. I love you." She choked up as she uttered the words and handed the phone back to the officer.

The officer asked a few more questions. Finally, Jake said, "Look, Officer, I know you're doing your job here, but there are two people at the Ottawa Police Department who will be interested to know you found us. Your superiors may have already contacted them, but I suggest you call them yourself. One is Maria Allard, Head of Missing Persons, and the other is Daniela Perez, Head of Homicide Division. Then I would like to call my daughter."

The officer replied, "It's because of them we were looking for you here. A bulletin came across our desks about an organization called the Guardians of Truth. We knew about them, and that they met here, but we had no reason to investigate. No one complained about them. When the bulletin came in that there might be a connection between the organization and your disappearance, I spoke with Staff Sergeants Allard and Perez. Allard gave all the credit to Perez. It was great police work making the connection. Then the fire was called in. We thought we should check the woods just in case you were nearby. I was praying you weren't in that barn."

Bannister handed the phone to Jake when a sudden knock on the driver's side window startled everyone in the car. A firefighter stood at the door in full gear with his face covered in sweat and soot. When Bannister turned the key in the ignition to accessory mode and rolled down the window, the firefighter leaned in, knocking his helmet on the car's roof. He said in a hushed tone, "There's something you should see."

Jake's heart sank. "Is it a body?" he asked from the back seat.

The firefighter glanced at Officer Bannister, who nodded. The firefighter continued. "We found a female's body in the barn."

Bannister quietly asked the firefighter if there were any identifying features.

"Her body is severely burned, but she's identifiable to someone who knew her."

Bannister turned to Jake with his eyebrows raised. Jake reluctantly nodded his agreement and climbed out of the car. Cassie remained in the car as the firefighter offered Jake some rubber boots, which he gratefully accepted. Not so much to protect his feet from getting wet, but more to give him time to prepare himself psychologically for seeing Grace's body. It was the longest walk he had taken in a long time. He had covered fires before, and the amount of water always surprised him. He trudged after Bannister and the firefighter through sodden grass and mud around the perimeter of the barn. The building was barely recognizable. They saw the moon shining through the remnants of the barn's roof when they approached the back. Six inches of water covered the floor. Scorched timbers dripped with water. Unrecognizable, twisted metal protruding from the mess resembled modern-day sculptures.

They didn't have to go further. What had happened became clear. The woman's body lay in front of the door between the area where Cassie and Jake were held captive and the space where the attendees sat. Ceiling tiles and larger pieces of wooden rafters lay on the lower half of the body. The woman's startled, wide eyes stared straight at the three men.

Jake looked away as he said with a voice tinged with sadness, "It's Grace. Weatherby's receptionist. She saved us, but obviously, she didn't make it."

CHAPTER FIFTY-FOUR

JAKE LET CASSIE eat most of the pizza, knowing that she needed it more than he did, but his stomach disagreed. Food, hot coffee, a shower, and bed sat second, third, fourth, and fifth on his list of priorities. Number one was seeing Dani, even though trouble was coming for failing to tell her where he was going. Bannister told them Dani insisted on picking them up. Jake remembered it took him and Weatherby about 50 minutes to reach the farm. He hoped she made it in less time.

Avery had, of course, been relieved to hear from him. It sounded like Dani had played down the possibility her dad might be in serious trouble when she'd provided Avery with updates. Jake didn't go into a lot of detail with his daughter, assuring her he would fill her in after he got some sleep. He would have to deal with her wrath as well.

Jake and Cassie filled in more details for Officer Bannister while they waited. The pizza hadn't lasted long, and Bannister produced another bottle of water each with the promise there was more.

Dani didn't disappoint. Jake smiled as he noticed flashing lights atop the dark outline of a fast-moving vehicle on the road well before 50 minutes expired. The dark shape with the Christmas light arrangement on top ate up the distance to the laneway in seconds and wheeled into the approach. The Ford Fusion shot into the yard and slid to a stop beside Officer Bannister's car. Dani and Haley got out.

Bannister let Cassie and Jake out of the police car. Haley rushed forward for a tearful embrace with her mom. Dani approached Jake more deliberately with a semi-frown. Jake felt like a puppy who knew his owner would be mad about a shredded pillow. He would be in trouble. He just wasn't sure what the consequences would be.

Dani stopped short of reaching Jake, and he wondered if she wanted to maintain her professionalism in front of Bannister, or if her anger prevented her from a more enthusiastic greeting. She simply said to Bannister, "If you're finished with them, I'll take them back to the city."

Bannister nodded. "I'll share the statement I took with you. We've already issued an APB on this Erickson character. We've warned that he's armed and dangerous. He's in the system for misdemeanors, but nothing on this level. We put one out on Weatherby, and the guy who calls himself Julian as well. Hopefully, we can nab them before the night is over."

"Let's hope so. Good job on the All Points Bulletins. It sounds like Erickson is a dangerous guy." Dani regarded Cassie and Haley, who still held each other tightly. "Are you two ready to go home?"

Both nodded vigorously.

Jake sat in the front seat of the Ford Fusion while Cassie and Haley occupied the back seat. A familiar odor reached Jake's nostrils. This time, it was chicken wraps and coffee from Tim Hortons. Dani distributed them to the group with a sullen apology. "You two need to eat something more substantial than this, but Haley and I didn't want to waste time getting here. Make the best of it."

Jake was grateful for the food. "We will. Thank you."

Cassie and Haley murmured in the back seat. Jake heard Haley say, "I'm sorry, I thought it was the media calling, so I didn't pick up your call." Cassie assured her daughter it was okay.

Dani stared straight forward as she accelerated down the dirt road. Her lips barely moved as she said, "What made you decide to attend the meeting without telling Maria or me?"

"I should have told you, Dani. In fact, I was about to call you when Weatherby showed up." It sounded like a weak excuse to Jake. "I just wanted to check things out. I didn't expect it to turn out the way it did. I didn't know who Julian really was, but I found out. In case you didn't know, his name isn't Julian." Jake described Julian removing the prosthetic make-up and noticing the identifiable feature on his arm.

"I know. The woman at the optician's shop in Weatherby's office building identified him as a regular visitor. She recognized the same thing on his arm."

"Oh, you mean Sally? Yes, she seemed pretty observant."

Dani cast a sideways glance at Jake but said nothing. As she did a moving stop before turning onto the highway, she said to Cassie, "I suggest you stay at your sister's place for a few days until we catch Erickson. We don't know what he might try, but we're confident he won't find you there. Are you okay with that?"

Cassie agreed, and Jake wondered what she had in store for him. He had nowhere to go where he would feel safe. A hotel, maybe?

Dani loosened up slightly as she drove. It seemed like she came around to Jake's thinking about attending a Guardians of Truth meeting, but she still simmered that he hadn't told her about his plans. As usual, the speed limit represented a mere suggestion to Dani, and the sign for the outskirts of Ottawa arrived swiftly.

She turned her head toward Jake, which to him seemed a major step forward. At least she spoke directly to him. "So, you're telling me Julian had everyone bamboozled into thinking a comet would obliterate the world, and he was the only one who could save them?"

"That's what I witnessed. Cassie had more involvement, so she'll confirm it. The crowd comprised professionals and blue-collar types. These weren't people who didn't know better. They should have realized it was bunk, but I guess he drilled it into them repeatedly in his dominant style, and they swallowed it. It's alarming."

"It sounds like a classic cult. Toss an appealing leader and some disenchanted people into a blender, and this is what you get." She peeked in the rear-view mirror, and her hand slid over to rest on top of Jake's for a moment before she pulled away. "I'm glad you're okay, but you're still in trouble," she whispered.

Cassie and Haley had dozed off in the back seat. Haley rested her head on her mom's shoulder as she snored faintly. Obviously, neither had had much sleep lately. Adrenaline and Dani's presence kept Jake going. Dani continued to quiz him about his time in captivity and the people involved. He told her everything. "I'm not sure what happened to Weatherby. Last time I saw him, he was standing beside Julian and Erickson. Erickson must have snuck up behind me and stuck a needle in my neck. Grace, Weatherby's receptionist, thought they got rid of him somehow. I don't know how or why, and there's no one except Julian and Erickson to confirm where he is. You have to assume he's alive until it's proven otherwise."

Dani nodded and told him about the break-in at Weatherby's office.

"When did that happen?" asked Jake.

"We can't be sure, but based on Sally's description, it was last night or yesterday sometime.

"It could've been Erickson, but he spent most of the last 24 hours setting the barn on fire and shooting at us. My guess is that Julian wanted to destroy evidence linking him to this. It would be records of Weatherby's clients since he seemed to be the recruiter."

"Yes, that makes sense. The computers were gone, and empty file folders lay on the ground. I don't think it was someone looking for drug money. It looked too thorough. The folders had only numbers. No names. Weatherby probably kept a master list linking the numbers to client names on his hard drive, which is now missing."

Jake agreed. "The only one I recognized in the audience was Grace, and she's no longer with us. We know who Julian is. We just have to find him."

Dani exhaled loudly and grumbled, "There is no 'we,'" as she pulled into Katherine's driveway. Haley had awakened moments earlier and shook her mom. A marked police car sat on the street. Dani said, "I'll walk you to the door, Cassie, and there will be an officer watching until Erickson and Julian are in custody. You can get a good night's sleep tonight."

Jake watched as Cassie walked shakily toward the house with Haley's support. Dani strode in lockstep right behind them. After Dani spoke to the officer in the car, she returned to her vehicle and climbed into the driver's side.

As she stomped on the accelerator, Jake asked, "Will there be a car outside my place as well?"

Dani stared straight ahead. "Nope, you don't deserve protection. You should have told me what you were doing. We're going to use you as bait."

Jake couldn't believe his ears. *Could this woman he thought he knew, actually be that vengeful?* He stared at Dani as he stuttered, "Bait? Uh… you can't be serious. Are you being serious right now?"

Dani finally burst out laughing. "I'm not letting you out of my sight. You're sleeping at my condo." She remained silent for a few seconds before adding, "On the sofa. And you're still in trouble."

CHAPTER FIFTY-FIVE

DANI AIMED HER parking permit at the scanner in front of the garage at her condo building. Her knee bounced until the large door slowly rolled up high enough that she dodged under it and down the ill-lit ramp. Jake considered the fact that he was going home with her. Nerves settled on top of the fatigue he already felt. He thought she had made a monumental decision about their relationship during his absence, at least until she'd added "on the sofa."

She wheeled into her parking spot on the second level and, as Jake grabbed the door handle to step out of the car, said "Just a second. I want to contact the officer at Haley's sister's place to make sure everything is okay. I'm sure it will be, but I want to be certain."

Jake rolled down his window. The sticky air in the garage barely registered as Jake's fatigue made him too foggy to think about anything. He was on autopilot and would do whatever Dani wanted. "Of course, take your time," he mumbled as he settled back into the passenger seat.

His head grew heavy and dropped to his chest as Dani made the call. He glanced up as the frown lines on her face deepened with each unanswered ring. She dialed again with the same result.

"I'm going to try Cassie's sister. Dani and Haley are probably already in bed and the constable could be checking the perimeter of the house."

Jake heard the concern in Dani's voice. She would roast the constable if he walked away from his phone. If he hadn't, something more sinister had happened.

"He might have just gone to the bushes to relieve himself," she said as she angrily keyed numbers. Cassie's, her sister, Katherine's, and finally, Haley's. No response from anyone. "Maybe they all switched off their phones for the night."

She called her daughter.

"Emilie, have you heard anything from Haley or her mom?"

Emilie said sleepily. "No, are they all right? Is Jake okay?"

"Jake's here with me, sweetie, and we're downstairs in the parking lot. I need to go to Katherine's to check on them. There is no need to worry. It sounds like I woke you. Sorry if I did. Go back to sleep. I know you have an early driving lesson tomorrow."

"Okay, love you, Mom. Hi to Jake."

Dani disconnected the call with one hand as she guided the car backward with the other. She changed gears and sped to the top of the parking ramp, narrowly avoiding the post holding the parking pass reader. Jake hastily fastened the seat belt he had undone a few minutes earlier. He latched onto the handle above the door, knowing this would be a wild ride. Dani was on the phone calling for backup. When she finished and sailed through an orange, turning red light, she said, "I should have sent you upstairs, but I didn't think you would mind coming."

Jake was wide awake now. "What do you think is going on?"

"I have no idea, but it seems like there's a problem." She slammed her right hand on the top of the steering wheel. "Dammit! I wonder if Erickson found them. I watched for someone tailing us. He could have changed cars, but I saw nothing suspicious. There was no one there. Katherine goes by her married name. How would Erickson find her?"

Jake thought for a minute before answering. "It's not your fault, Dani. Cassie and Weatherby were a bit of an item, and based on my personal experience, he's extremely good at eliciting information from people. Cassie could have revealed her sister's name during one of her sessions or on a date with him. He could've passed the information to Erickson or Julian. We don't know what happened to Weatherby. I'm sure everything will be fine."

But it wasn't.

It looked quiet as Dani roared down the street toward Katherine's house. The house sat in darkness, as if everyone was in bed. The police car sat exactly where it was when they left. But as they drew closer, they noticed the window of the car was open. The young constable's head rested against the back of the seat, as if he was sound asleep. A shiver ran through Jake.

Dani slid to a stop beside the police car. She drew her gun and tossed her personal phone to Jake as she ran past him to the front of the house. She yelled over her shoulder, "I don't have time to wait for the backup to arrive. They'll be here any second. You check on him. Call an ambulance. I'm going to see what's going on."

Jake hustled out of the passenger side of Dani's car into the sultry Ottawa night air. He hurried to the driver's side of the police car, glancing around the well-lit neighborhood as he did. Sudden movement across the street attracted his attention, and he swung his head around to see a white-haired woman in a plush bathrobe leaning on a cane in her doorway staring at the commotion on the street. Her body had a halo created by the light behind her. She shouted something, but Jake ignored it and continued to the police car.

Jake activated the flashlight on the cell phone and shone it on the officer's pale face. The officer's chest slowly rose and fell, but Jake could not wake him. A call to 911 assured him an ambulance would arrive in seven minutes. As he made the call, Jake stared over the roof of the police car at the gaping opening of the doorway leading into Katherine's house. He didn't know if the door was unlocked or if Dani had broken in. He wanted to hear what Dani found, but he needed to stay with the young officer.

A sound that Jake had become far too accustomed to in the last 24 hours shattered the night silence as sirens rose and fell. First responders, fire trucks, an ambulance, and the tactical unit arrived en masse, and the respective authorities piled out of their vehicles. Two heavily armed officers with their hands on their guns led paramedics to Jake's location. One officer spun Jake around and thoroughly searched him while the paramedics attended to the unconscious officer.

"You'll probably find a needle mark on his neck. He was probably drugged," Jake said as the officers handed him back his wallet with his identification. He heard Dani shout, "He's okay, he's with me."

Dani hurried to the officer in charge, who obviously recognized her. Jake listened to her with dread as she succinctly explained the situation on the inside.

"We have a male and a female victim tied up and beaten, but alive, inside." She explained they were Cassie's sister, Katherine, and her husband. "Two people are missing, a woman in her forties by the name of Cassie Wright and her daughter, 16, named Haley Wright." Using Katherine's description, she said, "They are believed to be with a man named Luke Erickson, about six feet four inches tall, well over 250 pounds, blonde, muscular, and extremely dangerous. We already have a BOLO out for him, but I want him found now! We don't know when he left the premises with the two victims, so we can't be sure how far he's gone." She looked at her watch and did a mental calculation. "It must be less than an hour. Let's cover all the areas we can within an hour's drive. Let's…"

Dani's voice trailed off when she heard someone shout her name and angrily turned toward the source. An officer stopped in front of her holding his notepad. He said, "The woman across the street says she saw a woman and teenage girl forced into a sports car by a large man." Jake hadn't had time to process the information when he recognized another officer running toward them as the constable who was at Mer Bleu bog when Jane Doe's body was discovered. The officer breathlessly slid to a stop a few feet from the gathered group.

"Detective Perez," he said. "I just heard a report on the radio about a hostage situation in Barrhaven. Negotiators are on their way, but the person says he has three hostages, including Cassie and Haley Wright. We don't know who the third person is. He's already made his demands. He says he wants money to replace what somebody stole from him and safe passage to a country where he can't be arrested."

Dani nodded. "So, a country that we don't have a reciprocal enforcement agreement with. Where does he want to go? Afghanistan?" She said sarcastically, "Sounds like an easy negotiation. And if we don't meet his demands?"

"He says he'll kill everyone, including himself."

CHAPTER FIFTY-SIX

BY THE TIME they arrived at the house in a middle-class neighborhood in suburban Barrhaven, the street lay covered in law enforcement vehicles. Officers knocked on doors on either side of the target house and gave homeowners two options: leave or shelter-in-place. Dreary-eyed neighbors on one side climbed into their Tesla with two small children and left, while a retirement-age couple living on the other side stayed to watch through a window. Yellow tape strung between side mirrors on police vehicles established the perimeter. Blue, red, and white light splashed intermittently off neighboring houses. An older model Mustang with a bullet hole in the windshield sat in the driveway.

House number 215 had a well-manicured lawn on a large pie-shaped yard, cheery summer flowers in a nice, raised garden bed at the front, and a teardrop-shaped area with a mixture of rocks and flowers at the head of the driveway. A porch ran about six feet deep from the house's left corner to the closed two-car garage. Two patio chairs sat on the porch, which was dark save for the spotlights aimed at the door and window. The two-story house was constructed of brick and vinyl siding. Erickson had drawn all the window shades. All that set it aside from the other houses on the street was the array of weapons pointed at it by a large contingent of men and women in tactical gear. That, and the drone buzzing overhead, and the menacing dark green armored vehicle with a solid-looking push bar on the front facing the house.

A search of the address in the police database had shown the house belonged to the third hostage, the man who called himself Julian. Dani looked at Jake as she pulled up, obviously mulling over a decision. Finally, she said as she climbed out, "I guess you can come with me. You have firsthand knowledge about Erickson, so you might be useful, but you'll have to wear Kevlar and stay well back. No surprise the Incident Commander has determined this is a major incident. The artillery and tactical vehicle confirm it. Besides, from what you've told me, this guy could do anything, including trying to shoot his way out. Promise me you'll stay back."

"Of course, I will."

Dani muttered something inaudible as she opened the trunk and tossed a vest to Jake. She put one on and zipped it up. She checked her gun and ammo and hustled past the tactical vehicle. Jake ran behind her in a crouch. He once wrote a story about the highly trained crisis negotiation team in the Ottawa Police Department. The tactical vehicle was a BearCat, first purchased in 2010, and the first of its kind in Canada. He had attended a hostage negotiation for his story and marveled at the negotiator's ability to communicate successfully with individuals who had, at least temporarily, lost touch with reality. His story had described the harrowing experiences the negotiators faced and their pride in having negotiations end without serious harm to anyone. He silently prayed that tonight would end the same way.

Their destination was a black Sprinter cargo van parked next to the BearCat. Dani put her hand out to stop Jake as they watched the BearCat creep forward. A mechanical arm extended from the vehicle as it crossed the lawn. The voice of someone inside the vehicle boomed through a loud hailer. "We're delivering the phone now. We'll break the window on your left side of the house and drop the phone inside."

Dani said, "It's an encrypted phone with a camera, so the negotiator can see and speak directly to the hostage taker."

Jake heard glass shatter and saw the Bearcat retreat on the lawn as Dani said, "We'll just stay inside the van for a minute. Just listen." When they climbed inside, they saw a muscular blond man in his early thirties wearing a black tee-shirt and jeans that wrapped around his thick thighs, sitting at a small table, holding a phone. A second, casually dressed man sat to his right scribbling something on a yellow sticky note, which he handed to the person speaking. The negotiator scanned the note in the light of a dim desk lamp on a flexible hose-style neck. The second man spoke into a headset, obviously updating an Incident Commander at the Command Center offsite on what Jake hoped to be progress. The sound of the Sprinter's door opening caused both to look up.

The secondary negotiator jumped from his chair and grabbed Dani by the arm to escort her back outside. "Who are you?" he demanded. When Dani showed him her badge, he apologized. "Okay, sorry Staff Sergeant, we can't have extra people in here. Any distractions could set Erickson off. I should have locked the door. Who's this?"

"His name's Jake Scott. Erickson held him captive with Cassie and Haley, and he would recognize their voices. He has firsthand knowledge of Erickson's violent streak. I thought he could be helpful."

"Okay, come in, but stay perfectly quiet. By the way, the third person in the van is a psychologist." Jake hadn't even noticed him.

When they re-entered, the negotiator spoke in low even tones, trying to calm the person on the other end, whom Jake presumed to be Erickson. He couldn't see the face on the phone without risking putting himself in front of the camera.

"I understand you feel like Julian robbed you of the money owed to you. We're looking into what we can do. Let's agree on a couple of things first, Luke. I'm going to be as honest with you as I can, and I need to know that you'll be honest as well. It's the only way this negotiation is going to work, right, Luke? So, while we look into replacing the money Julian stole from you, we need proof that all the hostages are okay, all right? As a sign of good faith, how about you send Haley out? That would be a good start."

Luke Erickson's agitated voice came through the speaker. "I can't do that. I'll put Haley and her mom on the phone. That'll be proof enough."

Everyone in the vehicle held their breath. The sound of a chair scraping across the floor echoed through the speaker. Then Cassie's feeble voice came through the speaker. "It's me, Cassie," followed by "It's me, Haley." Her voice sounded terrified.

Dani's head swung toward Jake. The negotiator looked at the pair. "I've got him on mute. Can someone confirm that's Cassie and Haley Wright? Anybody?"

Jake said, "I can. That's definitely Cassie and Haley."

The negotiator nodded and returned to the phone, as if he was about to converse with a friend at a restaurant. "That's great, Luke. I appreciate it. Can we see them? It would be helpful if we can see them."

"You heard them, that's enough."

"Okay, what about the man that's in there with you?" The negotiator appeared to be about to say the man's real name but realizing Erickson would relate to him as Julian, he used the fake name. "What about Julian? Can you put him on?"

"No."

"Why not?"

"He can't come to the phone right now."

"Is he dead, Luke?"

"He got what he deserved."

"We agreed to be honest, right?"

"Yeah, we did." Erickson's voice ticked up a notch. "You have said nothing about the tactical team you have on standby ready to break in and kill me. You have said nothing about the snipers you have outside trying to find the best angle to get a shot. I imagine their trigger fingers are getting a little itchy by now. What about the drone that just buzzed by the window? We haven't talked about any of that, so we're not being totally honest with each other, are we, Officer?"

The second negotiator scribbled something on a sticky note and handed it to the lead, who nodded and said into the phone, "Of course, you're right about all of that, but we don't want this to end badly for anyone. We're not here to use lethal force. It's the last resort. My job is to come to an agreement with you that will satisfy all of us. Can we do that?"

"I'll tell you what I want. I saw Jake Scott get into your van with a woman. Here's what I want to do. I want to talk to Jake Scott, and I want to talk to him face-to-face."

CHAPTER FIFTY-SEVEN

THE NEGOTIATOR HESITATED momentarily, glancing at his colleague beside him before looking at Jake and Dani. His colleague cocked his head as he listened in his headphones. Jake saw him scribble a large "NO" on a sticky note, underline it twice, and hold it up.

"We can't do that, Luke. You won't tell us whether Julian is dead or alive, so we have to assume he's dead. Sending Scott in would be foolhardy on our part, don't you think?"

"You have my word nothing will happen to him. I just want to talk to him."

"Well, Luke, I appreciate your promise not to harm Jake, but if Julian is dead, we just can't send Jake in. Why do you want to talk to him?"

"I don't know him, but he seems like the kind of man I can work out a deal with. Think about it. I'll call back in fifteen minutes."

The line went dead.

The negotiator stared at the phone before disconnecting.

"I want to go in."

All heads swung toward Jake, who leaned against the wall with his arms crossed. His eyes drooped from fatigue, and he still wore the same filthy clothes he had been wearing for days, but defiance was pasted all over his face.

"Look, this is an opportunity to at least get one of the women out. I don't know why he wants to talk to me, but try to trade Haley and Cassie, or at least one of them, for me. You're not going to get a better offer. He's probably already killed Julian if they aren't in this together."

Dani remained stoic while Jake talked. When he finished, she said, "That's exactly why we can't send you in. It's too risky. Why wouldn't he shoot you the minute you walk in the door? He shot at you in the woods. You said he tried to burn the place down with you inside. It's too risky, Jake."

"Of course, it's risky, Dani, but I thought about our ordeal, Cassie's and mine, on the way home. Why didn't Erickson just kill us before setting fire to the barn? I think he assumed we were unconscious, so it would have been easy. But he didn't. How did he possibly miss both of us when he shot at us in the woods? He had clear sightlines a couple of times. Is his aim that bad, that he missed from that range every time? I don't think so. He could've killed us but chose not to. I want to go in. If he didn't kill us then, why would he now? Go to bat for me with the Incident Commander, Dani."

"Your theories don't hold water, Jake," Dani said shaking her head. "I love what you're trying to do here, but it will end up in you getting killed." She raised her fingers as she counted off her reasoning. "First, he was sadistic enough to keep you and Cassie in a locked room with no hope of escape. Second, if Erickson killed Julian, he has nothing to lose. Third, when he shot at you in the woods, darkness was closing in and there would have been all kinds of shadows. It's difficult to hit a target under those circumstances. Finally, you told me the shots missed by inches, and Cassie was even hit by shrapnel. Do you think he's *that* accurate that he deliberately missed by a few inches?"

The negotiator, who had been listening intently with his elbow resting on the arm of his chair, said, "What am I telling Erickson when he calls? So far, the commander has given me a flat 'no.' Are we going with that? Erickson is calm now, but I don't know how long he will stay that way." He looked directly at Dani. "Are you going to talk to the Incident Commander, Staff Sergeant?"

Dani gestured to the second negotiator who handed her the headphones. She introduced herself and explained that she agreed with the decision not to allow Jake to go into the house. They discussed the possibility of Jake recording a message trying to convince Erickson to release the two women but concluded it would do no good. When she handed the headphones back to the second negotiator, three minutes remained until Erickson's 15-minute deadline expired.

And Jake was gone.

CHAPTER FIFTY-EIGHT

DANI STORMED FROM the van to find Jake talking to a uniformed officer behind a police car parked diagonally across the street. When she arrived in front of Jake, her face resembled a category five storm about to rain untold damage on the unfortunate victim in its path.

"What the hell do you think you're doing?" She pointed a steady finger toward her vehicle. "Wait in my car." She sounded like she was talking to a young child.

"Whoa, Dani. It was getting claustrophobic in there. There was no point in continuing the conversation. You made valid points. I'm no hero, and I wasn't about to make some grand gesture to walk into the house without everyone's agreement. The team needs to do their jobs without me hanging around." He gestured to the uniformed officer. "Besides, this guy wouldn't let me go anywhere."

Dani's features softened as she harrumphed. "I'm surprised you listened to me for a change. I still think you should wait in the car." She fished in her pocket. "Here are the keys. In fact, you should go home. We don't know how long..."

The door of the Sprinter van swung open. The second negotiator stuck his head out and shouted Dani's name. When he spotted her, he said, "Erickson says he'll send Haley out if Scott goes in. Otherwise, he's going to kill the two women. He just admitted he's already killed Julian. The commander wants a word."

Dani invited Jake back into the van, and he listened as she and the incident commander spent five more minutes discussing the situation. He heard her say, "I don't like the third option, but I guess it's all we have." When they concluded, she gave the negotiator three options in ascending order. The negotiator called Erickson. "Okay, Luke, here's the deal. We agree to an exchange of audio recordings between you and Scott. We'll drop a digital recorder in the same window we put the phone." He stopped speaking, waiting for a response.

Erickson's voice sounded more desperate. "That doesn't work. I want to see him in person. Your option isn't close to what I wanted."

Concerned faces stared at the negotiator. Erickson sounded like he could snap.

The negotiator said, "Okay, Luke. Maybe that wasn't fair. You can have a discussion with Jake on the phone. Would that be better?"

The sound of hurried footsteps echoed through the phone's speaker. Erickson shouted into the phone. "You're not taking me seriously. Listen!" The next sounds terrified everyone in the van. It sounded like a chair scraped across the floor and fell over, followed by muffled thuds and a blood-curdling scream. Cassie's voice came over the phone. *"Please don't hurt her! He's pointing a gun at Haley's head in the den. He's going to kill her. Do something!"*

Erickson came back on the phone. "Do you understand me now? Are you sending Scott in?"

The lead negotiator glanced at Dani, but she had already started for the door. He spoke calmly into the phone again. "Okay, don't do anything rash. Just relax and we'll figure this out. We'll let you speak to Scott, but there are a couple of conditions. That's fair, right? You already agreed you would let Haley go. That's great. It's the only way the discussion will happen. You need to be visible in the doorway without a weapon. Two members of the tactical team will accompany Jake. They will not attempt to harm you, but it's only fair that Jake has protection. You said you killed Julian, so we don't want that to happen to Jake. That's fair, don't you think, Luke?"

Erickson's voice came over the speaker system, sounding fatigued and distraught. "He needs to come inside. I want to speak to him alone."

The psychologist wrote on his notepad and showed it to the negotiator, who nodded. Jake only saw part of it, but it read something about Erickson escalating.

The negotiator said. "That's not going to happen, Luke. You have another option. Give it up. Let the two women come outside. Then you come out. I guarantee no one will harm you. Come outside after Cassie and Haley, and we'll end this."

"No, Cassie stays inside with me. I get what you're doing. You want me in plain sight so someone can shoot me."

"No one's going to shoot, Luke. It doesn't work that way here. Now, I gave you two options. Which one is it going to be?"

No hesitation this time. "I'll send Haley out. Send Scott up here."

The second negotiator scribbled madly on a sticky note and handed it over. The lead negotiator glanced at it. "Okay, but like I said, we can't send him up by himself. Two officers will accompany him. They will stand in front of Jake. It's a fair offer, Luke."

Silence hung thickly in the air. Everyone in the vehicle stared at the negotiator. Finally, one word from the speaker sent everything into motion.

"Okay."

A prickle formed between Jake's shoulder blades. He examined his shaking hands. With Erickson so unpredictable, he wondered what would happen in the next few minutes.

Dani opened the door and gestured for Jake to follow her outside. A tactical team member fitted Jake with an earpiece and tested it while Dani rested her hands on his shoulders and held his eyes with hers.

"Look at me. This has escalated beyond the point we can resolve it without the tactical team. You aren't going anywhere close. We can't put you in harm's way. The team tried to find out where the women were with the drone, but Erickson has the shades drawn. But Cassie told us Haley's in the den, so we'll have to assume they both are. You must stay behind the team members. Others will disperse gas in the back of the house to isolate Erickson from the women. Things are fluid in these situations but don't move a muscle. He's tired and irrational. Your job is to keep him talking. The tactical unit will take care of it. It will all happen fast. You've got this, Jake."

Jake wasn't sure if he could do it, but at least Haley would be released. He felt the ground shift beneath him. *Pull yourself together*. Voices rose behind him. "Watch the front door. Innocent coming out. Teenager. As soon as she's in the clear, a middle-aged man of about five feet ten inches tall will approach the front door with two officers to talk to the subject. His name is Jake Scott. Questions?"

Jake straightened, pushing his chest out and pulling his head up. He walked with Dani to the uniformed officer, and they all watched as the front door of the house gradually opened.

Two heavily armed tactical unit members nodded to Jake to pull in behind them. They watched the front door as Haley emerged into the blinding, high-intensity spotlight aimed at the house. She appeared tiny and vulnerable in her patterned pajamas. She held her hand over her eyes and bowed her head. Her body trembled. A shove from Erickson caused her to stumble. A lump formed in Jake's throat at the sight of her. Jake heard her turn and cry out, "Mom," as Erickson pushed her further from the house before slamming the door shut and latching it. Jake touched Haley's arm as she whimpered and darted past him into a female tactical squad member's outstretched arms. The officer led Haley away to a waiting ambulance.

So far, Erickson had kept his part of the bargain.

Jake hunched behind the two team members as they slowly moved forward with guns drawn. Erickson vanished for a few seconds and then reappeared, pushing Cassie in front of him. He had one arm wrapped around her neck and the other hand aimed a sawed-off shotgun at her head. She shook uncontrollably as Erickson hid behind her. A thin screen separated them from the assembled police resources outside.

Erickson had shut off the lights so as not to present a silhouette, but the floodlights lit them up, anyway.

Jake heard the negotiator in his earpiece. "This was not part of the deal. Tell him to let her go or the deal's off."

"Hello, Luke," Jake said as the group approached to within about thirty feet of the door. He stood on the stone walkway before a killer. The two tactical squad team members stood in a shooter's stance behind shields with their arms fully extended, their cheeks resting on their biceps and their legs staggered, maintaining a relaxed pose while offering a poor target. Jake was well hidden.

"Luke, this wasn't part of the deal. You need to let Cassie go. Why are you doing this?"

Luke's voice rose barely above a whisper. "I've gotten myself in a mess here, and I'm not sure how to get out of it. Someone has always told me what to do. I'm confused. I thought I had everything under control, but I've screwed everything up. All I wanted was the money Julian owed me, but he kept it all. What do you think I should do, Scott?"

"You told the negotiator Julian is dead. Is that true, Luke?"

"Yeah. I gave him a shot the same as I gave you and Cassie. I was so mad when he didn't give me the money. He deserved to die."

"You want my advice?" Jake shouted from behind the team members. "Give it up. The courts will be more lenient if you just stop this right now. Let Cassie go. Tell them everything about Weatherby and the Guardians of Truth. Things will go better for you."

"I can't do that, Scott."

Jake put his hands up in a gesture of frustration.

"Why did you want to talk to me, then?"

"Because I don't hold Cassie responsible for what's happened. She wanted to expose Julian, but we would have taken care of her like we did with Rosemary."

The thought of the woman in the bog flashed through Jake's mind, but he didn't let on.

"Who's Rosemary?"

"Rosemary didn't believe Julian, just like Cassie. We had to deal with her. Anyone who denied Julian's teachings had to be stopped."

Jake thought the police could deal with that. He had to focus on the situation at hand. He thought for a second about what he should say next as things developed in his peripheral vision. The spotlight now shone directly on the doorway where Erickson held Cassie. The rest of the front of the house was now in darkness, and tactical team members crouched in the shadows on either side of the doorway. Others hurried down either side of the house.

"Okay, so that still doesn't explain why you wanted to talk to me. You said you don't blame Rosemary and Cassie. What are you saying, Erickson?"

"There's only one reason for everything coming down the way it has. That's you, Scott. You're an investigative reporter. You would've brought down everything good the Guardians of Truth stood for. Julian did a lot of good for many people, and you want to destroy it. I can't let that happen."

A jolt of fear shot through Jake. *Where was this going?*

Cassie squirmed against Erickson and cried out as she also sensed something was about to happen.

A voice said in Jake's ear, "On my count of three, hit the dirt."

One…

Jake tried to warn Erickson one last time. "There are about twenty guns trained on you right now. Look at these two in front of me. I don't know what you're planning, but it won't end well for you if you try something stupid. I'm ending this conversation. You can go back to talking to the negotiators."

Two…

He heard Erickson shout, "I don't give a shit about how it ends for me, Scott, as long as it doesn't end well for you.

Three…

The night erupted.

CHAPTER FIFTY-NINE

TO JAKE, EVERYTHING unraveled in slow motion, but a hundred casual observers would each have a different version of events and a conflicting order in which they occurred. A future review of the mission by the Special Investigations Unit would determine that highly trained team members perfectly carried out their assignments under extremely difficult circumstances.

Jake later remembered it this way: on three, he dove for the ground as instructed. Just before he did, the spotlight lit a cloud of gas filling the hall behind Erickson and Cassie. Cassie bit Erickson's arm, and he shoved her sideways while aiming the shotgun at the threesome on the walkway. Based on Erickson's words, Jake knew he was the intended target.

The officers on either side of the step simultaneously rose from their crouching position, but the pair in front of Jake each fired two rounds from their Glocks. Dani would say it was the standard double tap used by police officers. Erickson pulled the trigger as he crumpled to the ground, firing pellets into the side of the doorway.

The two tactical unit members crouching beside the porch leaped onto the step, guns extended. One kicked the shotgun aside while the other trained his weapon on Erickson. Other tactical team members rushed in from all sides. A member of the squad spirited Jake away in the opposite direction toward a waiting ambulance. Jake's ears buzzed as if a swarm of angry bees had taken up residence in each one, but he still heard breaking glass and splintering wood as the squad breached the house from every entry point, screaming profanity-laced commands. As he ran the other way with the officer's guidance, Dani rushed toward the house with the others.

When Jake arrived at the waiting ambulance, he saw Haley sitting on the ground beside a paramedic. Fear for the safety of her mom was revealed by her face and drooping shoulders. The paramedic blocked her view of the house. As Jake stood safely in front of a second paramedic who checked his eyes and ears, a jolt of fear overtook him when he realized that contrary to what Erickson had said, Julian might still be alive inside the house, ready to shoot anyone who entered. He brushed the paramedic aside as he strained to see the activity at the house.

Relief replaced his fear when Cassie approached the ambulance between two members of the tactical squad. Shouts of "clear" echoed from inside the house, and Jake imagined the officers rushing from room to room. The ambulance attendant sat Cassie down and asked several questions. She was on the verge of collapse from fatigue, hugging her daughter as she responded with monosyllabic answers. A weak smile crossed her face when she spied Jake.

"It's over, Cassie," he said. "You don't have to worry anymore."

While the paramedics urged Cassie and Haley to go to the hospital for observation, they both declined. They simply wanted to go home. A discussion with the Incident Commander ensued, and he ultimately agreed and assigned an officer to drive them home. He did not confirm that Julian was dead, but he offered assurance they would be safe in their home. Cassie held up a finger to the officer before climbing into the squad car for the ride home. She walked to Jake and threw her arms around him.

"Thank you so much for everything you did, Jake. You risked your life to find me, and I'll never forget it. I don't know how I can ever repay you."

Jake returned the hug. "We saved each other. You were there for me, too. If you insist, you can do one thing. You can buy me coffee at the next ringette game. For now, be with your daughter and rest."

Cassie smiled and climbed into the squad car. Haley wearily waved at Jake through the back window as the car sped away.

Suddenly, the adrenaline that kept Jake upright dissipated like the air from a deflating balloon. He had no idea how long it had been since he'd slept. He collapsed on the lawn opposite Julian's house and closed his eyes until he heard a welcome voice and felt a hand on his shoulder.

"Jake. Jake, can you wake up?"

He opened his eyes to see Dani leaning over him.

"We need you to identify Julian's body. Can you wake up and do that?"

Jake pushed himself to his feet and trudged after Dani toward the house. "What time is it?" he asked.

"Just after 3:30 a.m," Dani replied as they lifted the crime scene tape to dodge under. They sidestepped the evidence markers on the lawn designating where the shell casings lay. Dani pulled on a pair of coveralls on the doorstep and handed Jake a pair. They stepped over Erickson's body draped in a blanket and wandered down a hall, past a living room/dining room. They avoided more evidence markers until they came to the den. Every light in the house blazed, and police officers opened drawers and examined every space, took pictures, and wrote on notepads.

Three dining room chairs sat in a row. A man occupied one, the other two remained vacant. Remnants of plastic ties lay scattered beside them on the floor. Jake assumed Erickson had tied up Cassie and Haley like the man who sat motionless in the third chair.

The man's chin rested on his chest; his wrists secured behind his back with plastic ties. An empty syringe lay on the floor under the chair. His body sat totally limp, and his eyes were closed. Although he could have been sleeping, Jake realized from the gray tinge on his thin face that he was dead. Jake stood staring at the tall man with an athletic build sitting in the chair. The man with the shaped eyebrows and thin nose, and the telltale birthmark on his wrist. The dead man sitting on the chair was the man who called himself Julian. But his real name was Noah Kirkland, Cassie's colleague from work.

CHAPTER SIXTY

"JAKE, ARE YOU sure you want to do this?"

Jake grimaced at the soreness in his ribs as he buckled his seatbelt and Dani shot out of his driveway. "Yes, of course. I slept well after paying attention to Oliver. He seemed to miss me a little."

"I'm sure he missed you a lot. You're possibly the only one who would put up with his temperamental disposition, and he knows it." Dani laughed. "He'll never let you know, though."

The sun shone through the back window as they headed towards the Queensway that would take them out of town. Dani wore a white shirt and black designer jeans. She wore her hair pulled back from her face the way Jake liked it. When Jake climbed into the car, he was greeted by a hint of lemon. He thought it could be her perfume or her hair product. Either way, she smelled great.

Dani had invited him to ride with her to the farm that was the location of the Guardians of Truth meetings. Dani had become suspicious when Jake told her about the bunker under construction. She didn't recall seeing anything resembling a bunker, although she'd admitted she might have missed it in the dark. She'd agreed to meet a member of the Ontario Police Force capable of handling an excavator at the farm.

They sat quietly in the car, as if recent developments had taken their relationship a step backward. When they reached the city limits, Dani said, "I realize now that some things led our investigation in the right direction for the wrong reasons. It had nothing to do with dating or revenge. It was all about money. We have two regular and two forensic investigators at Kirkland's house today. They discovered from yearbooks found at the house that he was an actor in his younger years. He loved playing someone else. They mentioned a picture of him as Cyrano de Bergerac, in which he was unrecognizable. He seemed to be a loner in school and university, but contrary to what he told you, he'd had a girlfriend, at least in university."

Jake blew air through his lips. "It's unbelievable. He even put on a show for me at the coffee shop. The person I met for coffee bore no resemblance to the one on stage at the farm. He was certainly good at disguising himself, but he forgot the birthmark on his wrist. It seemed careless."

Dani shrugged. "Maybe you're giving him too much credit. He might have become a little too comfortable. He didn't think anyone would notice."

"I guess. I also can't figure out why Erickson tried to shoot me right in front of an army of armed officers."

"We'll never truly understand his motivation, but I think he put himself in a situation from which there was no return. He probably hoped to take you with him, but it was basically suicide by cop. The Special Investigations Unit is involved, as they regularly are when an officer discharges a weapon, or there is a death resulting from police interaction. But you're aware of all that from your reporting days. I'm not telling you anything new. You, Cassie, and Haley will be called as witnesses to the shooting."

"I'm happy to say the officers did their job. Erickson gave them no choice. Has the cause of Kirkland's death been determined yet?"

Dani steered the car onto the road leading to the farm. Jake considered it more aiming rather than steering, as they blasted down the road like a guided missile. She said, "Not officially, but we both know it will be the same sedative they used on you and Cassie."

They traveled a few more miles in silence until Dani said, "We found a flash drive at Kirkland's house with a master list connecting the numbers on the file folders with names. Like a code book. We've contacted some of the people. Of course, they're afraid to talk because of the non-disclosure agreement they signed. We're telling them it's not worth the gunpowder it would take to blow it to hell. But there's something you should know. You mentioned Erickson brought up the name 'Rosemary.' A Rosemary McCutcheon is on the list. She's formerly from Thunder Bay, and the picture in the file matches our Jane Doe from the Mer Bleu bog. She moved to Ottawa about a year ago. Seems like she didn't have a job. No presence on social media. Kind of sad. If there are any living relatives, we'll find them. She must have been smart enough to see through the Guardians of Truth. Such a waste.

"My forensic guys also found a rather large shoe print on the boardwalk in the bog. It matched a pair of boots we found at Erickson's place. The person had to be strong to carry a body into the marsh. Erickson fills the bill. Another red herring was the fact that Rosemary and Cassie were similar in appearance."

Jake swallowed hard at the news of Rosemary McCutcheon. It would devastate someone, and they would miss a daughter, a mother, or a wife, forever. He turned to Dani. "Something else has been bothering me. Some of the people that attended the meetings were well-off, but others were like Cassie. Why would they recruit them? It's not like they would be flush with cash. Kirkland's entire purpose was to convince his flock, as he called them, to give up as much money as possible. People like Cassie wouldn't have a lot of money to give, would they?"

"Think about it, Jake. Everyone on the list seemed to have one thing in common. The ones we talked to own their houses or condos, and Weatherby convinced them to open lines of credit against their property. With the cost of housing these days, they collectively contributed close to a hundred million dollars. Cassie has a nice education fund for

Haley, but she didn't give it to Weatherby, thank God. We should be able to recover some of the money, but some will be long gone."

They got out of the car at the farm and walked to an officer wearing coveralls and a hard hat. Jake examined the area. He said, "The trees weren't there when Weatherby drove me here. The so-called bunker was there. I suggest that's where he should dig."

The man climbed into the excavator and began working. It didn't take long before he hit something. A little more digging and the sun glinted off the roof of Weatherby's blue BMW. When they removed enough dirt, two officers climbed into the hole with shovels to uncover the windows. One soon shouted that they had found the decomposing remains of a middle-aged male inside the car. Once again, Jake was called upon to identify a body—this time it was the late Robert Weatherby.

On the way back to town, Jake couldn't take it anymore. "Are we okay, Dani?" he asked, his brow furrowed in concern.

Dani put her hand on his. "I think so. If you do, that is. You and I are more alike than we know." She laughed. "Not that anyone would realize it by our respective clothing choices. We are alike in a lot of other ways. We both want justice to be served, and we will do everything we can to make it happen. I'll never stop you from getting yourself into trouble, and I guess I wouldn't want to, but please tell me what you're doing more often. We can overcome our respective personal baggage if we just make the effort. What do you think?"

Jake squeezed her hand. "I think I would like you to pull over."

"Here? On the highway?"

"Wherever you can."

Dani slid to a stop on the shoulder and activated the four-way flashers. Once the car rolled to a stop, Jake leaned across the counsel, pulled Dani close, and kissed her hard on the lips. A passing car whizzed by with its horn blaring, the driver obviously not amused at the youngsters sharing a kiss on a busy highway.

EPILOGUE

A FEW MORE PEOPLE than usual showed up at the Saturday breakfast two weeks later, which meant the group had to abandon their usual round table for a larger, rectangular one. A special guest sat at the head of the table. Eric Tremblay's pale face still bore dark circles under the eyes, and he walked like he had aged a few years. Still, his beaming face revealed how thrilled he was to be with his friends. The doctors had cleared him to leave the hospital a few days prior armed with stents in his narrowed coronary arteries as well as instructions for a new diet and exercise regime, and his wife, Lyla, who was determined to make sure he followed them.

Amanda's new server, Jeff, hurried over, coffeepot in hand, to take their orders. "Coffee for everyone?" he asked. All eyes turned to Eric, who said, "Just water for me, please."

Eric's wife, Lyla, who sat to his left, said, "Same for me." Identical orders came from the others.

"No coffee?" Jeff asked incredulously. Everyone shook their heads, so Jeff said, "Do you need more time with the menu?"

Everyone deferred to Eric, who asked for a yogurt parfait. Lyla said, "Yogurt parfait, please," as did Cassie and Haley Wright, Dani and

Emilie Perez, Ryan Cambridge, Pierre Chevrier, and Jake. Jeff stopped writing in his notepad about halfway around the table and wandered off, shaking his head. Eric's eyes widened as he observed each person order the same thing he had. Some of the straight faces had difficulty staying that way.

Finally, Eric said, "Okay, what's going on?"

Ryan had emailed everyone before the gathering to put them up to ordering the same thing as Eric. He said, "We wanted to honor you on your first day back by ordering the same thing as you. We didn't want to tempt you by ordering cinnamon rolls."

Amanda, who was in on the joke, sauntered over with the coffeepot she had taken from Jeff. "Who's for coffee today?"

Every hand went up except for Haley, Emilie, and Eric. Eric laughed heartily, plainly tickled by his friends' joke at his expense. Ryan whispered to Amanda, "Please scratch my order for the yogurt parfait. I'll have a cinnamon roll.

All eyes turned to Eric, who said hastily, "Don't worry about me. I have to get used to it. Please order whatever you like."

Amanda smiled while holding her pencil above her notepad. "Anyone else want to change their order?"

The first to raise their hands were Haley and Emilie. They ordered cinnamon rolls and everyone else asked for bacon and eggs except for Jake, who stuck with the yogurt parfait.

The group fell uncharacteristically quiet while they waited for their orders, as if a cloud had settled over them. Nobody knew what to say. Surprisingly, Pierre broke the silence. He normally said little unless it was to torment Jake.

"What an awful ordeal you went through, Cassie. You, Haley, and Jake. I read about it in the news, and they didn't reveal everything. I'm glad you and your daughter joined us this morning." Then, he glanced at Jake with a grin. "The worst part was probably being locked up with our friend Jake here."

Jake shifted in his seat to relieve pressure on his side that was still sore from Erickson's kick. As he did so, he noticed Ryan roll his eyes at Pierre's comment.

Cassie's face and hands bore the scratches and burn marks from her ordeal. A hairdresser had shortened her hair to remove the singed parts. A deep red scratch beside her eye remained where she'd been hit by the piece of tree trunk that had been shorn off by one of Erickson's bullets. A few hours of saline drip in the hospital had treated her mild dehydration.

"Actually, I wouldn't have made it without Jake. He kept me calm at the worst of times." She glanced at Jake. "I'll never forget what he did for me."

The conversation returned to normal subjects after that. Eric joked about the hospital food as he downed his light breakfast. Sports, weather, inflation, and the city's potholes each had equal time. Those that had coffee took their last sips as Ryan turned to Emilie.

"Jake tells us you're quite the artist."

A crimson color crept from the neckline of Emilie's shirt to her hairline. "Thanks, I like to draw," was all she could manage.

Jake held Dani's hand, the two of them agreeing to drop any pretenses. He jumped in to relieve Emilie. "She's an incredible artist. In fact, I'm going to commission her to draw something for me. I have a large space on the wall in my sunroom. Or at least I will have shortly. I want one of Emilie's drawings to hang there. We can invite her to bring her portfolio to next Saturday's breakfast. One of you cheapskates might be interested in commissioning her to draw something for you."

Jake winked at Emilie, who stared at him wide-eyed. Dani squeezed Jake's hand under the table. "What space? I didn't think you had any wall space left," she whispered.

Jake said out of the corner of his mouth, "Remember that big clock? It's going to Value Village this afternoon."

Everyone went their separate ways when the conversation stopped, and the coffee ceased flowing. Hugs and pats on the back followed as everyone was delighted with the outcome for Eric, Cassie, Haley, and Jake. Dani and Jake walked hand-in-hand back to his house with Emilie chattering eagerly about ideas for the wall art. When they arrived at the house, Dani noticed a signed lottery ticket lying on the table, along with assorted dishes. Jake had apparently scrunched the tattered ticket in a pocket. She thought he had probably won a free ticket and thought nothing more of it.

Emilie wandered into the sunroom to check out the space where the drawing would go, with Oliver following inches from her feet. Jake and Dani sat at the kitchen table. Jake said, "I need to go to Toronto, and I'm hoping you'll join me. We can visit Avery and Nick for a couple of days. What do you think?"

"Sure, that would give you close to five hours to explain why you failed to tell me about the meeting and why you joined that dating site." She smiled. "I'm just kidding. I would love to go."

"We need to make a side trip to cash in that ticket. I checked it last night, and it's a winner, so I have to go to the Lottery and Gaming Commission office in Toronto to cash it in."

Dani's eyes widened. "Oh, really! I don't know anyone who has ever won before. How much?"

"It's $11,000."

"Whoa! Well, that's certainly better than nothing. And what will you do with your newfound wealth?"

"That's easy. I'll use some of it to pay for our trip. Then, I want to stop at the shop where I bought the ticket on our way back. There's a woman named Jing Wei who deserves the rest. You may have to bring your gun, though. I have a feeling she may be difficult to convince."

Thank you for reading *The Guardians of Truth*.
If you like what you read, please consider leaving a review
at your favorite online book retailer.

QUESTIONS TO START YOUR BOOK CLUB DISCUSSION

1. How did you experience *The Guardians of Truth*? Were you immediately drawn into the story? How did the story make you feel?

2. What motivates Jake Scott? Dani Perez? Julian? Robert Weatherby?

3. How do the characters grow or change during the story?

4. Is the story plot or character driven? Do events unfold quickly or is more time spent developing characters' lives?

5. Do you think the cover reflects the storyline?

6. Were there any questions left unresolved in the story?

7. Have you read Barry Finlay's other books? Can you discern a similarity in theme or writing style between them? Or are they completely different?

ABOUT THE AUTHOR

Barry Finlay is the award-winning author of the inspirational travel adventure, *Kilimanjaro and Beyond – A Life-Changing Journey* (with his son Chris), the Amazon bestselling travel memoir, *I Guess We Missed The Boat* and five Amazon bestselling and award-winning thrillers comprising The Marcie Kane Thriller Collection: *The Vanishing Wife, A Perilous Question, Remote Access, Never So Alone,* and *The Burden of Darkness*. His new Jake Scott Mystery Series debuted with *Searching For Truth*. He is now following that up with *The Guardians of Truth*. Barry was featured in the 2012-13 Authors Show's edition of "50 Great Writers You Should Be Reading." He is a recipient of the Queen Elizabeth Diamond Jubilee medal for his fundraising efforts to help kids in Tanzania, Africa. Barry lives with his wife Evelyn in Ottawa, Canada.

Contact Barry Finlay

Author Website: **www.barry-finlay.com**

Facebook Page: **https://www.facebook.com/AuthorBarryFinlay**

Twitter: **https://twitter.com/Karver2**

BOOKS BY BARRY FINLAY

THE MARCIE KANE THRILLER COLLECTION
The Vanishing Wife: An Action-Packed Crime Thriller
(Marcie Kane Book 1)
A Perilous Question: An International Thriller & Crime Novel
(Marcie Kane Book 2)
Remote Access: An International Political Thriller
(Marcie Kane Book 3)
Never So Alone
(Prequel novella to the Marcie Kane series – Book 4)
The Burden of Darkness: A Marcie Kane and Nathan Harris Thriller
(Marcie Kane Book 5)

THE JAKE SCOTT MYSTERY SERIES
Searching For Truth: A Jake Scott Mystery (Book 1)
The Guardians of Truth: A Jake Scott Mystery (Book 2)

NON-FICTION TITLES
Kilimanjaro and Beyond: A Life-Changing Journey
I Guess We Missed the Boat

**FIND THEM ONLINE OR AT YOUR
FAVORITE BOOK STORE OR LIBRARY**

Read the first book in the exciting Jake Scott Mystery Series

SEARCHING FOR TRUTH

Former journalist Jake Scott relies on his weekly breakfast gatherings with friends and a temperamental tabby cat named Oliver to keep his spirits up. He has lost his wife, retired from his job, and watched his daughter move to Toronto with her boyfriend.

Things change when one of the breakfast attendees, a beautiful and tenacious police detective with a troubled teenage daughter, suggests Jake should write a book. When he takes her advice and researches a convicted murderer's case, he finds out something is terribly wrong. Could a member of the breakfast group be hiding a secret deadly enough to commit murder?

Jake follows leads that uncover a mysterious and disturbing roller-coaster ride of clues, all while his attraction for the detective grows. An attempt to force the true murderer out of hiding results in a terrifying ordeal on the coldest night of the year.

WWW.BARRY-FINLAY.COM